THE SECRETS OF SAUNDER

ARIELLE HADFIELD

DESERT WEST PUBLISHING

*To all the girls who come from hard places—
Keep looking for your crown*

CHAPTER 1

The Kingdom of Barlow
Under the Rule of His Majesty King Herrick II

*L*iviya determined that Tish had two days left to live. She could tell based on the sound of her coughs. For the past few days, Tish's coughs had grown coarser, deeper, more frequent. Her skin yellowed. Beneath her eyes turned a bluish gray. The coughs jolted her body, each one spraying out droplets of blood and forcing out more life. This was always the worst day of Guernsey Fever. Tomorrow, Tish's coughs would finally subside. She'd lie silent and still in bed. The next night, she'd die. Liviya had seen it too many times.

Outside, the bitter wind blew violently, like it, too, hated Barlow and was eager to escape. It sent freezing drafts between the loose boards of the shack that two dozen young maids called home. The winter had been cold and icy, but no snow had fallen. It hadn't fallen in years. The dry riverbed cut through the land like a thick scar. Without fresh rain or snow, everyone in Barlow drank dirty water, most got sick, and many died.

Tish coughed again, a series of powerful rumbles that left her breathing shallow. In the next cot, Bicka looked at Liviya. The thin blanket rested beneath her chin. Bicka had spent the day sleeping, but the coughing must have woken her up. Or the cold. Beads of sweat formed above her wide eyes. She coughed, a hoarse wheeze that matched the pitch of the screaming wind, just like Tish's coughs a few days earlier.

Bicka was the youngest of the maids by several years, another child taken away from her family when her parents couldn't pay the king's taxes. Soon King Herrick would be stealing away the babies. Bicka's forearm was still scabbed where King Herrick's branding iron had marked her with a P, identifying her forever as one who had been purchased. Liviya looked at her own forearm and at the same scar burned there only days after being dragged away from her family. She hardly remembered them now.

Across the room, Mrs. Wilde, the house mother, tossed the last of the softened potatoes into a pot of dirty water. The girls had decreased the rations for several weeks to ease into starvation. Finally, they had run out of food.

The aroma of thin stew filled the room. Mrs. Wilde scooped half a ladle into each bowl and passed them around to the girls. Liviya lifted the chipped bowl to her lips.

Mr. Wilde cleared her throat. "Must you always be so unruly?" She passed Liviya a spoon.

"Tish don't mind," Liviya said, exaggerating the peasant drawl that Mrs. Wilde's strict rules had long since erased.

Bicka lay in bed without moving, her bowl untouched beside her. Liviya dipped the spoon into the bowl and held it against Bicka's lips.

Bicka took a few sips until Tish's coughing stole her attention. "Is she gonna die?"

"No, she's not gonna die." Liviya lifted the blanket from her own lap and spread it over Bicka. "Tomorrow she'll feel better, you'll see. She won't cough anymore." Liviya smiled as she smoothed Bicka's sweaty hair, softly humming. Bicka coughed again, and Liviya winced. She offered another bite of soup, but it dribbled down Bicka's chin. After a few more attempts, Liviya returned to her own cot. She stirred the watery broth in her bowl, unable to eat though starved. Around her, the other girls dressed for bed and settled beneath their thin blankets.

Across the room, Mrs. Wilde held her glare until nobody was listening. "It doesn't do these girls any good for you to lie to them. It'll be even harder for her now when Tish dies."

"When Tish dies, Bicka will be unconscious in bed, burning with fever," Liviya said.

Mrs. Wilde shook her head. "No. She's just coughing from all the cold air."

"It's Guernsey Fever," Liviya replied. "She's got about five days."

Mrs. Wilde's small frame swayed. She grasped the back of one of the bent chairs. Shaking her head, she turned to the fireplace. A few orange embers lifted above the cold ashes. The wind tossed them around the stone hearth before they faded and fell.

Liviya lay down on the damp straw and closed her eyes. The bed rustled as bugs scattered beneath her weight. Tish and Bicka coughed again, a chorus of agony and death. Liviya squeezed her eyes shut and cursed King Herrick for killing them.

Tish died two days later. Her soul slipped away as the sun slipped beneath the horizon. Liviya waited by her side for her final exhale before stepping outside, pausing only to tuck Tish's thin blanket around Bicka's burning body.

Outside the air was no fresher than inside the cottage. The stench of death followed them everywhere. Though Liviya mourned the loss of Tish, no tears fell. Her eyes had dried up long ago, just like the river. Inside, the girls had nothing. No food, no water, no hope.

Mrs. Wilde stepped outside, the door creaking closed behind her. She sat next to Liviya on the leaning stoop and rested her hand on Liviya's knee.

"It's not your fault," Mrs. Wilde said kindly, somehow knowing of the guilt that ate away at Liviya's heart. Guilt that Liviya couldn't save the sick girls, guilt that she was still healthy, guilt that she couldn't cry.

"There's still time for Bicka," Liviya said without any emotion.

"Oh, Liviya." Mrs. Wilde wrapped her arm around Liviya's shoulders. "Just love her till she goes. That's all you can do."

Liviya pulled away from her embrace. "If we found food—"

"There's nothing," Mrs. Wilde said. "The fields have all been picked over."

"Not King Herrick's fields," Liviya said. "There's food there."

Mrs. Wilde grabbed Liviya's upper arm. "These girls need you. Don't you do anything stupid."

Liviya pulled away before bruises formed beneath Mrs. Wilde's fingers. She dropped her face against her hands, hiding the agony etched into her eyes.

"You couldn't save her if you stole the king's crown," Mrs. Wilde said.

"If I had the crown, I could buy medicine, a blanket." Liviya paused to listen to Bicka's barking cough. "A field to bury her body." Her voice broke, which was fitting, because heart was broken, too. Liviya lifted her head and stared across the land. She wouldn't let her spirit break. Those girls needed her. There was still food out there. She'd find it.

Mrs. Wilde grabbed Liviya's arm again, as if she were able to read her thoughts. "Swear it. Swear you won't steal from the king."

"I won't steal from the king. I swear it." The lie crossed Liviya's lips easily. In Barlow, the truth was too difficult to speak.

CHAPTER 2

The kingdom of Barlow always seemed dark, but Liviya lay awake until the darkest part of night. It was safer to sneak around King Herrick's fields when there was no light at all. Liviya leaned over Bicka to be certain she hadn't died in the night. She was alive. For now. Liviya opened the door, sneaking through the narrow crack before too much wind blew inside and woke the girls, or worse, Mrs. Wilde.

The rough road jarred Liviya's joints as she ran, but she didn't stop until she reached the edge of the village. A leaning fence divided the village from the king's fields. Beyond them, the palace loomed. Even that had crumbled under King Herrick's reign. The large white stones were now gray, and the whole building sagged as if it sighed in despair. Liviya had seen paintings of its earlier splendor. How far it had fallen. How far they had all fallen.

In the past, fertile fields had covered the land. Now they grew mostly weeds. Yellow stalks of corn lined the fence. Vines wound around the wide leaves, threatening to drag the stalks to the earth. They barely grew tall enough to produce any ears, and they dried up months ago. Each breath from the wind made them creak. Liviya crept through carefully, stopping every few feet to look for corn.

The guards walked between the rows and along the fence in straight lines. Their uniforms were faded and their weapons tarnished, but it was enough to keep away most of the others. Liviya watched carefully, inching forward when the guard closest to her turned his back. Lying down, she pulled herself forward on her elbows. She moved slowly to keep the dry stalks quiet.

The corn thinned to an open field with no place to hide. It was a long run back to the fence, but Liviya wouldn't return empty-handed. A boulder in the tall weeds offered a shadow to hide in. She accepted it gratefully.

Liviya crawled forward again, careful to keep below the weeds. She looked at the plants in the next rows. Probably beans of some sort. Like the corn, they had only dry leaves. With a stick, she scratched the ground in case something remained below the icy soil. Nothing. Every root of every plant had been dug up, and every tree's boughs were bare. Others had run out of food long before she had. Suddenly Liviya wondered how many people had died in King Herrick's field trying to find enough food to live. However many there were, they had taken it all.

Nearby, something rustled. Liviya held her breath, pressing her stomach against the dirt, wishing the ground would swallow her. Another rustle, and a rabbit appeared. It hopped forward, stopping in front of Liviya's face, its eyes level to hers. The rabbit was so close Liviya could have touched it. She wanted it badly. A rabbit was food. Meat. She froze, afraid to move, afraid to breathe, pleading it would stay. Liviya sucked air through her teeth. A single move would send the rabbit hopping away.

Moving only her eyes, Liviya scanned the area around her for anything she could use to catch it. The rabbit paused, long ears twitching as it listened to the dark night. It took two hesitant hops forward and out of her reach. Liviya closed her eyes, the only expression of frustration she could afford. The grass rustled again. Suddenly, an arrow pierced the rabbit. Its body shuddered, and blood oozed from the wound. Liviya looked away, her stomach heaving. After a final lurch, the rabbit grew limp.

Shouts sounded across the field as the guards converged toward the commotion. Liviya looked across the field and saw him first. Several yards away, a man hunched in the grass. He was one of the few fortunate ones who possessed a weapon and the knowledge to use it. Leaves on his head and back disguised him in the field, but not enough.

"Ay!" a guard shouted. "Stop there!"

The guards ran toward the man with their swords raised. He leapt from the grass and ran for the fence. The other guards fell into formation. They were practiced in catching poachers, that was certain. The man would never make it. Neither would Liviya. Instead, she stayed still beneath the sparse weeds.

The guards raced after the man. In only a few steps, they tackled him. One of the guards struck him in the temple with the hilt of his sword. The man fell silent, blood trailing down his face. They tied his hands and feet and tossed him over the fence where other guards loaded him into a barred cart. He would be taken to the king and killed. King Herrick always killed.

Other guards fanned out across the field looking for others. As they drew near, Liviya scooped up the rabbit, not even minding the blood that smeared on her palms. Holding it by its ears, arrow extending from its neck, she snuck toward the fence. Each move brought her closer to freedom.

"There's another!" a guard shouted.

Liviya jumped up and ran. Feet thundered behind her. She scrambled under the fence, scraping her shoulder on the bottom slat and tearing her sleeve. An arrow sailed by her, landing a few feet ahead. She clambered to her feet and continued running. The village's earliest risers were leaving their houses. Liviya sprinted past them, rabbit in hand. The guards closed in behind.

"Stop her!" they shouted.

"Good morning, Liviya," the baker replied as he hobbled past. More than once she had stolen him some eggs and earned herself some bread in return. He pushed a cart filled with buns. "You better hurry." He paused to fix the buckle on his shoe. The slope in the road called to the unmanned cart. It started rolling, wobbling back and forth until it fell, spilling the bread and tripping the guards as they passed.

Liviya rounded the corner. "Guards this way," a woman whispered as Liviya passed. Skidding to a halt, Liviya dived into an alley. Her heart pounded and her legs burned, but she kept moving. Her home waited just up the street. She'd probably arrive before any of the girls had awoken.

The guards yelled behind her, but she pulled away with each step. A grin warmed her cold cheeks. She had escaped.

Behind a shed, Liviya stopped to catch her breath. She inspected her hands and dress. Her hands were dirty, and her dress was torn, but that should be easy enough to explain. Everyone was always dirty, and her dress was already torn. Holding the rabbit in her apron, she wiped away the dry blood on her hands.

When her breathing settled, Liviya tucked her hair behind her ear and practiced a calm smile. Peeking around a corner, she waited until the guards weren't looking. She crossed the street and returned to the servants' quarters.

As Liviya reached the door, Mrs. Wilde threw it open. She stood with her arms crossed, toe tapping, gray eyes staring.

Liviya pushed past her to Bicka's bedside. Her fever was so hot it nearly heated the room. Liviya knelt beside her and patted her cheek.

"How are you?" Liviya asked, knowing that Bicka wouldn't answer. Like Liviya had predicted, Bicka was unconscious.

The other girls eyed the rabbit. "Did you poach that?" one asked.

"Of course not," Liviya replied. "That's illegal. Besides, I can't shoot a bow." She held up the rabbit with the arrow still stuck in its neck. "I found it."

The rest of the girls rose from their cots and swarmed around Liviya.

Any lecture Mrs. Wilde had would have been unheard over the excitement, but her piercing eyes said it all. *Stupid. Careless. Dangerous.*

Liviya smiled. It was the most alive she had felt in weeks, and the food would keep them alive even longer.

Mrs. Wilde continued to grumble, but she sliced the meat into chunks and tossed it into a pot. She poked at the coals, easing them to life enough to boil the water. The sweet aroma of meat filled the cottage and made Liviya's stomach rumble. The girls feasted on the rabbit. With stomachs full, the girls dressed and left to the palace for their duties, faces lifted with small smiles. Liviya lingered for a few more minutes with Bicka, easing soup into her chapped lips.

When the cottage was quiet, Mrs. Wilde stood over Liviya with arms crossed. "I suppose you intend to try that again tomorrow."

Liviya stood up, towering over the small woman. "Yes, ma'am." She crossed her arms, too.

Mrs. Wilde's lips quirked, not with disappointment, but with pride. She dumped an extra serving of broth into Liviya's empty bowl. "Then you best keep up your strength."

Liviya waited until Mrs. Wilde turned her back, then brought the bowl to her lips and drained it. They'd live. She didn't know how, or for how long, but they'd live.

CHAPTER 3

The Kingdom of Saunder
Under the Rule of His Majesty King Josiah

In the kingdom of Saunder, all maps were torn off above the northern border, entire chapters were removed from history books, and anyone who even spoke of the kingdom of Barlow was hanged as a traitor. At least that's what was written in the law. Michael rarely heard anyone speak of Barlow. When they did, they said very little and said it very quietly. Almost twenty years ago, in a war with Barlow, the kingdom of Saunder lost their beloved Prince Nathan. His father King Josiah returned home with a crippled leg and grief severe enough to cause fits of delusion, which worsened with age. Prince Nathan left behind his infant son Daniel, the sole heir. Today was a celebration of Daniel's eighteenth birthday. He would become king— if he would show up to receive the requirements.

In Saunder, before a new king was crowned, he had to prove his worthiness. To test his bravery, he had to defeat an enemy. To test his wisdom, he had to complete a challenge, a riddle handpicked by the king. He also had to be married, but that was often the least concerning part. Receiving the requirements was an event as highly anticipated as the coronation itself. Michael and most of the kingdom had never seen it.

The wealthiest and most noble men and women had arrived hours before, as well as the priests who would officiate the ceremony and the scholars who would document the challenge for generations to read. Outside the ballroom, peasants gathered in the courtyard, hoping for a glimpse of the king or to hear even a whisper of his words. The entire kingdom was present. Everyone except for the prince.

Michael leaned back in his chair and glanced around the table at the untouched banquet. Several people met his eye. They looked at him with gazes that seemed to ask if he knew where the prince was. He did not. Last night, the prince, several of the noblemen's sons, and quite a few other friends with neither nobility nor character, had gathered to celebrate his eighteenth birthday. Michael didn't go. It wasn't his crowd. Neither was the crowd in the ballroom, but King Josiah had insisted he attend. Michael politely argued that he had much more important things to do, such as assist the fifteen stable boys who had taken the flocks to better fields. Michael had offered to go with them, but the king refused to allow it. They discussed it for weeks leading up to the banquet, but in the end, the king won, because the boys were gone. In an annoying irony, Michael was present, but the prince was missing.

Michael fiddled with the gold buttons on the cuff of his sleeve. The strict formality in the ballroom began to lighten as the people grew tired and impatient. Some people conversed quietly. Those who didn't fidgeted in their chairs.

The maids passed each other strange looks, standing awkwardly alongside the tables, unsure of what to do if they weren't serving food. Mrs. Maude, the plump, middle-aged head cook, glared at her plat-ters, daring the food to grow cold before it was eaten. She turned a glare to Michael, probably suspicious that he had snuck food before dinner was served. Michael winked. Mrs. Maude turned away grumbling.

A small commotion caught the attention of the crowd when the youngest maid, Chancey, dropped a platter of buns. Mrs. Maude shooed away the nearby maids, a sure sign that Chancey had been tripped. Soon enough, the scene was forgotten, and people whispered again about the prince's whereabouts.

King Josiah rested his hands on the cane between his knees. Wisps of gray hair stuck out from above his ears. The crown sat lopsided on his head, with the centerpiece, the Heart of Saunder, resting over his left eyebrow. He grimaced as if in pain. His breath came out in forceful exhales. Someone needed to help him rest. Besides, Michael could use a break from the ballroom.

Michael leaned over the empty chair between him and the king. "Your Majesty," he began.

"You'll stay," the king replied.

Defeated, Michael slumped back into his chair. With a sigh, he looked through the arched window. The sun quickly moved toward the horizon. It sent its rays through the colored pieces of glass, forming ribbons of rainbow along the floor.

The nobles around him talked about their noble things, their money and estates and lineage, conversations Michael couldn't contribute to. He had been raised in the boys' home outside the city, the orphan son of his peasant mother. When he was seven, King Josiah had come to the boys' home in search of a boy who he determined held promise. In the group of fifty dirty, dark-skinned boys, the king chose him. It was an incredible opportunity that saved him from a life of poverty, but it also required him to attend banquets where the guest of honor never arrived. Most days, Michael longed for the simple life of the stables.

"There are a hundred beautiful women here," the king said. "Go dance."

"No, thank you," Michael replied. The girls stood in a colorful group, the loudest ones in the ballroom. They were the daughters of the noble men. They could all do far better than Michael, and for that he was grateful. Beautiful? Yes. Wealthy? Beyond belief. Interesting? Not in the slightest.

Michael eyed them again. "I'll go mingle," he told the king.

The ladies' laughter grew louder as Michael approached. He greeted each of them by name, kissing the hands they offered him. He stole a glance over his shoulder at the king. As soon as Michael was sure he was beyond the king's line of sight, he excused himself and stood along the back wall.

"Michael," someone whispered. "Michael." The voice was muffled behind the velvet curtains that divided the preparation areas from the ballroom.

Reaching a hand behind him, Michael eased the curtains apart. Prince Daniel stood in the cavity covered in filth alongside several wide-eyed kitchen maids.

"There's some trouble at the cathedral," Prince Daniel whispered.

Irritated, Michael rubbed his face. Prince Daniel lived his life with an air of carelessness that was contrary to the way the king raised him. He had offended more visiting diplomats and dignitaries than each of Saunder's old princes combined. When he led his troops into battle, he returned with an alarmingly high casualty rate. Mothers wept when their sons were stationed under the prince's command. Everywhere he went, disaster followed. Unfortunately, the complaints of the people followed him home. Arrogant. Aggressive. Irreverent. And today, they would add tardy.

"Everybody's waiting for you," Michael hissed.

"Quick, give me your coat."

Michael glanced around the ballroom, then side-stepped into the curtains. He peeled off his coat and gave it to Daniel. He grabbed a towel from a nearby cart and tossed it to the prince. "Wash your face."

Prince Daniel wiped his face and ran the towel through his hair, smoothing the pieces that stuck out. "How do I look?"

He looked like a man who had spent the night partying with pigs in a fallen cathedral, and he smelled even worse. But the king wouldn't notice.

Michael clapped him on the shoulder. "You look great. Good luck."

Michael walked with Prince Daniel back through the kitchen and servants' corridors until they reached the ballroom doors. A startled page jumped to his feet and pulled the doors open. "Presenting His Royal Highness, Prince Daniel."

The audience rose. A collective sigh of relief was audible above the sound of the squeaking chairs. Michael watched Daniel just long enough to be grateful again that Daniel would become king and that Michael could leave. He turned down the hallway.

Mrs. Maude stood at the end, hand on her hip and wooden spoon pointed in Michael's face. "The king'll have your hide if you leave."

Michael patted her cheek. "I'm just getting another coat."

"You better be right back!" Mrs. Maude called as he left.

Michael walked out the back door of the palace. He followed the stone path across the courtyard to the cathedral. The entire west side had fallen into a pile of crumbled stones. Dust still floated atop the debris.

Michael ran his fingers through his hair then returned his hand to his pocket. The wind bit his cheeks. The air forced ice inside his lungs. It had been a strange year with an early frost and record cold temperatures, but there was no snow. Luckily for the people, the Sepes River ran along the border of Saunder and Barlow before it took a sharp turn back into Saunder, filling a reservoir. Saunder had plenty of water; it was just colder than the people were used to.

Michael jogged closer to the cathedral. Empty cartridges were littered across the lawn. The area reeked of sulfur. Several of the stones in the heap were stained black. Michael dipped his fingers into the black powder and sniffed it, but couldn't identify it.

With the wind roaring in his ears, Michael inspected the burnt wall. It could probably be repaired, but it'd take weeks to complete. Months if they tried to replicate the original workmanship. The city would be without a place of worship. The people would be angry, and more complaints would come.

Michael moved his gaze along the wall. Someone else had been here already. On the far corner, a symbol was written in the dust: three vertical lines inside a circle. Michael didn't recognize it. That made him wary. It was a message, but a message only a few were intended to understand. Michael ran his fingers along the lines, hoping to glean information from the wall it was written on.

Suddenly, Michael became curious about a lot more than the symbol and what it meant. What would happen if King Josiah died before Prince Daniel completed his requirements? Surely the prince would become king regardless. There was no other heir. Most people, like Michael, would serve the prince. However, some might find his incompletion of the requirements an easy excuse to serve another. Disagreements like that led to civil war.

Someone placed his hand on Michael's shoulder. Turning around, Michael saw Geoffrey. Geoffrey had been the king's adviser for as long as he could remember. He had accompanied the king to the boys' home all those years ago. Geoffrey's coat pulled tight over his gut. He stroked his graying whiskers. "Storm's coming."

Geoffrey was right. The signs had been there for a while, but Michael was just beginning to recognize them. There was a rebel group in the kingdom. Some weren't loyal to the prince.

Michael pulled his hand away from the wall. "I want to be very clear where I stand. I serve my king, and I'll serve the rightful heir. I'll serve him faithfully, until I die, giving my life if necessary."

Geoffrey's smile was small, but not so small that it hid his amusement. "I'm talking about the weather."

Michael followed Geoffrey's gaze to behind the palace. Dark clouds billowed. They sat on top of each other above the valley where the boys had taken the sheep.

"No. My boys are out there," Michael choked out. They didn't have the supplies to survive such a storm.

Geoffrey stepped in front of Michael and held up his hand. "Allow me to also be very clear where I stand. I stand with my people. I stand with the man who serves them, and I stand with my sword lifted against the man who does not." He patted Michael's shoulder. "We can save them. Let's go."

As Michael and Geoffrey reached the stables, the snow arrived. They each mounted a horse and raced for the palace gates. White flakes dusted the ground, faster and fuller than Michael had ever seen.

In minutes, mounds of snow covered the trail. The wind howled. Michael's frozen fingers struggled to hold the reins, but his horse trudged forward. He cursed himself as he plowed through the snow. He had spent the entire evening among the kingdom's fancies while his boys and flocks had suffered. The snowflakes whipped across his face like tiny swords. Everything was white, camouflaging the landmarks, even the palace, which on clear days could be seen miles away. Only feet away, Geoffrey was invisible.

Michael used one hand to shield his face and brought the other hand to his mouth to blow on his frozen fingers. His body shook, making each inhale hurt.

In the distance, shadows moved slowly through the storm. The boys! "One. Two. Three…. Twelve. Thirteen. Fourteen." Someone was missing.

Michael dismounted and stood in front of each boy, shaking the snow from their hoods and scanning their faces. They were cold and confused, but they were alive. "Where's Jacob?" he barked.

One of the boys sank to his knees. Geoffrey pulled him onto his horse. Michael stomped into the snow a few times, driving the blood back into his feet. He peered over his shoulder, trying to estimate the distance to the palace. He peered back into the storm.

"Get these boys home," Michael said. "I'll go get Jacob."

"It's a fool's mission alone," Geoffrey warned. His words were muffled beneath the freezing, white blanket.

Michael looked to the boys, their blue lips and wide eyes. They wouldn't make it back alone. "Get them home," he said again. "Have supplies ready for when I return." He wiped the snow from the saddle, remounted his horse, and galloped deeper into the blizzard.

Each step forward brought more ice and more chance of getting lost on the way home, but he wouldn't return without Jacob.

The horse, head down, fought through the thick snow. Struggling to hold the reins, Michael put them down and let the horse walk. The horse had as much chance of finding Jacob as he did. He reached to pat the horse's neck, but was unable to remember its name. This realization brought another one. He wasn't shivering anymore.

In a panic, Michael stumbled off the horse. He needed to find Jacob, and soon. He'd dig through the snow with his hands if he needed to. With a deep breath, Michael tried to clear his mind and think like a boy. Where would he seek shelter? Michael spun in a slow circle, stopping when his intuition hummed. He didn't know which direction he faced, but he knew Jacob was there. He lunged through the snow and found Jacob crouching in the slim shelter of a snow-covered tree.

"Jacob!" Michael shouted.

The near-frozen boy stumbled toward him. Struggling to hold him, they both sank to the ground. Michael had fought in countless battles, but for the first time, he stared into the eyes of death. The horse was gone, Michael was lost, and snow continued to fall. But he was satisfied. He had found Jacob. At least the boy wouldn't die alone.

Michael put his arm around him, doing his best to offer protection from the storm. It seemed ages ago that his biggest worry was leaving a banquet. More ice formed in Michael's chest, a different kind, as he remembered the banquet, the prince, and the fallen cathedral with the marking on the wall. The memory brought a surge of urgency. Michael sensed a war was coming. This time, there would be no enemy advancing and no attacks on foreign cities. This was the worst war of all, a war within the walls of Saunder, a war against the prince.

"Get up," Michael ordered. He pulled Jacob to his feet. "Ten steps. Give me ten steps."

He counted each step as he and Jacob fought to move forward. When he reached ten, they both sank down, unable to go any farther. In all the whiteness, darkness started to close in on him.

Suddenly, a hand above pulled him to his feet. "He's here!" a voice called. It was Geoffrey. He lifted Michael onto a horse. Slapping the horse's flanks, he sent it flying toward the palace, following closely behind with Jacob.

At the palace steps, Michael slipped off the horse. The wind blew the front doors open and snow swirled around the room with an icy scream. Geoffrey helped him inside. Mrs. Maude rushed toward him with a blanket. That was all he saw before he passed out.

CHAPTER 4

*M*ichael awoke in his room with a pounding head and haunting memories. He threw off the blankets that covered him. Flames crawled up his chest and across his cheeks. He pried open his dry lips. "Where's Jacob?"

Mrs. Maude placed a cool rag on his forehead. "Rest now. He's doin' just fine."

Michael blinked until his vision cleared. Mrs. Maude moved slowly. Her dress was wrinkled. Graying hair fell from her bun and into her face. She smiled, but her eyes showed the exhaustion of someone who had sat beside a bed for several days without sleeping. Michael reached for her hand and squeezed it. "And the other boys?"

"A lot better than you," Geoffrey said. He was unshaven and unkempt, but he looked relieved. He stood beside the window where Michael guessed he had been pacing. "Some of their mamas fixed you a plate." He motioned to the table beside the bed where an assortment of baked goods waited.

"Bless those boys and their mamas." Michael sat up slowly, head spinning. He pulled the rag from his forehead and ran it across his face, a weak defense against the fire engulfing him.

Across the room, he caught the gaze of King Josiah. Someone had moved his chair into Michael's room. While Michael had slept, the king had aged another decade. His skin was an unearthly gray. He stared across the room with empty eyes. His hands rested on his cane, bearing the weight of his hunched upper body. Without a word, the king lifted a finger.

Mrs. Maude took the rag from Michael, dropped it back in to the bowl, and dried her hands on her apron. Geoffrey moved toward the door. As he passed, he squeezed Michael's shoulder. They left the room, pulling the door closed behind them.

The room was silent for a long time.

"Attend the banquet," the king said finally. "That's all I asked you to do."

The king asked Michael to do far more than that. Most things, Michael did without question, but that was an argument for another time.

"My boys needed help." Groaning, Michael sank against the pillows.

"Any number of men in that room could have saved the boys. Give the order, and watch them run. But you." The king pushed the end of his cane into Michael's chest. "You were there to receive the requirements for the throne."

Michael studied the old man wistfully. Once strong and wise, his mind was now muddled.

"You mistake me for Prince Daniel," Michael explained gently.

"No." The king's gaze was focused and intense, not at all like the faraway stare when he was confused. King Josiah knew exactly what he was saying.

Michael shuddered. He had feared that some wouldn't serve the prince. He had never imagined that King Josiah would be among them or that Michael would be asked to rule instead.

"You'd deny your own grandson his crown?" Michael asked, unable to hide the contempt in his voice.

King Josiah scoffed. "The crown is not rightfully his nor has it been denied him. As stated in the legends, the crown will go to whomever first completes the requirements. You'd do the kingdom a great disservice if you didn't try."

With a slow exhale, Michael offered a weak excuse. "I don't have royal blood." Fingers fumbling, he found the ring that hung on a chain around his neck. It was the only token he had from his mother.

"If we both spilt our blood, it would look very much the same," the king replied.

Michael considered leaving the king alone in the room. His stiff legs made him think better of it. He wasn't sure they were strong enough to carry him away. Instead, Michael shifted against the pillow and closed his eyes.

The king sighed as if he had already said the words he had wanted to speak and was too weary to speak them again. His disappointment filled Michael with an ice more bitter than the blizzard.

With a groan, King Josiah struggled to his feet. Michael moved to help him. The king pushed him back against the pillow again with his cane and turned to the door.

"You're confused," Michael called out, desperate to have the last word.

King Josiah turned slowly. "And you're a coward."

MICHAEL FELT WELL ENOUGH TO BE OUT OF BED THAT EVENING, BUT Mrs. Maude kept him down until the next morning before she finally let him go. "King's orders," she had insisted when he protested. "And I don't disobey the king." She said the last part with a raised eyebrow of judgement.

Mrs. Maude also refused any visitors, insisting Michael needed rest. Thankfully, Geoffrey had moved the king's chair back to his room. Michael hadn't seen him since.

When he finally got permission to leave, Michael pulled on a clean shirt. He sat on the edge of the bed and rubbed his head, waiting until he was certain he could bend to put on his boots. It seemed that while he had slept, the entire world had changed, leaving him unsure of his place and purpose. Uncertain as he was, he knew he didn't belong on the throne. No matter the reason he was offered it, Michael didn't want the crown.

The longer he sat, the more clearly he could think. As King Josiah had said, the crown hadn't been denied to Daniel. He simply had to earn it. As soon as he did, all would be right with the world again. That was Michael's place. To help the prince, as he always had. He would help him defeat an enemy and complete the challenge. And when Daniel was king, Michael would serve him faithfully. It was a perfect plan. The only problem was that Michael didn't know what challenge had been given. He was annoyed to find that the king had been right. Michael should have attended the banquet. With his plan decided, Michael pulled on his boots, stiff muscles complaining with each movement, and went to find Daniel.

CHAPTER 5

$\mathcal{M}$ichael left his room, stopping by the kitchen just long enough to tug gently on Chancey's braid. When she saw him, she squealed and jumped into his arms, nearly knocking him backward.

"You're all anyone's been talkin' 'bout," Chancey said. She was eight or so. Much younger than any of the other maids in the palace. She didn't have anywhere else to go. The king's compassion had found a place for her here.

"They all said that you were 'bout near froze walkin' back in and that no one else ever would of did that."

"They're all exaggerating," Michael said. "Lots of other people would have done it. Geoffrey would have, but he brought the first group back. And King Josiah sure would have if he could walk."

"Maybe," Chancey agreed slowly.

"Prince Daniel, too. He's brave," Michael said.

Chancey wrinkled her nose. "The prince don't really like getting dirty, and you were real dirty when you came in. Wet, too. You're lucky Ms. Maude didn't gripe at you for mussing her floors."

Michael smiled just long enough to make Chancey smile, too, then he furrowed his brows. "The prince does a lot of good for his people. You always remember that."

Chancey shrugged then continued with things she found far more interesting. "I think you died a little and the king saw your ghost." She lowered her voice to a whisper. "He ain't really recovered from it much. And Mrs. Maude said she ain't seen him that sad and scared since the day he lost his son."

"Well that's because he needs someone to watch his horses," Michael said. "And I'm just about the best there is with those horses."

Mrs. Maude appeared around the corner. "You're far more replaceable in those stables than you think. You're lucky he lets you fool around in there so much instead of doing anything useful around here." She removed the wooden spoon from the pocket of her flour-dusted apron and pointed it at Chancey. "Back to work before I start thinking 'bout replacing you in the kitchen."

Michael snuck Chancey a wink before she scurried away. He left with Mrs. Maude still muttering about wasted time. Whistling brightly, Michael walked to the king's study where he found the prince.

Prince Daniel looked up when Michael entered. "Ah, you're awake."

A map covered the table. Torn corners still marked the spot where it had once been attached to the wall. Tokens representing Saunder's armies lined the northern border.

"What are you doing?" Michael asked.

"Defeating an enemy," Prince Daniel said. "I've declared war." He motioned for Michael to close the door then whispered, "Against Barlow."

Michael cloaked his surprise with a cough. He rarely heard that name spoken aloud. It sounded harsh and alarming, like the word itself was a curse. Head spinning, Michael slid a chair up to the table and sat down before the floor came to him. The day at the fallen cathedral with the strange graffiti seemed long ago, but Michael knew better than to ignore past fears simply because new ones arrived. There may be a question of the people's loyalty to Daniel. If there weren't dissenters now, an unprovoked war would create some the minute it was announced.

"It's extreme, Daniel. Declare a duel against a rival or avenge the death of a friend. That's all the king is expecting. But an entire war?"

"We'll win," Prince Daniel replied.

Of course they would. Barlow was a disease-ridden, half-starved, tyrant-ruled plot of land that would be entirely desolate in a matter of years. Even still, fighting a war would cost Saunder lives. War always cost lives.

"And the king has approved this?" Michael asked. If King Josiah gave his permission to march to Barlow, the world really had changed while Michael was sleeping. King Josiah was content to let them slowly starve. He would never allow his men to step foot there.

Prince Daniel straightened the tokens along the map's border. "I have determined that due to the king's age and failing health, he doesn't need to know."

The prince's expression invited no arguments. Michael guessed that the near loss of his life didn't endear him to the prince enough for him to disagree.

"What's your challenge?" Michael asked, trying to sound as uninterested as possible. The challenge had been, at least in part, intended for Michael. Inside, he fought a fear that it was something he could do.

Prince Daniel motioned to the king's crown on a small table across the room. The large ruby had been pried from the golden prongs and sat among tools and brushes. "The Heart of Saunder," the prince said. "I have to make it clear."

Michael looked at the ruby, gleaming bright red in the dark room. It was impossible. Impossible for Daniel, and impossible for Michael. Relieved, Michael laughed. He cleared his throat when Daniel glared.

"It's a riddle," Michael said. "But you'll figure it out." At least he hoped he would. Michael certainly had no ideas. He never did well with riddles. Michael turned his attention back to the map and the gathering armies. He could help Daniel defeat his enemies, though, both outside Saunder and within her walls.

"Suppose," Michael began, speaking slowly to allow time for the thought to fully develop. "Suppose you secure an alliance instead. That's defeating an enemy, no? And it prevents a war." He cleared his throat and looked down to his scuffed boots. "The people will love you."

"An alliance." Prince Daniel formed a triangle with his fingers and brought them under his chin. He thought for a long time.

"We'd save the money and resources that war requires." When Daniel made no reply, Michael added, "And think of the power of our lands combined."

Prince Daniel lifted his eyebrows, then shook his head. "The king would never allow it."

The prince was right. King Josiah lived by the creed that some wrongs were too wrong to ever be righted. Even if they were wrongs that only he remembered.

Michael shrugged. "Maybe the king wouldn't need to know this either." The words dug into his heart. They sounded dishonest. Treasonous. But they weren't. They were spoken only out of loyalty to his prince and the crown that belonged to him.

A smile stretched across Prince Daniel's face. "Make them allies, and I will have destroyed an enemy."

Inside, Michael's senses started to hum. This was a bad idea. Prince Daniel liked it a little too much. But Michael didn't know what else to do. He pulled a dagger from his belt and tossed it onto the table. "Keep this in your boot, and promise me, Daniel, if anything goes wrong, we kill their king and leave."

Daniel slapped his hand against the table. The tokens toppled over. "Very good. We march in the morning.

MICHAEL AND PRINCE DANIEL QUIETLY PACKED THEIR BAGS, SADDLED their horses, and left first thing the next morning so as not to leave any whispers behind for the king to hear. After several hours of hard riding, they stood at the edge of the canyon that divided the kingdoms. The canyon, a hole in the earth four hundred feet deep, could have been a wall a thousand feet high and a thousand years old. It blocked all communication, all trading, and any form of friendship between the lands. The only connection between them was a weathered bridge that neither side had bothered to repair. The horses balked at the idea of crossing it. Michael let them rest before pushing them forward.

The canyon sliced between the two lands, earth eaten away by the Sepes river. Centuries ago, the river forked, delivering half of the water to each of the kingdoms. But legend told how the earth herself lifted up, damming Barlow's river as punishment for their cruel and barbaric ways. Barlow was left with only the rain that fell to water their fields. There was never enough. It kept Barlow weak. Every year, their people starved. With Saunder's army of men and some shovels, Barlow could have water, too. It was an offer their king would be unable to refuse, no matter what grudge he might hold.

Michael and Daniel sat in the shade of a tree and let their horses drink freely from the water and graze on a few blades of grass. It was the last of both they would have until they returned. Michael rested, too, lying back in the damp grass with his eyes closed. His head was starting to pound. He began to wonder if he should have remained at home. No, he told himself. It was just fatigue talking. Maybe a little bit of fear. He'd be home soon enough, back in bed. Prince Daniel would be one step closer to his crown. A few hours of discomfort were well worth it.

Michael wiped his face and signaled to the prince. "Let's finish this."

In Barlow, the horses' hooves were loud on the frozen ground, crunching chunks of ice and splintering frozen puddles of mud. The sun began its descent, but it still offered enough light to see the wasting kingdom of Barlow.

The land was empty—poorly formed roads, no houses, no travelers. Tall weeds grew together in patches. In the distance, trees reached out bare branches like fingers threatening to ensnare the men. Michael's worry grew louder now. He and the prince had traveled to an enemy country to meet with a stranger in order to seal an alliance that their king had not approved. Michael would be punished, he was sure of it. He might even hang. But if he did, at least he would die an honest man, loyal to the throne, doing what he felt was best to help the prince succeed.

The palace loomed in the distance. With each step, it showed more of its age and deterioration. By the time they arrived, Michael was surprised it was standing at all. At the palace gates, two sleepy-looking guards hopped to attention and crossed their swords across the entrance.

"Stop, by order of King 'errick!" one shouted. Scabs covered his face. His mouth housed only a few teeth, all of them rotten. He wore what was once a red uniform that had either faded to brown or had been covered in layers of dirt. Michael surveyed them with a smile. King Herrick's moth-eaten men looked more like half-witted highway robbers.

Michael dismounted and held up one hand. With the other, he placed his sword on the ground, far enough away to please the guards, but close enough to retrieve it again should a fight ensue.

More guards approached. They held their dented swords toward Michael and Daniel.

Prince Daniel dismounted as well and presented his hand with the seal of Saunder on his finger. "I am Prince Daniel of the kingdom of Saunder. I seek an audience with your king."

A guard cackled. "That's an unfortunate 'eritage. We kill all trespassers from Saunder. Except royalty. They's to be taken to King 'errick so 'e can kill them in ways that ain't as quick or pretty." Snickering. the rest of the guards moved their swords a few inches closer. Their leader motioned to Prince Daniel. "Take the prince. Kill the other."

With swords in his face, Prince Daniel allowed his hands to be tied. The guards hoisted him into the saddle. With a slap to the flanks, the horse moved forward. Several of the guards followed.

Michael studied the remaining two men. They were inadequately armed, and over-eager to kill. He could fight both and win with minimal effort. He took a closer look. Maybe medium effort since he wasn't at peak health. But defeating the guards wouldn't get him into the palace with Daniel. Once inside, Daniel would be severely outnumbered, and his hands were tied. Michael needed to stay with him. He needed to get into that palace. He had only one idea.

"He's lying," Michael called. "I'm the future king of Saunder."

The guards exchanged puzzled looks. The man leading the horse that carried Prince Daniel stopped. He looked from Daniel to Michael.

"I came to declare an alliance with Barlow. Included among the terms are shares of water."

Even King Herrick's most deft guards couldn't ignore that point. The swords lowered slightly.

"I demand that my message be delivered to the king and my companion freed. If we seal no alliance, we will signal to our troops waiting on the border to attack. Your land will be leveled in hours."

There was no waiting army, but the guards had no reason not to believe his lie.

"Take 'em both," the leader said. He turned to Michael. "We'll spare your lives for now, but King 'errick will kill you both, and one of you's gonna be wishing you let us do the deed."

Michael slowly moved his hands behind his back and allowed the soldier to tie them together. Another soldier thrust his foot into Michael's stomach. He folded, and while he coughed, the soldiers threw him on top of a horse.

CHAPTER 6

Over the next few days, Liviya stole a handful of frozen apples and a sack of weevil-infested flour. Both times, the guards nearly caught her, following her through the village square, around the palace grounds, and into the outskirts of the city before she finally escaped them. All the while, Bicka grew more ill. Liviya guessed she had only hours left. She spent every spare moment by Bicka's bedside. More desperate every day, her thievery grew even more dangerous.

Today, Liviya stood at her station in the palace kitchen polishing silver. It was her least favorite chore. The cold weather kept her fingers stiff. She had to pause often to stretch them out. Usually Liviya complained the entire time she polished, but today she was simply too tired. Although the stolen food gave her and the girls energy, waking up in the night to steal it stole the energy right back.

Mrs. Wilde passed by a few times, once with a large stack of platters, later with a pile of pressed linens, and finally with another load of silver to be polished. Liviya groaned as Mrs. Wilde clinked the pieces into the tray. She'd be here all day. Maybe into the night. Mrs. Wilde left, turning back after a few steps. "I could use your help."

Liviya agreed gratefully and left the silver. Mrs. Wilde pointed to a bucket of dirty water. "Help me get this upstairs."

They walked through the dining room and into the hall where a great set of stairs wound to the second floor. Liviya's duties rarely took her from the kitchen. This was a new adventure. Mrs. Wilde walked up with the mop in her hands. Liviya followed with the bucket, sloshing water on more than one step.

Mrs. Wilde and Liviya started at the front of the corridor and cleaned the bedrooms. Most were empty and had been for years; King Herrick haunted the entire place by himself. There were dozens of rooms, but the cleaning was simple. They mopped the floor and dusted away the cobwebs that claimed the corners. It was a pleasant reprieve from the monotony of the kitchen. Each door unlocked a window to a world Liviya had never seen.

A single door remained at the end of the hall. The door was worn, like it had been opened dozens of times. Jewels encased the doorknob, like it protected a treasure inside. Mrs. Wilde eased it open.

It was another bedroom. Unlike the others, long ago, someone had stayed there. It appeared nothing had changed since the occupant left. The winter air blew inside, but nobody closed the window. The drapes, once a yellow silk, were tattered. The bedding had faded over the years, but the bed remained made. Mrs. Wilde fluffed the pillows.

A mirror hung over a table that held silver combs with jeweled handles. Bottles of perfume filled a tray. One of them was open. The contents had evaporated long ago. The top drawer was pulled half open. It contained a tiara placed lopsidedly on a velvet pillow. Someone had removed it in a hurry and never put it on again. There was also a small bowl filled with coins. Not the brownish bent bits of metal, but gold coins stamped with the seal of Barlow. Liviya reached her hand out. Mrs. Wilde slapped it down.

"Careful. The king inspects everything in this room every day. He'll know if anything is missing."

Liviya turned away from the table and the temptation it offered, focusing instead on a portrait that hung above the bed. It showed a young woman. The tiara in the drawer crowned her head. She wore a rich blue gown that matched her eyes. She smiled so sweetly that Liviya smiled back.

"That's Barlow's princess," Mrs. Wilde said.

She was gone before Liviya had been born, but Liviya had heard the stories. Almost twenty years ago, a foreign prince came and married the princess. Unexpectedly, the king died. The prince became king in his place, even taking his name, becoming Herrick the Second, who was nothing like the first. Those who questioned it died also, outspoken barons, gossiping maids. That's when the water stopped, some said.

"Did Herrick kill her, too?" Liviya asked.

"No one knows," Mrs. Wilde replied. "Some say she escaped with her baby."

Liviya looked at the portrait. The princess was a good woman. She could see it in her eyes. If she were alive, she would have ruled differently. She would have raised her baby to be a better king.

"I think they're alive," Liviya said. "And I think they'll come back."

Mrs. Wilde shook her head. "Don't waste your dreams. People who are lucky enough to escape aren't ever stupid enough to come back." Mrs. Wilde turned to wring out the mop. "She's gone. Herrick will always be king."

When the room was clean, Liviya returned to the kitchen and the pile of waiting silver. The shining handles showed pictures of a princess beside her dead father, a girl married to a murderer, holding a baby that had her eyes. Liviya rubbed the silver furiously. No matter how much Liviya stared, the silverware was clean and put away before she was able to see the rest of the story within it—the story where Barlow's princess and baby prince escaped to safety and returned later for the crown to save them all.

AFTER HER WORK IN THE PALACE, LIVIYA TURNED THE DIRECTION opposite of her home. The wind whistled outside, screaming cold curses. The freezing air was no deterrent. Liviya needed food. She pulled her shawl tighter around her cheeks, almost grateful for the wind and the excuse to hide herself among the guards. She had stolen too many times. The king had responded by doubling the watch.

Liviya walked along the road until the guards thinned slightly. The bent chicken coop waited at the corner. Head down, she reached inside for eggs. She grabbed two when someone spotted her.

"Thief!" A guard ran toward her, but two eggs wouldn't feed all the girls. Liviya fumbled around until she found another. It wasn't a feast, but it was better than nothing.

With the guard only steps away, Liviya kicked in the side wall, releasing a group of startled hens and an angry rooster. The flapping chickens slowed down the guard for only a moment, just enough time for Liviya to start running. More guards came from their posts. Liviya weaved between the sheds and stables until the entire barnyard was awake. The squawking animals caught the attention of those nearby. Any guard who hadn't seen her yet saw her now and joined the chase. Liviya raced outside the palace grounds and into the city. She crossed the roads back and forth between the houses and shops. The guards yelled behind her. After a quick turn, Liviya entered the first door she found. She shut the door behind her and leaned against it.

The first thing she noticed inside was the smell. It was clean. Fresh. Drying herbs hung from the windows. Some she recognized, like the dark green leaves of mint and the purple sprigs of lavender. Most she had never seen before. Some grew in pots and others hung upside down in the window. Mismatched jars filled with oils and creams lined the shelves. She recognized the shop as an apothecary. Something here could heal Bicka. Liviya was sure of it.

Nearby, a man sat at a table, grinding dry leaves with a mortar and pestle. "What can I help you find, miss?" He had a trim, triangular beard and a starched rectangular apron.

"My friend is sick. Guernsey Fever," Liviya said.

The man's eyes crinkled apologetically. "The only cure is Seabalm, and it doesn't grow here." He opened an old book and showed her a faded picture of a small, white flower. "But we've got this." He reached for a bright green plant with heart shaped leaves. "Ruttamon can alleviate the symptoms, prolong life a few weeks. Months if they're lucky."

Liviya hung her head, but only for a moment. Maybe the Ruttamon would keep Bicka alive until Seabalm could be found. And if not, at least it would make her more comfortable in her final hours. "I'll take it."

The man crushed the herbs and poured them into a pouch. "Boil it in water until it's fragrant. Mighty bitter, but she needs to drink it all."

Tucking the pouch into her pocket, Liviya whispered a prayer of gratitude to the heavens beyond the hazy Barlow air.

"Two pieces of gold." The man held out his palm.

Liviya stared, mouth refusing to form words. "I haven't got any money," she said finally. A shout from outside reminded her of the stolen eggs. She reached into her other pocket. "But I've got these." She set down two eggs. One oozed its white through a crack onto the clean counter.

The man was polite enough to not laugh. "My son is at the academy. These won't pay his tuition. I need money."

"A child is dying," Liviya snapped.

"One less person to share water with," came his reply.

Liviya's temper flared with a familiar fire in her core. She pressed her lips together to hold it in. There were guards outside. She couldn't risk making a scene.

"You're a greedy pig," she spat. She turned to leave, slowing when he spoke again.

"One gold coin. I'll hold it for you in case you find one."

It was better, but still impossible. "Where would I find it? Money's not setting in the streets."

The man lifted an eyebrow. "Where did you find the eggs?"

Liviya licked her lips. She was a thief, and the man knew it. He needed money. The coward wanted her to steal it. Liviya considered it. Only King Herrick had that kind of money, and stealing from his palace was far more dangerous than stealing from his fields. Liviya looked from the herbs back to the man, then back to the herbs. She thought of Bicka who deserved the medication, who deserved far more.

"Hold it," Liviya said. "I'll get the money."

CHAPTER 7

As Liviya raced back to the palace, a voice in her head tried to discourage her from robbing the king, but the voice sounded just like Mrs. Wilde, and Liviya had grown so accustomed to ignoring her. Liviya snuck in the back door of the palace. All the maids had already returned home for the night. The kitchen was dark and eerily quiet. She tiptoed up the marble stairs, creeping down the corridor to the very last door.

The room was empty, just as she and Mrs. Wilde had left it. The bowl of coins sat in the drawer, untouched, inviting her to take them. Guilt stalled her steps. After a swallow, she moved forward. If King Herrick took care of his people, she wouldn't have to steal from his princess. The rug muffled her feet, but her heart pounded in her ears. She tucked a few coins in the folds of her skirt. A sound moved down the hall. Liviya shook off the shudder. Everyone was sleeping. She paused just long enough to take a deep breath before stepping out of the room.

Liviya walked down the hallway toward the stairs. Across the corridor, another door opened and a man appeared. Though his face was half hidden in the shadows, the horror stories described him accurately. After five years of working in the palace, for the first time, Liviya looked into the face of King Herrick.

"Fetch me some water," he barked.

"Yes, Your Majesty." Liviya slipped into a precise curtsy, grateful for Mrs. Wilde. Her strict training had taught Liviya to comply immediately.

Liviya rose and walked toward the stairs, hardly daring to lift her feet for fear the jingling coins would betray her. She felt the king's eyes on her longer than she would have liked. She quickened her pace, eager to put distance between them.

"Wait," King Herrick called.

Liviya froze. He couldn't have known she had stolen anything. He probably only had another request. She turned slowly, trying to remain calm.

"Come closer," he said.

Liviya's feet refused to move, until, on their own, they started running.

"Stop her!" he called. "Guards!"

Guards appeared from the other end of the corridor. Liviya twisted between them and raced down the stairs. Their fingers brushed against the back of her dress. Straining, she pulled free.

"Halt!" Two more guards stood at the bottom of the staircase.

Liviya tried to stop, but the marble floor offered no traction for her worn shoes. Instead, she slipped, falling on her backside. Scrambling to her feet, she ran past one door, peering in to see if it offered an escape. It didn't. She kept running. If she could reach the front door, she'd be free. More guards pulled it open from the outside and chased after her. Liviya turned into the dining room, slipping through a servant's entrance and into the kitchen. She toppled over a pile of pans as she passed. The clanking echoed against the stone walls. The guards hollered more orders. Men blocked the exit.

With guards approaching on each side, Liviya jumped over the table, spilling a cruse of oil onto the floor. Slowing just enough to watch the guards slip, she turned back toward the door leading to the dining room. She shut the door behind her and turned to run again, but crashed into King Herrick's chest. The force hurtled her backward. With a growl, he reached for her hair and pulled her to feet.

Liviya whimpered and slapped at his arms, standing on the tips of her toes to relieve some of the weight on her scalp.

"Pretty bold to steal from the king."

"You're the only one with any money," Liviya spat, clinging to his arms.

King Herrick dragged her back into the kitchen. Lifting her by her collar, he dumped her on the table. He pinned her down with his hand on her face. Screams muffled, she tried to wiggle free. King Herrick reached for a knife hanging on the wall, the knife that halved entire hams in a single stroke. Snarling, he raised it above his head. The light glinted off the edge of its blade. Liviya was sure she would die. The knife hung in the air for what seemed an eternity. Then urgent shouts sounded from the corridor. Two guards burst into the kitchen.

"Your Majesty," the first one called, pausing a little when he witnessed the scene. "Men from Saunder is 'ere."

The color drained from King Herrick's face. He lowered the knife. "Josiah?" he whispered.

"The prince and 'is companion," the second guard reported. "They says they here for an alliance."

Fear gone, King Herrick laughed, a long, deep guffaw that echoed around the quiet kitchen. "An alliance! Kill them both. Bring me the prince's head."

The guard nodded slowly and eyed the knife in the king's hand before he continued. "I don't know who's who, sir. They both says they the prince."

King Herrick took his hand from Liviya's face and spun around. Liviya scrambled off the table, hiding in the corner behind a toppled pot. She brought a hand to her tender scalp. King Herrick stroked his graying whiskers. Liviya watched the different emotions color his face. Anger. Confusion. Fear. "Bring them to me. Let us meet this other prince."

The men nodded and left. King Herrick motioned to the guards in the kitchen. "Lock her in the cellar. Keep her alive for now."

The guards pushed a screaming Liviya outside and into the cellar, locking the door above her. It stank of mold, mice, and death. The space was so small that her knees pressed against her face. The door scraped against her back. Liviya screamed and screamed and screamed. Even when she became aware of her hysteria, she couldn't stop. Throat raw, her screams became shallow gulps of air. Finally, she was able to breathe deeply. Then somehow, maybe a cloud that covered the moon or a candle blown out above, the world became a little darker, and Liviya knew that Bicka had died. Liviya hadn't been able to get the medicine, and she hadn't been able to say goodbye. She had failed. Soon, she'd die, too. And still, no tears fell.

CHAPTER 8

King Herrick's soldiers deposited Michael and Daniel at the steps of the crumbling palace. It was dark, without even blinks of light from the stars. The wind was fierce. It burned Michael's eyes, but he welcomed the coolness against his fevering body.

"Wait 'ere. King 'errick be killin' someone else," the guard said. "'e'll need to clean 'is blade." He tugged each of the ropes around their wrists before leaving them outside.

Lying on the frozen dirt, Michael and Daniel were silent until the guards were gone.

"You got your dagger?" Michael asked.

Prince Daniel twisted his ankle in his boot and nodded. In the bustle, something had knocked his nose. Blood drew a red line across his lips. He wiped his face on his shoulder.

Michael rolled to his knees. "Scoot closer. I'll get it out."

The men scooted together until their backs touched. Michael leaned to the side and twisted his hands, reaching for the hilt of the blade.

"Come here. I'll cut your ropes," Michael said.

Prince Daniel grabbed for the dagger. "I'll do it."

Michael released the it into the prince's bound fingers. He to move it right side up and pointed the blade toward Michael's back.

"Easy," Michael said, tensing when the blade brushed against his hand. After a moment of sawing, and a few nicks to his fingers, his ropes fell loose.

"Stand up." Michael took the dagger and cut the prince free. "Listen, we gotta get out of here. Go inside. Kill the first guard you find. That'll be your enemy."

Prince Daniel shook his head. "I'm killing the king."

"We don't have time for that!" Michael snapped.

"I'm not leaving till he's dead," the prince replied. He touched his nose to check that the bleeding had stopped.

Michael exhaled through clenched teeth, trying to find the delicate balance between obeying the prince and telling him he was an idiot. If they left now, they'd leave with only bruises to Daniel's ego. Any longer, they'd find themselves with a lot more wounds to lick.

"Fine. Two minutes. If you can't get him, just kill a guard." Michael reached for Daniel's arm. "But promise me, Daniel. Promise me you won't tell them who you are." The last thing they needed was a bloodthirsty king certain about whom to kill.

"I promise." Daniel tugged his coat into place and stretched his neck from side to side. They climbed the stairs, and Michael reached for the doorknob, counting down with his other hand.

Before they could move, the doors flew open. A group of guards stood in the entry. They were surprised to see Michael and Daniel loose, but quickly they pointed their swords toward them. Outnumbered and unarmed, Michael raised his hands above his head. Daniel discreetly tucked the dagger into his belt and raised his hands also. With swords against their backs, the guards led them through the palace.

The palace was old. Everything was faded—the walls, the curtains, the portraits. Brown ivy clung to the exterior and tried to climb inside. Candle ends offered a small amount of light in the rusted sconces above them. It flickered with the draft from deep within the castle that filled the air with a dank smell.

The guards stopped at a door and opened it. King Herrick sat on his throne, flanked by two guards on each side. They held their weapons at ready. King Herrick's sword waited in its sheath at his waist. He held up a hand, stopping the guards while Michael and Daniel were still well out of his reach. "Which one of you is the prince?"

Daniel still had the dagger. If Michael could keep the king's attention on him, then Prince Daniel could lunge forward.

"And which one of you is the king?" Michael asked. "It's hard to tell when you're all crawling with fleas."

The guard behind him knocked the back of his head with the hilt of his sword, making Michael's vision spin.

King Herrick kept his gaze on Michael as he spoke. "Give me the prince and the companion goes free. Only one of you need die."

Neither one responded.

King Herrick looked between his guards with a smile like they shared a joke. "Which is worse, a coward or a fool? One man too afraid to die alone, the other a fool who will follow his prince even to the grave."

Michael wasn't a coward. He was loyal. A tyrant king like Herrick wouldn't know the difference. Regardless, Michael made sure to hide his discomfort.

"Die as a king, and I'll see your body returned to your people," Herrick offered. "If not, you'll rot away in a peasant's grave, soon forgotten and forever unknown."

Daniel adjusted slightly, pride pierced by the king's careful words. Michael resisted looking at him, hoping Daniel remained expressionless.

"We bring an alliance," Michael said. "Included in the treaty is shares of water."

Moving only their eyes, the guards behind King Herrick looked at each other. Michael made no reply, but noted their change. When Prince Daniel did lunge forward with the dagger, the guards might choose to defend their king slowly, after his heart had been pierced.

"Liar," King Herrick whispered. "This alliance is nothing more than a scheme to destroy my kingdom. It's the same ploy Josiah presented twenty years ago. My kingdom won't be fooled again."

King Herrick must have seen the confusion Michael tried to hide, because his eyes twinkled. "Oh, then there's a lot you don't know." He stood up and stepped closer. "Are you the prince? Come with me. I'll tell you all your grandfather's secrets."

Michael spat in Herrick's face.

King Herrick wiped his cheek. "There are ways of making men speak. Let me tell you my favorites." The guard behind Michael kicked the back of his legs, forcing him to kneel. The chain around Michael's neck fell from his shirt. His mother's ring twisted slowly in front of his face.

King Herrick watched it for a long time, hypnotized. Then he spoke. "It's unfortunate this alliance is but a farce. My people need this." He returned to his throne. "I have no son, no heir to take my crown." He looked between Michael and Daniel, teeth showing through his smile like fangs. "My people need a lot more than water. They need a king."

Daniel turned to Michael with excited eyes that tried to communicate his idea. Whatever it was, it was stupid. Michael knew that already.

Prince Daniel stood up taller. "Let us seal this alliance, combine our lands, and your people will come under the rule of the king of Saunder."

King Herrick raised a brow. "Then the alliance is real?"

"I swear on my life," Prince Daniel said.

King Herrick leaned forward with a poisonous whisper. "I won't seal an alliance with a boy too afraid to speak to me king to king."

Prince Daniel extended his hand, showing the ring. "I am Prince Daniel, grandson to King Josiah, and heir to the crown of Saunder."

The guards moved their swords closer.

"He's lying," Michael said in a weak attempt to protect him. The guards looked to their king and shifted their swords to Michael.

"This charade is over," Daniel ordered.

Michael closed his mouth and hoped that Daniel was bluffing.

Maybe, just maybe, when the guards removed their weapons, he'd reach for his dagger and kill the king.

"I recently received the requirements to earn the throne," Daniel said. "I have come to defeat an enemy, not by shedding blood, but by sealing an alliance."

"How wise. You, sir, will long be heralded as one of Saunder's greatest kings." Herrick motioned to his guards. They took another step back and returned their swords to their sheaths. With a smile, he stepped toward Michael, close enough for Michael to kill him if had been holding the dagger.

"And you are?"

Prince Daniel answered for him. "This is Michael, Captain of the Guard."

King Herrick raised a brow. "Impressive title for someone so young. You can't be much more than, what, twenty?" He reached for Michael's necklace. "What's so special about you, I wonder, to earn such a position?"

Michael was an expert swordsman, a brave soldier, a respected leader, and he was clever, clever enough to not be fooled by Herrick. He remained silent.

"The king found pity on him," Prince Daniel replied. "He's nothing but the orphan son of a peasant woman."

"When did she die?" King Herrick asked.

When Michael didn't reply, King Herrick pulled on the chain.

"When did she die?" he hollered.

"I was a child," Michael replied, only because he didn't want the chain to break.

"Ah," King Herrick said. "And your father was?"

"Absent." Michael didn't know anything about his father. Even if he did, he wouldn't tell Herrick. Herrick had found the prince. The shift of his attention to Michael was disconcerting.

"Probably a thief or a drunkard," Daniel muttered.

King Herrick studied Michael for a moment then turned back to Daniel. "Your companion plays a convincing king. Be wary of him.

Like blood, once those words of power touch your lips, the thirst is impossible to resist."

"Like blood, I have no thirst for power. I only act to protect my prince," Michael said. He looked to Prince Daniel, making sure he heard the words.

"Your loyalty is admirable." King Herrick smiled at Michael. "But I'd wager you would drink from that cup if that was what was required to save your prince, or better, your kingdom."

Michael made no reply, unsure of what response was correct. Would he never take the crown? Or would he do whatever was required to protect his prince?

King Herrick turned back to the prince. "You'll have to forgive the rude welcome you received from my guards. We are unaccustomed to visitors, especially friendly ones." He pointed to a chair beside the throne. "Come, sit."

Michael remained standing, guards' swords still pointed into his back.

A maid emerged from the shadows with two cups and a teapot. She placed them on the table. A raised scar on the inside of her wrist caught Michael's eye.

"P," King Herrick said when he saw Michael looking. "For purchased. I mark my slaves with a hot iron." He crushed bright green leaves and dropped the powder into his pot. "Then everyone knows they're mine."

"Yes," Michael said slowly, "I'm familiar with branding. We use it for our cattle." The thought of burning human flesh left a foul taste in his mouth.

The maid poured the tea and left quickly. Prince Daniel pulled the treaty from his pocket and passed it to the king. King Herrick sliced the seal and read through it carefully.

"These terms will save my land. You promise food, water, and the aid of your armies." He tapped his fingers against the table. "But years ago, Josiah made other promises, and I expect those to be met as well." With a wave of his hand, a guard left. He returned with a yellowed paper. King Herrick passed it to Prince Daniel.

Michael leaned forward and tried to read over his shoulder, elbowing against the guards who held him back.

"The prince of Saunder must marry the princess of Barlow," King Herrick said while Daniel read. "Josiah promised this."

"Certainly," Daniel replied.

"You might want to meet her first," Michael warned. "She could be mighty ugly."

King Herrick glared at Michael, but continued. "Before she becomes queen, she, too, must defeat an enemy and complete a challenge. As an honest man, I'll hold her to the same challenge Josiah set forth twenty years ago. The princess of Barlow must fill the canyon that divides our lands."

Michael shook his head. "That's impossible. She'll never be queen, and the alliance will never be sealed."

King Herrick raised his eyebrows and looked to the prince. "I had thought to converse with a king. Instead I speak with your nursemaid."

Prince Daniel glowered at Michael. "He's tired from our travels. Perhaps there's a place where he can rest."

King Herrick motioned to his guards. The guard held up a rope and waited for Michael's wrists.

"Your Highness," Michael pleaded to Daniel as the guard tied his hands together.

But neither King Herrick nor Prince Daniel offered any other order. The guards pulled Michael toward the door.

"When you're done with him," King Herrick called, "wake Mrs. Wilde. Tell her to assist the princess in dressing to meet our prince."

"Your Majesty?" the guard asked. His Adam's apple bobbed up and down.

"I believe she's still in the kitchen," King Herrick said slowly, "where you left her before our guest arrived."

The guard whispered something to the other, who shook his head fearfully. Then they left, dragging Michael behind them.

MICHAEL WAS GETTING REAL TIRED OF BEING DRAGGED AROUND BY unpolished guards. They couldn't tie a decent knot, and they didn't even stand up straight in their suits. He only found one of those particularly annoying. The other was an advantage. He twisted his hands free from the knot and walked with the guards until they stopped him in front of a door.

"Listen," Michael said when they opened the door, "you let me go, and I can make it well worth your time."

"What you got?" the guard asked.

Michael took the moment to lift his foot between the guard's legs and drive his elbow into his face as he fell forward. He grabbed the guard's sword and turned it toward the other. "Have a seat."

Both guards sank down. Michael tied their hands together. "Now you just lay there nice and easy. Try not to make too much noise. I'm gonna sleep for a bit." Michael took off his coat and laid it on the stone floor across from the guards. There wasn't much he could do right now. He might as well rest. Michael crawled onto his coat, cursing his headache, cursing the prince, and cursing the entire kingdom of Barlow. Once he left, he'd never return.

Michael awoke with the sunrise. He rubbed the sleep from his eyes and tried to ease away his headache. He inspected the guards tied up in the corner and nodded his approval of their miserable-looking condition.

"You wait here," he said. "I'm going to go get some breakfast." Whistling, he left. While he was out, he was going to learn as much as he could about Barlow.

CHAPTER 9

*L*iviya remained tucked in the cellar for hours. Her throat was raw from screaming. She hated the feeling of panic swelling in her chest. King Herrick wouldn't keep her in there forever. At least she hoped he wouldn't.

Finally, Liviya heard footsteps. Someone rattled the knobs above her and unlocked the chain. Liviya leapt out of her dungeon, barreling toward the doors open ahead of her. She sank to her knees, the hysteria threatening to return even though she was free.

A guard stood at the doors with Mrs. Wilde, who wrung a handkerchief between her hands. She looked nauseated, face pale and eyes wide. She wrapped Liviya in a hug, not speaking. The guards grunted and led them back inside.

The sun had long since set. Unlike the quiet earlier, the entire palace was awake. Maids rushed into the kitchen. Others hurried through the halls with clean linens. Everybody whispered. The guards led Liviya and Mrs. Wilde up the stairs and down the hall. They stopped at the door with the jeweled handle and let Mrs. Wilde and Liviya inside.

"What's happening?" Liviya asked when they were alone.

Mrs. Wilde explained things slowly, like she didn't quite understand. "Saunder has come for an alliance. Our princess will marry their prince."

Liviya looked to the portrait and the smiling princess. "Has she returned?"

Mrs. Wilde shook her head. "No. King Herrick is playing a game. He has decided that you will be the princess."

Head spinning, Liviya stepped back until she touched the wall. She hadn't been saved at all. She was simply sentenced to die another day and in another place, after King Herrick had used her to gain whatever he thought this lie would give him.

Mrs. Wilde looked from Liviya's eyes to her feet and back again. She offered a weak but optimistic smile. "Well, you can't wear that. And you'll need a bath." She pulled the tattered dress over Liviya's head and pushed her toward the tub that maids had already filled with hot water.

When she stepped in, dirt clouded the water. Drops splashed over the side, splattering the floor.

Mrs. Wilde remained silent. Her brow was deeply furrowed. Liviya felt the same tension pulling at her own eyes. Without warning, Mrs. Wilde dunked Liviya's head under the water. Liviya surfaced with a cough. Suds stung her eyes.

Stepping from the bathtub, Liviya wrapped a towel around her shoulders and walked toward the fire, leaving a trail of wet footprints across the stone floor. She slipped a chemise over her head and sat in a chair.

Mrs. Wilde stood behind Liviya and brushed her hair. The comb caught painfully on the knots where King Herrick had pulled her hair. Liviya kept her complaints to small whimpers. She had brought this on herself.

When the comb moved smoothly through Liviya's hair, Mrs. Wilde set it aside and began pinning pieces of Liviya's hair to her scalp in a painstakingly slow manner. Finally, all her hair was piled on her head. Mrs. Wilde stretched her aged fingers with a tired sigh.

A deep green gown waited on the bed. Mrs. Wilde lifted it over Liviya's head and laced the back with more force than Liviya thought possible from an old woman. Each pull pressed more air from Liviya's lungs and threatened to break her bones. The long sleeves extended to the middle of her hand, covering the scar on her wrist. No matter how Mrs. Wilde tried to dress her up, she had been marked as a slave. Nobody would truly believe she was anything else.

When her work was done, Mrs. Wilde wiped her brow. "The king is waiting to introduce you at breakfast. The guards are busy downstairs. The maids are in the kitchen. You can still escape." She smiled sadly, but there wasn't time for goodbyes. "Good luck, my dear."

As soon as Mrs. Wilde left, Liviya reached behind her back and untied the laces. She needed to escape. Quickly. Stepping out of the gown, she reached for her old dress and cloak. She pulled the hood over her carefully combed hair. Remembering the coins, Liviya grabbed a handful. By the time King Herrick saw it was missing, she'd be gone. With quiet steps, she crossed the room and pulled open the door. Then she ran.

Outside, Liviya walked along the side wall of the palace grounds, watching for a hole in the ground large enough for her to crawl through. When she found one, she lowered herself to her hands and knees and slipped through.

In the village, a different world welcomed her. The rising sun burned through the fog. The excitement burned through the despair. Change was coming. Even nature knew today was different and treated the people to a hint of spring. The people spread the news that Liviya had already heard. "Saunder is coming. They want an alliance."

Liviya heard new information. "Saunder will share the water." But there were things they didn't know. They whispered about them carefully. *What princess? Who is marrying the prince? Who is saving us?*

Nobody. There was no princess. Liviya was leaving. There would be no alliance. There would be no water. Liviya pulled the hood closer and hid her face.

Carts overflowed the city square, parking wherever they found a space large enough. Eager salesmen yelled at those passing by. Liviya pulled away from their clutches and ignored their cries. She passed woven baskets, hanging meat, gleaming jewels, and pens of live animals. She fought through the crowd, looking up only often enough to search the area for any guards that might recognize her. Up ahead, Liviya saw the hanging herbs of the apothecary. Her feet moved themselves toward him until she stood at his cart. Bicka was dead, but other girls would get sick, too.

Liviya slammed the coins on his cart, much more than he needed. "Give me the Ruttamon."

The man reached for herbs from the same bundle that had hung in his shop and ground them in a bowl. He dumped the powder into a pouch. "Boil this in—"

"I remember." Liviya tucked the pouch in her pocket. He slid a single gold coin toward him, leaving the others on the table. Liviya shoved them all toward him. "You take care of the girls in the palace, you hear? Give them all the medicine they need. Food and water, too. Clean water."

"Yes, miss," the apothecary said meekly. "I'll keep them alive and well."

Liviya smiled beneath her hood, enjoying the sweet taste of power for the first time.

Behind her, several guards jogged past in a single line, swords jangling and boots clapping against the ground. Liviya froze and waited till they passed. More approached from the other direction, fanning themselves out. Once again, Liviya found herself surrounded by the king's guards. They couldn't be looking for her. Mrs. Wilde was keeping them distracted. But the fear still ate at her. She stepped away from the cart and hid in the largest crowd she could find.

The crowd erupted into cheers. In the center, a magician disappeared into a cloud of smoke, only to appear again on the other side of his table. The people gasped. Liviya pushed between their shoulders, desperate to be entirely hidden. In the tight swarm, she remained on the outside. The magician held out a closed fist. When he opened it, a yellow bird escaped, wings raising it to the sky. With another puff of smoke, there were two birds. Now they were blue. The birds landed on his table.

The magician rubbed his hands together, blew away the magic, and disappeared in another cloud of smoke. Whatever magic he used, Liviya wished she possessed it also so she could disappear and never be seen.

Liviya fought to move forward again. A man in front of her peered around at the guards and then at Liviya. He smiled, like he somehow knew she was hiding and found it entertaining. He was obviously no lover of King Herrick's guards, either, because he stepped back and allowed Liviya to take his spot. With a breath of relief, Liviya moved forward, remaining close enough to hide in the cover of the man's broad shoulders. She looked at each of the guards, relieved to find that none had spotted her.

"I've learned his secret," the man said. Dark hair curled around his ears. His long white sleeves were rolled to his elbows.

Liviya lifted her hood just enough to look at him.

His dark eyes held a gleam. "I'll tell you," he offered, "but you'll owe me a dance."

Liviya pretended she didn't hear him, but the heat rising in her cheeks confessed that she had.

"I'm Michael," he said.

"Liviya." A puff of smoke dissipated in the chilly air. The crowd screamed.

Michael cocked his ear toward her. "Livvy?"

"Liv-ee-ya," she said impatiently.

"My apologies, Miss Livvy."

Liviya turned, exasperated. "I said Liviya."

Michael winked. "I heard you."

Murmuring her annoyance, Liviya pulled the hood tighter around her face. She looked at the guards again, eager to continue her escape.

"Shall I tell you the secret?" Michael asked.

"No, thank you," Liviya replied with plenty of attitude.

Michael's laugh came easily, like he laughed often. That was a rare trait in a place like Barlow. The sound was refreshing. Energizing. It almost made Liviya smile.

"Another time then," he said.

"Never." Mostly because Liviya didn't know how to dance, but also because there would be no other time. She was leaving today. The first pang of homesickness struck, and she had yet to leave.

"Who's next?" the magician asked. He spun his hat up his arm and around his shoulders. "More birds are in here. What color shall we make them?"

The people applauded, but no one delivered a coin.

The magician called again. Michael stepped forward and placed a coin in the man's palm. "A blue bird, and a flower for the lady." He held out his hand toward Liviya.

"A blue bird, and a flower for the lady!" the magician repeated for the crowd. He pulled Liviya to the center where everyone could see her, except for the guards. The magician looked inside his hat. Face somber, he held it up to the crowd and tipped it upside down. Nothing came out. Everyone booed.

Finger to his lips, the magician brought the hat to his ear. "I hear them." He reached in his hat and pulled out a yellow bird, then a red one, followed by green and pink and white.

"Blue!" the people cried. "It's supposed to be blue!"

The birds flew in a circle above the crowd, then perched on the table in a line. The magician set his hat on the table upside down. One by one the birds hopped onto the rim, turned blue, then hopped inside.

The people applauded and cheered.

Liviya waited, trying to look unimpressed even though she marveled. "And the flower?"

The magician pointed to Michael who held out a flower. When Liviya reached for it, he closed his palm. With a smile he opened his fingers, revealing a gold coin. "A coin to play again," he said.

Liviya stared at the coin. Pure gold. It was her need for gold that had led to her arrest. It was another reminder of life's cruelties.

Things would be entirely different if only she had met Michael yesterday.

"What's your wish?" the magician asked.

The rest of the crowd waited eagerly.

Her wishes were simple. Food. Water. Freedom from Herrick's tyranny. But those things couldn't be bought with a single gold coin, and they certainly weren't in the magician's hat. Even if the alliance were real, it wouldn't free her land. Saunder could send all the water they wanted, but Herrick wouldn't put it in the people's hands.

Staring at the gold coin reflecting the rarely seen sun, another thought began to form. Maybe she could go to Saunder and survive just long enough for the lost prince to return to Barlow and claim the throne. He could march with an army, kill Herrick, reign in his place, and save them all. Liviya knew that eventually Saunder would discover her lie and then she'd die, but many others would die as well if she didn't at least try.

The guards ordered a shout and jogged away to different posts. Liviya watched them, relieved. She turned back to find Michael watching her.

"Do you need help with something, Miss Liviya?" Michael looked around at the guards then peered underneath her hood.

Liviya looked into his eyes. He appeared to be sincere. Part of her wanted to tell him her story, but how could she explain her situation and what help could this stranger offer?

"I'm just late returning home." She held the coin back toward Michael.

"Keep it," Michael said. "You might need a little magic some day."

Liviya tucked the coin in his shirt pocket. "I don't believe in magic. I've got to go now." She took a few steps.

"Liviya," Michael called.

She turned back. He reached into his pocket and pulled out a flower. With a smile, he handed it to her. Liviya brought it to her nose. "Thank you, Michael."

Michael tipped an imaginary hat. "It was my pleasure."

CHAPTER 10

*L*iviya raced back to the princess' room. No. It was her room now. Her heart pounded as she took off her old dress and stepped back into the green gown.

Mrs. Wilde's voice sounded down the hall along with the heavy thump of a guard's boots. "She was here just a moment ago. Must have snuck out the window. It was wide open."

Liviya pulled the laces as tight as she could and sat in a chair to hide the open back of her gown.

Mrs. Wilde opened the door. Her eyes widened.

Liviya offered her most innocent smile. "Just stepped out for air."

The guard seemed annoyed to have been dragged away from his post for nothing. "Get downstairs. The prince is ready." He shut the door behind him.

"Why are you still here?" Mrs. Wilde asked.

"I'm going to do it," Liviya said. "I'm going to play the princess."

Mrs. Wilde shook her head. "The prince will know you're lying. He'll kill you."

"Probably," Liviya replied. She leaned forward with a whisper. "But they'll send us water. Maybe we can survive until the rightful prince returns." Liviya stared at the old housekeeper, the friend with whom she had disagreed with so many times over the years.

Mrs. Wilde's face softened.

"I'll die anyway," Liviya argued. "At least let me die warm, well-fed, and trying to save the others.

Mrs. Wilde threw her hands to the heavens. "Oh, Liviya." She motioned for Liviya to stand and pulled the laces much tighter than necessary.

Dressed again, Liviya handed Mrs. Wilde the pouch of medicine. "For the next girl who gets sick."

Tears filled the woman's eyes. "I'll tell them you say goodbye. Know that they'll miss you." Sniffling, she pulled Liviya into a hug. Then Mrs. Wilde held her at arm's length and shook her head. "Well, this won't do at all."

"Do I still look like a maid?" Liviya may have been bathed and dressed in silk, but she was still a beggar in disguise.

Mrs. Wilde turned her toward the floor-length mirror that hung from the far wall. "You look scared, Liviya, and that won't do at all." She put her arm around Liviya's waist and stood beside her in front of the mirror. Even with her gray hair piled into a high bun, she didn't reach Liviya's shoulder.

Curls framed Liviya's face. The laced bodice showed a figure that had hidden for years behind a servant's smock. The green in the gown highlighted the honey in her hazel eyes. Staring at her reflection, for the first time, Liviya saw how beautiful she was. She blushed again, realizing Michael must have noticed the same thing.

"If they had asked me who to send, I would have chosen you." Tears glistened in the woman's eyes. "You're capable. That's why I've always been the hardest on you." She pulled Liviya into a tight hug. "Liviya, stay alive. Then come back and save us all."

Mrs. Wilde took Liviya's arm and led her down the corridor. With each step, her heart beat louder. They paused in the doorway to the dining room.

"That's the prince," Mrs. Wilde said.

A man sat across King Herrick at the table. A blue ribbon secured his blond hair at the nape of his neck. He was handsome with bright blue eyes that Liviya could see from across the room. He chatted with King Herrick as if they were old friends, one ankle crossed over his other knee.

Liviya inhaled slowly and walked through the door. The room was large with dark red walls trimmed in gold. It was the perfect representation of Barlow—citizens' blood and King Herrick's gold.

"Here she is," King Herrick called, rising as she entered.

Liviya sailed across the room and kissed both his cheeks, pretending she always had. She sat in the seat he pulled out for her and rubbed her silk sleeve against her raised scar.

Prince Daniel also rose and bowed. "A pleasure to meet you." He kissed her outstretched hand. "Your father was correct in describing you as his most beautiful possession."

Liviya hid her grimace behind her goblet and glared at King Herrick. *Possession.* How accurate. He had imprinted his possession of her into her skin.

King Herrick returned to his seat and motioned for the maids to fill his plate. He tucked his napkin into the collar of his shirt.

The maids scooped large servings onto Liviya's plates and passed her looks of encouragement. Liviya ate while the men talked, too scared to savor the bites. Still, she ate. She was smart enough to know she needed the food even though her stomach was in knots. King Herrick and the prince spoke about money and wars, water and women. And they spent a great deal of time discussing a ruby and the final requirement.

Prince Daniel shrugged. "Every king who's ever ruled Saunder has been assigned a challenge. It's simply a way to form a legend about me for future generations."

"Ah, yes," King Herrick replied. "Josiah and his legends. They are, after all, the heart of Saunder." He lifted his goblet. "Long live King Daniel." He brought the goblet to his lips, but paused. "Assuming, of course, that nobody steals your crown."

The color drained from Prince Daniel's face. Liviya watched him try to control his temper.

King Herrick smiled. "Oh, yes. I hear the rumors from here. Not all serve you. One leaf blown in the wrong direction will start an uprising. Somewhere, there is a man pumping his bellows in hopes of gaining from your fall." King Herrick dipped his finger in his wine and drew a pattern on the table like he wrote in blood. Three vertical lines inside a circle.

Prince Daniel slammed his fist against the table. Liviya jumped. King Herrick smiled, like he had expected that reaction and approved.

"You only know Saunder from the rule of Josiah, a man so near death he pleads for it in his sleep. When I'm king, my people will serve me."

"I'm certain you'll do what it takes to make it happen," King Herrick said. "When your land is one, you can rule Barlow as well, but not until then. Think of it as. . . a challenge." King Herrick hoisted his goblet again. "Let us share this meal as friends and allies, nay, as family."

Liviya raised her goblet and clinked it against the others, fear making her insides freeze. King Herrick was planning something, probably the destruction of Saunder. That was fine. The kingdom of Saunder could fight in a civil war until the end of time. She didn't care. She just needed someone to fight King Herrick first.

Michael left the magician and continued his exploration of the streets while he waited until an hour when Prince Daniel would be awake.

Outside town, dying men buried the dead in shallow graves. Feral dogs spread waste down the rutted roads. The people were filthy, and oh, the stench. Dead cattle spotted the fields. Scavengers flew in lazy circles with bits of bloody meat hanging from their beaks. The city was filled with dirty, broken people who needed more help than the alliance could provide. Most of the people had accepted this as their fate and waited to die. Except for one. In this kingdom of poverty and need, Michael had found a small ray of light in the eyes of a girl fighting to survive. He hadn't seen her since, but he'd been looking.

Michael reached into his pocket and counted his remaining money. He stopped by the baker for small loaves of bread. He also purchased some dry meat and little bags of nuts. He was smart enough to avoid drinking the water and found a jug of wine instead. A lot of the people were sick with Guernsey Fever. It was a shame. Most countries had eradicated it with basic water hygiene. Barlow was well behind the rest of the world in many areas.

As he walked around the village, Michael spotted the people with the most need and shared what little provisions he had. Hunger was evident in people's eyes. He read the suffering in their spirits. A mother walked, dragging a dirty child behind her. Neither wore shoes. An old man lay on a pile of tattered rags on the side of the street. His bones protruded from his skin. Michael gave the man a roll and the woman and child some nuts.

Across the street, Michael felt an older woman watching him. When he looked closer, he realized she was blind. She sat with a dog covered in pus-oozing sores. Michael sat next to her for a moment.

"Good day, madam." Michael reached for her hand and placed a roll into her palm. She tore it in half and gave a piece to the dog at her feet.

"I'm looking for a girl named Liviya. Do you know her?"

The woman eyed him warily. "Don't much like people asking about Liviya."

"Just want to get some food to her," Michael replied.

The woman reached out her withered hands and touched his face. Michael let her explore his features.

"You're not a guard?" she asked suspiciously.

"No, ma'am," Michael replied. Not a guard of Barlow, at least.

"And you ain't upset with her over anything? Got no orders to take her to the king?"

"No, ma'am," Michael said again, this time with a chuckle.

The woman lowered her hands. "Haven't seen her. Could be she's gotten herself in a mite of trouble." The woman shrugged. "She does that a bit. When she escapes, I'll tell her you was lookin' for her."

Michael reached into his bags and scrawled a note onto some paper. He tucked it into a bag along with some food.

"I won't be around much longer. When you see her, give her this." Michael rose, clasped the woman's hand, and patted the dog on the head.

The woman nodded and began humming. Michael wished her farewell, then returned to the palace.

When he opened the door to his room inside the palace, the waiting guards pulled themselves to sitting. Still bound, they only watched Michael.

A few minutes later, a page knocked on the door and entered, eyes widening when he saw Michael free and the guards bound.

"I'm to escort you to the border where you'll meet your prince," the page stammered. "The king's orders."

"You have new orders," Michael said. "Take me to my prince or I'll slice you into pieces and feed you to the dogs."

The page looked to the bound guards then back to Michael. "He's dining with the king."

Michael rustled the boy's hair. "There's a good lad. I'll follow you." He saluted at the guards in the corner. "Good day, sirs." The guards mumbled a response, which Michael took to be a kind farewell.

AFTER BREAKFAST, KING HERRICK ASKED FOR A PRIVATE MOMENT TO wish his daughter farewell. Prince Daniel offered a warm smile and a bow to the princess, then stepped out of the room, leaving Liviya alone with the king.

Liviya waited until the door was closed. "I won't kill anyone."

The king raised a single eyebrow above his goblet before emptying it in a few noisy gulps.

"And I'm not a spy," she added.

King Herrick scoffed. "I wouldn't trust you to relay the secrets."

"Then what's your game?" Liviya asked.

"We're sealing an alliance," King Herrick said simply. "It was their king who suggested these terms. I'm merely meeting them the best way I'm able."

"Then you'll have me be queen?"

King Herrick nodded. "After you complete your challenge, of course."

Liviya waited for him to explain, not willing to give him the satisfaction of asking what it was.

"Fill the canyon," he said.

"Fill it with what?"

King Herrick shrugged. "Rocks? Water? The bodies of all our dead? You decide. I don't know what the old man wants."

Liviya pondered for a moment. She glanced to the back wall and the mural that depicted the great chasm she had never seen in real life. "They'll know I'm lying."

"Good," King Herrick said, turning back to his food. "Then you'll be tried as a traitor and Josiah will kill you. A fitting end for a thief."

Liviya looked away, determined not to show the king her fear. "Suppose I succeed?"

"If you have any love for your people, you'll pierce Josiah's heart and bring the kingdom of Saunder to its knees."

The fire inside her ignited immediately. "Josiah's not the tyrant. You are."

Herrick reached for her gown and pulled her close to his face. His rant was interrupted by a fit of dry coughing. His skin was pallid, his eyes sunken into his cheeks. Looking around the room, Liviya recognized the Ruttamon leaves near King Herrick's tea kettle.

Liviya was ecstatic. "You have Guernsey Fever." She motioned to the leaves around him. "These won't keep you alive but for a few months. You're dying!"

King Herrick offered a resigned nod. "Yes. But I'll live long enough to see peasant filth rule Saunder." He was strangely calm for someone discussing his impending death. Liviya may have unearthed one clue, but there were more pieces to this puzzle. Herrick took another drink from his teacup. "Maybe I'll even live long enough to watch you come crawling home a failure."

"I will come home," Liviya said, "and I'll kill you myself."

King Herrick reached for her wrist. Squeezing it, he hoisted her off her feet. He poised his lips, ready to spit curses laced with poison. A knock at the door interrupted him.

"I said take him to the border," King Herrick growled.

"You'll have to forgive him," a strangely familiar voice replied. "I didn't want to leave without saying goodbye. Where's my prince?"

The king released Liviya. Rubbing her wrist, she turned toward the door. Michael, the man from the streets, wore a soldier's coat from Saunder. He scanned the first half of the room and stopped when his eyes landed on her. "Liviya?"

Liviya offered a weak smile. "Hello, Michael."

CHAPTER 11

*K*ing Herrick ordered that a carriage take his new allies to the border. If the alliance wasn't a trap to lead them to their death, the carriage certainly was. It creaked and rattled as it rolled to the front of the palace on uneven wheels. Like most of Barlow, it was garbage.

Michael loaded a single trunk of the princess' belongings onto the back of the carriage. Of all the surprises he had been unprepared for in Barlow, this was the most jarring, making him question his intuition. He had watched Liviya in the streets and felt drawn to her. In their brief conversation, he had liked her immediately, yet she was King Herrick's daughter. All of his carefully practiced and well-worded arguments to convince the prince to leave the princess in Barlow left his mind. He stood, stammering like an idiot. There was nothing Michael could do to stop it. The prince wanted her to come, and here she was.

Princess Liviya waited at the top of the stairs outside the palace. She stood in a ray of light. Holding her hand to her eyes, she blocked the sun and gazed at the crowd that had gathered. She seemed surprised at the number of them. Prince Daniel stood with her and offered his arm. The crowd stood still and silent, with the solemnity of a family at a funeral. It was a startling change from their excitement in the streets earlier that morning.

As they began their descent, the people bowed. Every man, woman, and child knelt on the ground and remained down long after they arrived at the carriage and rolled away. Michael had discovered a striking number of differences between Barlow and Saunder, but this was the most profound. The people in Saunder didn't love Prince Daniel like the people in Barlow loved their princess.

In the carriage, Michael sat next to Daniel. Liviya sat across from them. She kept her eyes on the road for the first hour, only looking away when the palace spires were finally hidden behind the haze. Her face was hard to read. Michael wondered if she would have cried had she been alone.

With a groan, Michael shifted against the hard seat. Each breath formed a vibration in his lungs. He felt winded, even though he was only sitting. Next to him, Prince Daniel dozed, lulled to sleep by King Herrick's lies and wine. That made Michael all the more frustrated. He leaned his head against the back of the seat. The miles rolled by slowly. Michael was hot. His throat screamed with every swallow. Even though he tried not to, he stole a look at the princess. A stubborn piece of hair kept falling into her face that she repeatedly tucked behind her ear, where it stayed only until the next bump jarred it loose. She was beautiful. This time, it was not his throat that made it difficult to breathe.

"When will you send the water?" Liviya tugged on her sleeve.

"We're not," Michael replied.

"But the alliance—"

"There is no alliance, Highness." The words came out harsher than Michael had intended. He blamed it on his pounding head. He spoke again, softer this time. "There's only an alliance if you marry the prince. That's unlikely to happen. King Josiah won't let one of Barlow's barbarians into his palace."

"We're not barbarians," Liviya argued. "My people are good people."

Michael scoffed. "What do you know of your people? You sit on a bed of gold while they starve."

Liviya's mouth gaped open. Michael wondered if she was struggling to find the words she wanted to say or if she knew exactly what words she wanted to say and was trying not to say them. Her reply was interrupted by the sound of a harsh whinny and the carriage skidding to a stop. They had reached the border. Their ride in Barlow's wagon was done. Liviya pushed the door open, slamming it against the side of the carriage. She stepped out, shimmying through when her wide dress caught on the door.

"Allow me." Michael reached for her skirt.

Liviya ripped it from his hand and muttered a curse.

Prince Daniel stirred awake. If he was startled to see his princess storming away from the carriage alone, he showed no sign of it. Daniel stepped outside and lifted his face to the sky.

"Look at that sun. It's a good day to be crowned."

Michael looked at the sun. It was bright. It was warm. But there was lightning in Liviya's eyes, the rumbling of thunder in Michael's chest, and ominous clouds following them from Barlow. Yes, the sun was shining, but not for long. A storm was coming. It was coming quickly.

OUTSIDE THE CARRIAGE, THE CANYON AWAITED. IT WAS A LANDMARK Liviya had only seen depicted in murals on the palace walls, but they did little to capture its beauty. The ground became a hole so deep it made her head swim. The walls were lined in layers, each a different shade of brown and green. At the bottom, the river wound through. From the top of the canyon, it was only a blue line. It was the largest body of water Liviya had ever seen. Liviya stared. It was all clean. She had thought that water would soon flow into Barlow. Unfortunately, she'd have to stay alive a lot longer than she thought in order to offer her people any help at all.

Prince Daniel stepped out of the carriage, rubbing his eyes. He walked a few meters away to a group of trees. Michael untied his horses from the back of the carriage. Liviya continued to glare at him. His accusation still stung. She was no barbarian. And she had lived every minute of suffering with her people.

Michael pulled a canteen from his bags. After taking a drink, he splashed some onto his hands and wiped his face.

With the carriage empty, the driver turned back to Barlow, leaving Liviya alone with a strange prince and a man she had met in the streets.

Hardly looking her direction, Michael tossed the canteen to Liviya. "Take a drink. We'll leave in a few minutes."

Liviya opened the canteen and peered inside. She poured the water in her hand in a thin stream. It was perfectly clean.

"I don't have a goblet for you, Highness. You'll have to drink it like that."

His callous words were more sparks on her terribly flammable temper. Liviya had never seen a princess before, but she was quite sure she wasn't being treated like one. She placed a hand on her hip. "The introductions happened so quickly, you'll have to forgive my confusion. Are you the king, or are you a common man?"

"I think that's obvious," Michael snapped.

Liviya had hoped to offend him. She was pleased to see how much it did. "You speak like you outrank me. I feared I had mistaken who you were." She flicked water in his face. "Allow me to remind you that I'm a princess. I demand respect."

Michael raised his eyebrows. "You're not my princess. Until you complete the requirements, you have no power here. Now get on your horse. Let's go."

Even dressed in fine silk, with jewels in her hair and a crown on her head, she was powerless. Liviya indulged in the disappointment for a small moment, then made a decision. She may not have as much power as she would have liked, but she still had some power.

Liviya straightened her crown and lifted her chin in what Mrs. Wilde always called defiance. "No."

"No what?" Michael asked

"I'm not getting on the horse."

Michael's eyes darkened. "So help me, Highness, you'll get on that horse or I'll hoist you up there and tie you to its back."

Liviya saw his bluff immediately. This was the same man who gave her a flower and teased her in the streets. He may have been in a foul mood, but he was no threat to her. She held out her wrists in an invitation.

Michael muttered his annoyance. Like she expected, he had no response.

Prince Daniel returned from the trees. He clapped his hands. "Let's go!"

"I've got a terrible fear of horses," Liviya said. "I'd much rather walk."

Prince Daniel paused and turned questioning eyes to Michael, who stared in disbelief.

"This horse is real nice," Prince Daniel said, gently patting its neck.

Liviya looked at the horse and clicked her tongue apologetically. "It's a terrible fear."

Prince Daniel struggled to keep a smile. In fact, he looked quite annoyed. He shifted his eyes to Michael.

"She doesn't want to go," Michael said. "Let her walk back to Barlow."

Prince Daniel shook his head. "King Herrick wants her in Saunder."

"You don't have time to walk her all the way back to the palace," Michael replied. "Your challenge is waiting."

Prince Daniel stood up and dusted off the seat of his pants. "You're right. I need to get home. Michael, walk with her and keep her safe."

Michael rubbed his face with his hand. He hated the idea. That was clear from his expression. But he said nothing. He was very obedient. Mrs. Wilde would have loved him.

The prince left with one of the horses. When he left, a cloud hid the sun, blanketing the mountain in a cool gray.

Liviya walked to the edge of the canyon and peered inside. The sight made her stomach heave. The canyon would never be filled. But it wouldn't hurt to try. She picked up a small rock at her feet and hurled it into the abyss. She watched it bounce against the edges until it disappeared, leaving the canyon just as empty. Another rock lay at her feet, a bigger one this time. She threw it with so much force it pulled her forward.

"You're scared all right, but not of horses," Michael said, voice heavy with the accusation. "You don't want to stand before my king."

Liviya crossed her arms. "I'm not scared of any king." She had stood before King Herrick. There was nobody in the world as cruel as him. Despite her courage, her heart pounded. She wasn't afraid of being punished, even if it was death. There was a deeper fear inside her, something she hoped for and hoped against with equal energy. What if they never knew about the lie? What if she truly became queen of Saunder? What if she never saw her home again?

"This way." Michael pointed to the overgrown path. He led the horse. Liviya followed behind.

"I'm sorry," he said after the first few steps.

Liviya looked into his eyes to gauge his sincerity. He didn't look at all apologetic. Instead, his eyes twinkled. "I'm sorry I asked you to dance. I had no idea you were so difficult."

Liviya hated him, she decided. Her cheeks pulled into a smile, a smile she was glad he couldn't see. She kept walking. The kingdom of Saunder was waiting. The people of Barlow needed her there.

CHAPTER 12

he mountain was dark, the path lit only by stars and a sliver of moon. Crickets chirped in the bushes. In the distance, coyotes howled. The crisp air carried the scent of a cool night and the princess' perfume.

Liviya walked mile after mile without complaint, without hardly a word spoken at all. They stopped alongside the river to let the horse drink. Michael was exhausted and annoyed. He should have been home by now. In fact, he never should have left. Every few steps he offered an invitation to ride the horse. Liviya refused each time. He tried threats. She ignored them. He even tried gentle encouragement in case she truly was scared of horses. But nothing. Liviya was the most stubborn girl he had met in his life. In the back of his mind, he wondered if a sincere apology would convince her to ride the horse. Michael straightened his shoulders and kept walking. He couldn't speak the words. That left him walking alongside the road wondering if he were the more stubborn one.

Liviya looked up and caught him looking at her.

"Could be that we'd be there by now," Michael said.

"You can ride," Liviya offered.

Michael rolled his eyes. The prince ordered him to escort her home. Leaving her alone on the mountain was not an option. He continued walking, kicking the stones as he passed, lost in his thoughts.

With the snow mostly gone, Michael recognized the area as the place he had found Jacob in the storm not too many days ago. The land held no signs of its earlier tempest, but there were more changes to his world. Now Michael had refused a crown that wasn't his, sealed an alliance that would keep his kingdom at war, and traveled home with a princess who would marry his prince.

At the sound of a horse's hooves, Michael looked up the trail. A shadow moved alongside the trees.

"Hello," a voice called. It was Geoffrey. He pushed his horse into a trot and pulled him to a stop beside the weary travelers.

Geoffrey looked around. "Well now, isn't this where I found you last time? How come I have to keep dragging you off a mountain?"

Michael liked to think that he had outgrown the need for Geoffrey. Obviously, he was wrong. No matter how hard he tried, Michael kept finding problems that he couldn't solve alone.

"We've been waiting for you. Daniel arrived hours ago."

"She wouldn't get on the horse," Michael replied. "Said she's afraid."

Geoffrey held up his lantern until the light showed on Liviya's face. The hem of her dress was muddy. Her shoes were entirely caked in mud, as if she had intentionally stepped in every puddle along the way.

Geoffrey arched an eyebrow. "So, the rumors are true. Michael brought home a princess."

"This is Daniel's princess, and if he had any sense, he'd march her right back home before the king finds out."

Liviya kicked flecks of mud at Michael. He resisted the urge to throw her into the river.

"Oh, he knows already," Geoffrey said. "Been stewing about it all evening."

"And the people?" Michael asked.

Geoffrey chuckled. "Every hired hand in the palace left to spread the word the minute the prince arrived with the announcement. The whole city is lined up to greet her."

Michael narrowed his eyes. "What do you mean by 'greet'?"

"Protest," Geoffrey replied, matter-of-factly, which was what Michael had guessed. "There were rumors circulating that she had killed you. Others thought you ran away with her." He nudged his elbow at Liviya, who wrinkled her nose.

Michael shifted his weight in the mud. This alliance was turning into a bigger disaster than he had thought. "Will the guards be there to escort us inside?"

"Well, I don't know where the guards are, Michael," Geoffrey said. "The king sent me to fetch you, like you're some wayward child." He rubbed his nose, leaving Michael suspicious that Geoffrey thought the very same thing.

Liviya blew stray hairs out of her face. A streak of mud lined her cheek. She looked tired, but she didn't look remotely close to giving up, nor did she look scared. "When are we leaving?"

Michael threw his hands into the air. Now she was eager to be at the palace? The horse pawed nervously in the dirt. Michael's head pounded with every beat of his heart. He pressed his hand to his head to ease the pressure.

"Whenever you give the order, Your Highness," Geoffrey said with a bow. He held out his arm. "Allow me to offer you a ride."

Liviya lifted her skirts well above her knees, then grabbed Geoffrey's arm. He gently lifted her onto the back of the horse. Michael fought a smile as they trotted away. Liviya was so unlike any woman he had ever met. He'd never admit this to anyone, but he liked her. He liked her a lot.

THE HORSES LEANED FORWARD AS THEY CARRIED THEIR RIDERS UP THE hill that housed the palace. In the distance, navy flags waved a welcome in the dark night. Guards stood at perfect attention at their posts on the wall. In the black, the palace appeared. The spires on each end stretched into the sky. Despite the late hour, lights showed from every window. People spilled from the palace into the city square and lined the road.

At the palace steps, they gathered in a frenzied herd, hurling rocks and spoiled food. They held torches and screamed angry epithets that made Liviya cringe. Michael, however, wasn't surprised. Had anyone else arrived with a princess from Barlow, he might have been in the same crowd himself. The horses fought against the command to ride forward, stepping side-to-side and shaking the reins. Michael dismounted and moved to help Liviya, but she had already slid off the back of Geoffrey's horse and moved to the other side where the horse would offer some protection.

"You ready to go home?" Michael shouted over the crowd.

Liviya shook her head and shouted a reply he couldn't hear.

Michael handed the reins to the stable boy. "Take these horses around back."

From somewhere deep in the crowd, someone threw food so rotten Michael couldn't identify it. It splattered against the side of the horse and sprayed into Michael's face. Michael slowly brought his hand up and wiped the waste from his lips. He turned around slowly, all of the day's annoyances bubbling to dangerous anger.

He stepped forward into the crowd, shaking his head slightly. These people were angry about the alliance, and he was, too. But Michael wasn't their enemy. He fought wars for these people. He played with their children in the streets, plowed fields with their fathers, and nearly died saving their boys from the mountains. These people might be angry, but he wouldn't let them throw garbage at him. Not when he was following orders. Besides, the sooner they got her to the king, the sooner King Josiah would send her home and they could be free of her.

Michael stared into the crowd. Most of the people fell silent. The things in their hands dropped to the ground. They looked away in shame or offered apologetic glances. Except one. One boy still held a rock over his head. His jaw was tight and eyes dark.

Michael met his stare. "So help me, William, put that down and let us pass or I'll lock you in the dungeon and leave you there until you dig your way out or die."

William lowered the rock but still clenched it in his fist. Michael cocked his head slightly. William bit his lip. Those nearest him murmured their advice, tugging discreetly at his sleeve. Michael took a step forward, and William dropped the rock.

Michael smiled. "There's a good lad." He offered his arm to a wide-eyed Liviya, who, for the first time, accepted it. Despite his spinning head, he noted how comfortable it felt. He found himself wondering what would have happened if they had met under different circumstances and what it would be like to escort the princess into a palace that was his. But he shook that thought away. The crown belonged to Daniel. Liviya belonged to Daniel.

The crowd parted as they walked through. They didn't bow like the crowd had in Barlow, and he didn't expect them to, nor would he ever ask it. His only request was to get Liviya to the palace in peace.

Michael led Liviya up the stairs leading to the palace entrance. The guards heaved open the heavy, wooden doors. They stood up straight. If they had any opinions about the princess entering the palace, they didn't show it on their faces. Michael praised them with a curt nod of approval. The lights were all on inside. The king was probably awake. They could finish this mess this evening.

Michael adjusted his collar and smiled at Liviya who looked a lot less nervous than he felt. "Shall we?"

～

THE PALACE OF SAUNDER MADE BARLOW'S PALACE LOOK LIKE A peasant's cottage. The spires were so tall, even craning her neck all the way back, Liviya couldn't see the top. Early spring flowers sprang from around the palace, dotting the world with color, even though the sky was dark. They winked encouragement at her.

She stepped into the palace behind Michael. Prince Daniel sat in a chair. He leaned his head on his hand. "It's about time," he said when they entered. "Been waiting here for hours."

"Thankfully the princess overcame her fear of horses a few miles in. Otherwise you would have been sitting there for days." Michael looked around for the king. "Is he mad?"

"What do you think?" Daniel snapped. He shifted his weight against the wooden chair. "I told him this was all your stupid idea. We should have just attacked. This whole ordeal would have been over by now, and I'd be celebrating my crown."

Liviya's stomach lurched, like it had been sliced through with a sword in a battle she didn't know had come so close to happening.

"You still have to complete your challenge," Michael said, unperturbed by the prince's outburst. "Besides, without an alliance, you'd never have met your princess." He winked at her. "She's delightful, I must say."

Liviya ignored the heavy sarcasm in Michael's voice and spun in a slow circle, admiring the palace splendor. It was full of wealth and riches she had only ever dreamed of. Padded furniture filled the room, colorful tapestries covered the walls. Everything was clean. A fire roared in the hearth. As she spun, she caught sight of a man waiting in the corner. He cleared his throat. Michael and Daniel fell silent.

The old man sat in a simple chair. He wore his night clothes. Bare feet stuck out of the end of the blanket that covered his lap. A gnarled scar ran up his leg. Despite his plain appearance, something about his presence identified him as the king.

"Your Majesty." Michael and Daniel bowed. Behind them, Liviya sank into a curtsy. Either the king couldn't see her or didn't care to look at her. She rose slowly and took a step back.

King Josiah turned his gaze to Michael. "An alliance? What in the blazes gave you that terrible idea?" The king's voice was weak, but he spoke with an unmistakable power far more fearful than anything Herrick had ever screamed.

"I thought—" Michael began

"You thought I was confused," the king said.

"I'm sorry." Michael dropped his gaze. "I'll make things right."

The king's eyes turned to ice. "No, you won't. You've made that very clear on multiple occasions."

Liviya didn't know what they were talking about, but whatever it was, Michael didn't like the reminder.

"Now, as for this alliance nonsense, let me say this twice so my words won't be brushed away." The king looked slowly from one man to the next. "Barlow is an enemy, this alliance is nulled, and you will never step foot there again."

"Yes, Your Majesty," Michael replied with a small nod.

"Is it clear?" the king said again.

Michael wavered slightly before answering again. "Yes, Your Majesty. I understand."

"Good. Now get that girl out of my land."

After only a few moments in Saunder's palace, Liviya's adventure as a princess ended. Angry tears threatened to pool in her eyes, but she forced them away. She knew before she tried this that it wouldn't really work. She wouldn't waste any tears on such a far-fetched plan.

"I have the horses ready," Michael said. "I'll take her back home immediately."

"Don't bother," Liviya snapped. "Nothing has changed. I'd rather walk."

Liviya was hoping for some angry remark, but Michael only nodded. This made Liviya even angrier. She should have run away in Barlow when she had the chance. Now she was being sent home. Just like King Herrick had predicted, she would go crawling home a failure.

She took a few steps toward the door, before whirling around with one last jab. "You're a coward to bring me all the way here just to make your king send me home. If you knew he'd say no, you should have saved us both a miserable journey. Furthermore," she added, emphasizing each syllable, "you didn't think me so threatening on the streets when you asked me to dance!"

The king held up his hand, interrupting Michael's reply. "You met him on the streets?"

Liviya nodded.

"And he asked you to dance?"

Liviya nodded again.

"I didn't know she was the princess," Michael said quickly. "She was dressed like a peasant." He turned to Liviya. "What were you doing, anyway?"

The king looked at Liviya, waiting for an answer to Michael's question. There was something in his face that made Liviya certain he wasn't interested in a lie.

"I was running away. But I came back," she added quickly, "because I wanted this alliance. And if coming here and marrying the prince is what saves my people, well, that's a small sacrifice to make."

The king pursed his lower lip and nodded slowly, looking toward Michael.

"Besides," she added, with the hope it would irritate Michael, "I heard the prince was handsome."

The king chuckled, all the intensity from earlier melting into a goofy grin. Serious again, he said, "You were sent by your king."

"Yes, Your Majesty," she replied.

"Last time there were two. Are you the princess of Barlow or are you the one he wants to be queen?"

Moving only her eyes, Liviya looked to Michael for help. Michael shrugged and shot her a look that said he wasn't interested in helping her.

"My name is Liviya," she said, hoping that would adequately answer his question.

He studied her with a gaze that seemed to peer into her soul and read all her secrets. "You understand your challenge?"

"Fill the canyon," Liviya said, even though she didn't have a clue how to do it.

"Fill the canyon," the king repeated. "The divide between our lands. Do this and you'll become queen of Saunder. Then we will seal an alliance with your people and send them water."

"Yes, Your Majesty," Liviya said again with a smile. She was staying! She would have hugged the old man if he were anyone other than the king. After years of misery, her people had hope for survival. The chance of success was slight, she knew that, but at least it was there.

The king returned her smile. "Welcome to Saunder, Princess. And, Michael," the king said, "get yourself in bed and stay there."

As if on cue, Michael coughed.

Obeying an unseen signal, a woman rushed from the other room. "Michael! What did you do to this poor thing?" She dusted the mud from Liviya's cheeks and wrapped her in her arms. "Don't let Michael bother you none. He can be such a brute." She shot Michael a look of severe disappointment. "I'm Mrs. Maude. I keep things up 'round here."

Her introduction was interrupted by a crash as a rock flew through the window. Mrs. Maude screamed. Michael and Prince Daniel drew their swords. Liviya froze and watched the rock fall to the ground as if in slow motion. On the flat surface of the rock, someone had crudely painted a symbol—three parallel lines inside a circle. It was the same symbol King Herrick had painted in wine during breakfast with the prince. Daniel's face darkened.

"Guards!" he shouted. "Find him!"

The guards left in a flurry of pounding boots and clanking swords.

"Let's get you to your room," Mrs. Maude said, gently pulling on Liviya's arm. "Chancey!" she hollered. A small maid with bunches of dark hair billowing from her braid appeared. "Clean this up."

Chancey nodded three quick nods. She returned into the corridor, stumbling over the foot of another maid.

As Liviya followed Mrs. Maude, she looked over her shoulder one more time at Michael. He watched her walk away with an expression that was difficult to read. She got the sense that whether he knew it or not, if he wanted her gone, she'd be gone. But here she was. When their eyes met, she offered him a small smile. "Thank you."

Every available guard spent the night trying to find the man who had thrown the rock in the window—everyone except Michael. The king insisted he stay in bed. Michael only protested slightly before going to his room and falling asleep fully clothed on his bed. He slept well into the next morning and awoke feeling considerably better. When he was dressed, he went to get an update on the night's searches.

Prince Daniel had scheduled a meeting with the barons of the land and the top advisors to discuss the rebel group. The maids tiptoed through the corridors. The top advisors whispered to each other in the hall outside the study. Beside the door, the king leaned on Geoffrey's arm. Everyone seemed content to let Michael walk in first. They slowly followed behind him.

When Prince Daniel was angry, the people cowered for days, but not Michael. In all Prince Daniel's unpredictability, one thing was constant; he was loud, but harmless. But this—this was unusual. Today, Prince Daniel remained composed.

"I have but half a land." The words were even and slow, like the heavy drums from an advancing army, and they were equally foreboding. The prince stood up and paced in front of the men, hands folded behind his back. "One leaf blown in the wrong direction will start a rebellion. Someone is pumping his bellows in an attempt to gain from our fall."

Under the table, Michael tapped his foot. Prince Daniel was angry, that was certain, but he was calm. Too calm. Like the few seconds of silence after a flash of lightning before the thunder roared. Michael preferred his screams.

"I want that traitor found and punished," Daniel said.

"We won't find him," Michael replied. Hundreds of people were in the crowd that day, many of whom had rocks. They were only wasting time and money by having the guards search.

Prince Daniel nodded slowly as he considered Michael's words. "He'll pay for that window, even if it means that we take the money from every person in the kingdom."

"Your Highness—" Michael began.

"Fifty tilots each," Prince Daniel said.

One of the barons offered a low whistle.

Michael studied the map of Saunder that covered the far wall. Time had begun to fade the thick lines that marked the boundaries. Other things were also fading in Saunder—morals, leadership, loyalty. The lines on the map could be redrawn. The rest of the things were far more difficult to restore. Without them, the shape of Saunder would change.

Everyone was silent. Some studied their hands or gazed absently across the table. Geoffrey picked at his fingernails. Even the king said nothing. He simply stared at the wall in front of him. Was he even aware what was happening? Among the silent men, Michael didn't speak either. Who was he to disagree with the prince?

"And from whose pockets will come the funds to replace our cathedral, I wonder," Baron Van Cleef said finally. "Perhaps we should fix our catastrophes in the order they occur."

Prince Daniel glowered. Baron Van Cleef was a wealthy man, carefully bred from generations of Saunder's most elite. He had a unique style, hats with large feathers and clothing in bold colors with graying facial hair that he trimmed in sharp angles across his cheeks. He strummed his fingers on the table. Across the table, he met Michael's eyes. They had far more in common than Michael would have guessed.

But nobody else spoke, and the Baron's words were easy to ignore.

"By royal decree," the prince began. The scribe held his quill and wrote the words on the page. When he finished, he held a cube of wax against the flaming wick of a candle. Red drops spilled on the parchment like drops of blood. Prince Daniel pressed his ring into the wax, marking it with the seal of Saunder. As quickly as it hardened, the words were law.

"Then it's done," King Josiah said, suddenly alert. "Michael, go gather the fine from the people. And take Liviya with you. It will be good for her to see the affairs of our land."

The meeting adjourned. Geoffrey helped the king leave. The barons filed behind them. Michael slowly gathered his papers, waiting for the room to clear, specifically King Josiah.

"I've been thinking about the ruby," Michael said. It was a terrible idea, but it was all he had.

The prince raised his brows. "I'm listening."

Liviya woke up the next morning with the disappointing realization that being a princess wasn't much different than being a maid. First, she still had to follow orders. Second, it was cold. Third, there was a lot of poverty.

Liviya had been ordered by the king to travel with Michael to collect the fine for the window from each household. It didn't matter that she didn't want to spend the day with Michael or that she had no interest in collecting money. The king insisted, so here she was. Princess or no, she had to follow orders. With begrudging help from some of the maids, and some creative squirming to hide the seal on her arm, Liviya got dressed. The two girls didn't say a word. At least not to Liviya. There was a lot of snickering between them and quite a few thoughts communicated through eye rolls, which Liviya translated easily enough. They didn't like her. No amount of fire would warm their chill. *They're just maids*, she tried to tell herself. Still, their coldness stung more than she cared to admit

When Liviya was dressed, she met Michael downstairs. After some sarcastic comments about her preferred mode of travel, for which she had no witty reply, they climbed in the front of a wagon. As they journeyed outside the palace, she realized that poverty didn't end at Barlow's border. She was no stranger to want and could see it in the faces of the dirty children in the streets, the weary eyes of women hanging laundry, and the haggard faces of the men as they led their animals through the rocky fields. Poor people lived in Saunder, too.

Michael and Liviya stopped in Baron Van Cleef's home first. He, too, wasn't able to hide his dislike of Liviya, though he was better at pretending amiability than the maids. He was a large man dressed in colorful silks. He wore the most flamboyant hat Liviya had ever seen, with long feathers that stuck out like a rooster's tail.

He shook Michael's hand when they entered. "Always good to see you, Captain." He offered Liviya a stiff bow and a curt "Princess," by way of greeting.

Baron Van Cleef invited them into his study, a room decorated with shelves filled with colorful books. In the center was a table carved into perfect corners, shining with carefully applied polish.

The baron removed a wide ledger from the drawer and flipped through the pages. He marked on a line and handed Michael a leather bag. "You know my people," he said to Michael, "so I'll be frank. Some families will struggle to pay the fine and still afford food." He handed Michael a much larger bag. "For the ones who won't eat after paying."

"I can't accept that," Michael said. "The orders are that everyone pays."

Liviya tried to estimate how many coins waited in the bulging bag. Certainly more than fifty. "Take it," she said. "The prince gets his money and the people keep their food."

"The prince doesn't want money," Michael explained with visible annoyance. "He wants to punish the man who broke the window. He can't be certain he's been punished unless he collects money from everyone."

Liviya crossed her arms. She had more opinions on this, but she'd wait until they were alone. She didn't want Baron Van Cleef to witness her outburst. He disliked her enough already. He had stopped his inspection of the ledger and studied Liviya instead, his fingers running along his jaw.

"Rumor says you've received your requirements," Baron Van Cleef said.

"Yes, sir," Liviya replied awkwardly, not certain how a maid should reply to a baron, and not certain how a princess would either.

"There's a reason for the requirements," Baron Van Cleef explained. "Legend tells of a king of Saunder long ago who had twelve sons. As was custom, the king offered the crown to his eldest. To the king's surprise, and utter disappointment, his eldest son refused." He threw up his hands. "Refused the crown. Can you imagine?"

Michael, behind him counting the coins, stiffened.

Liviya tried to look equally surprised, though she knew very well how someone could refuse a crown. She had nearly done the same thing herself.

Baron Van Cleef continued. "The king would have to pass the crown to another. To his dismay, he found that none of his other sons had been prepared for it as the eldest had. If the crown came not to the eldest, then to which son?"

He paused, allowing a moment for Liviya to ponder this.

"This great king of Saunder devised a way of determining who was most worthy to serve. He gave his remaining eleven sons two requirements that must be fulfilled. Whoever completed them first would be king. The plan was successful. From among his eleven sons, the king found his successor. The tradition continued throughout all the generations of Saunder's kings. King Josiah defeated an enemy and completed a challenge prior to becoming king and issued these same requirements to his son, Prince Nathan, who, sadly, was lost before completing them."

Baron Van Cleef took off his hat and bowed his head. "Rest in peace, Prince Nathan," he and Michael murmured together.

Liviya brought a fingernail between her teeth. "Then it's a race. Winner takes the crown."

"In the past it was a race," Michael clarified. "But Prince Daniel is the only heir. One day he'll be crowned even if the requirements aren't met."

"Don't be so certain," Baron Van Cleef replied. "The king's not dead yet. He might find love and have another son." He blew onto his fingernails and brushed them across his lapel. "Besides, where in the legend does it say the new king must be an heir?"

Michael coughed like he was choking, though he was neither eating nor drinking.

The baron wound his finger around the room. "Somewhere in this kingdom, there's a man who will one day realize he has a chance to be king. He just might complete the requirements first." He bowed to Liviya and kissed her hand. "Welcome to Saunder, and best of luck on becoming queen." He looked to Michael. "And, Captain, good luck to you as well. On your journey today, of course."

CHAPTER 14

Traveling to Saunder with Liviya was difficult. Traveling around the city to collect the fine was far worse.

Few families had a surplus of fifty tilots. Those who were able to pay the fine only did so with immense sacrifice. Liviya, no matter how often Michael repeated the prince's orders, refused to understand that the expectation was that they collected fifty tilots from each family. There were no excuses, no arrangements, no exceptions. Fifty tilots. Every time.

"But how much is fifty tilots truly worth?" Liviya asked.

Michael rubbed his face. "About a week's worth of food."

They stood on the dirt floor of a simple cottage in front of a young couple, Jane and Dmitri. Like others, they didn't have money. They had recently spent it all on seeds, which waited in bags on the table in front of them, about fifty tilots worth. Michael insisted they should take the bags in place of the fine. Liviya, like always, had other ideas.

"See, if we take all their seed, we're taking away an entire year's worth of food, and that's more than anybody else had to pay."

"That's because nobody's really paid yet," Michael reminded her. The wagon outside was full of alternative forms of payment. Bottles of milk, a few eggs, a wooden rocking chair, and Michael's least favorite, a baby goat.

"The fair thing to do would be to take only the amount of seed that would produce a week's worth of food." Liviya pulled open the bag and dumped the wheat into her palm. "About this much should do it."

Jane and Dmitri's eyes darted from Michael to Liviya to their fifty tilots' worth of seed that would provide for them for a year. Even their toddler sensed the unease and fussed on the floor.

"I'm not returning to the prince with a handful of wheat as payment," Michael whispered harshly.

"Why not?" Liviya asked. "He doesn't want the money. You said so yourself."

Michael made no reply. He had already noticed his exact words being repeated and used against him.

"I'm certain taking only this much seed punishes them enough, even if they are the real perpetrators."

The logic was so flawed but so honest that Michael had a hard time refuting it. "I suppose next you'll be offering fifty tilots for the little one's blanket."

The little girl held a well-loved blanket in the same hand as the thumb in her mouth.

"Oh, I'd pay much more than fifty tilots for that," Liviya answered. "That's quality knitting." She reached out and touched Jane's arm. "You're very talented."

Jane reddened and stammered her thanks. Like many of the people they had visited, Jane and her husband had met the new princess with hesitation and poorly hidden disgust. But, like the others, they warmed up to her quickly. It wasn't just because Liviya argued against them paying a fine for a crime they didn't commit. The princess was simply pleasant to be around, as long as you weren't trying to make her do something she didn't want to do.

Michael and Liviya walked back to the wagon with a handful of wheat to add to the rest of the "fines" they had collected. The baby goat bleated when it saw them. Even the animals liked Liviya immediately. Liviya picked him up and set him in her lap in the front of the wagon.

Michael looked at his ledger. The day was nearly done. They had only one more stop. He flicked his reins. The horses carried them forward. Liviya cradled the baby goat in her lap and buried a kiss into his coarse hair.

"Twelve sons is a lot."

Michael only responded by glancing in her direction. She looked at him with wild, curious eyes spotted with flecks of gold. The fresh air tinged her cheeks with pink.

"Why is there only one now?"

"Because you killed Prince Nathan before he had others," Michael said.

"I didn't kill him. King Herrick did."

"King of Barlow, princess of Barlow. It makes no difference to me."

Liviya scratched the goat's head. "What about Daniel's mother? Where is she?"

Michael paused. "She died." At least he thought so. That's what he seemed to remember. He tried to think back. Now that he thought on it, he couldn't remember ever being told that specifically.

"How tragic," Liviya said, and for one blessed moment she was silent. "How long ago?"

"I don't know," Michael said. "A long time ago."

Liviya cocked her head. "How do you not know?"

"I was a child, maybe a baby," Michael said. "I don't remember it, and I never cared to ask." He clicked his tongue. The horses pulled them toward the left in a fork in the muddy road.

Liviya wrapped her shawl around her arms, though Michael felt plenty warm. The snow was nearly all gone, only clumps of gray remaining in the shadows of boulders and trees.

"And what about Prince Nathan's mother? How long has Josiah been alone?"

"I don't know, Highness." Michael dropped the reins to his lap and turned to face Liviya, sucking in a short breath when their eyes met. "How about for every question you ask, I ask one in return? You owe me several. Where is your mother? How long has Herrick been alone? Are you the only heir, or were there eleven more of you wandering the streets dressed like diseased vagrants? How come you haven't been married yet, or at least betrothed? Why was your father so eager to be rid of you, and who else is he planning to murder with this alliance?"

Liviya, taken aback, was silent again. Satisfied, Michael turned his attention back to the horses. "I see you don't know your history near as well as you think I should know mine."

"I do know my history," Liviya said. "Allow me to teach you a few key points, because you keep getting it wrong." She continued without taking a breath. "My people are good people, and once we were ruled by a good king. His daughter was a saint, and she had a pure soul. Everyone loved her. She would have made an excellent queen. The man you hate so much is King Herrick *the second,* a foreign prince who came and stole away everything Barlow had. He killed the king, stole his daughter, and dried up the river that ran through our land. And at some point, he killed your prince. For that, I'm sorry. But I didn't wield that sword, so watch what accusations you throw at me."

Michael opened his mouth to apologize, but Liviya kept talking. "Since you're so curious, the queen is dead, but there is another heir. King Herrick had a son who was hidden away in his infancy to protect him from his father. He'll return one day and save my people. He'll rule as rightful king and return my land to our powerful and prosperous state." She pointed her finger into Michael's chest. "Be careful. One day, Barlow will have something you want, be that power or armies or money, and then you'll wish that we were truly allies. Did that answer all your questions?"

Liviya's finger was still pressed against Michael's chest. He lowered her hand slowly, taking the time to think of a reply. "I suppose that's a good start."

Liviya's information raised a lot more questions. Michael wasn't sure he wanted to know the answers. The kingdom of Barlow had a dark history, worse than he had thought.

Liviya rubbed her face into the goat's neck and looked up at

Michael, completely innocent. "I think I'll call him Arthur. Do you suppose the king will let me keep him?"

"I imagine so," he said, avoiding the look of delight on Liviya's face. "He seems to be developing a soft spot toward strays."

If Liviya recognized his words as an insult, she offered no reply.

Michael pulled the carriage to a stop outside a leaning cottage. The door hung open. The roof was sparsely thatched. Weeds grew along the path leading to the house. The earth in front of the home rose in uneven hills. It was the girls' home, where the poorest of the poor were kept. These were no ordinary orphans. They were the daughters of criminals and traitors. Their futures held little hope. Neither did their present circumstances, judging by the looks of the exterior.

Michael knocked on the door and greeted the woman who answered. "Good day, Ms. Luther." He held up the prince's declaration. "We've come to collect the fifty tilots for the window."

The color drained from the woman's face. "We haven't got fifty tilots. Not even close."

Michael cast a quick glance around the cottage. They had several mats pushed against the walls to make room on the dirt floor where several girls sat. They had a crooked chair and a table that held a few bent plates and rusted spoons. Not even Liviya could find something to take and pretend it was worth fifty tilots, though Michael knew that she was going to try.

Lips pursed, Liviya surveyed the home. "They shouldn't have to pay."

"Everyone pays," Michael said as he marked the ledger. Why did he have to explain this so many times? "We need to make certain he's punished."

"*He*," Liviya repeated. "This is a girls' home. Your criminal isn't here. They shouldn't have to pay."

Michael's hand froze, mid-mark.

"Unless you think the criminal was a woman. Some of the best ones are, you know." Liviya pulled on her sleeve.

Michael had no argument against Liviya. Honestly, he didn't want to think of one. Even though he wouldn't admit it, he enjoyed sparing the people unjust punishments as much as Liviya.

"You're right," he said. "Let's go."

He had thought that Liviya would be happy to have won an argument again, but she put her hands on her hips. Michael dropped his head back. She had a lot more to say, and she was going to say it.

"These girls need help."

"I'll be sure to mention that to the church. They distribute supplies to the needy."

"We have supplies in the wagon."

"Those aren't ours to give!" Michael said.

"The prince doesn't need them, and these are his people. It's all the same except now we've collected from potential criminals and helped the needy."

"No," Michael said firmly. Supposing he took supplies today, then tomorrow he might take money, and soon enough he'd take the crown. "This is the prince's responsibility."

"This is everyone's responsibility," Liviya replied. "Especially when the prince fails."

"Careful, Highness," Michael said, his voice heavy with enough warning that for the first time, Liviya stopped talking. Her shoulders slumped.

"Listen," he said finally, "talk to the prince. Maybe he'll send them more supplies."

Liviya sighed, unhappy and defeated, but Mrs. Luther smiled, another friend among Liviya's growing fans. Michael wished Mrs. Luther and the girls a good day and walked with Liviya back to the wagon.

Michael and Liviya left their wagon at the gate where the treasurers took inventory of the fines they had collected.

"Fifty tilots per family. Or the equivalent," Michael added when the man eyed the baby goat. He handed him the ledger. "It's all documented here."

Michael was quick to leave for other duties. Liviya suspected he wanted to be rid of her, which was fine. She was eager to be rid of him as well.

Alone in the palace, she wandered around, trying to find enough courage to talk to the prince. Every second she stood before him was another opportunity for him to learn her lie. She couldn't die yet. But she couldn't just hide the entire time, either. She had come to save those in need. There was nothing she could do for Barlow yet, but she could help the people of Saunder. She'd talk to him, Liviya decided. She'd just be very brief.

Liviya found the prince in his study. He sat at his desk with the Heart of Saunder in the center. The rest of the table was cluttered with stones, tools, and open books. He slowly scratched along the surface of the ruby with the edge of a dagger. It shrieked as the blade passed over it.

"Your Highness," Liviya began.

Prince Daniel didn't look up.

Liviya took another step into the room. "Michael and I just returned from the girls' home in the city. They're in dire need of supplies."

"The priests send them food every month." Prince Daniel set down his dagger and reached for a pick. He placed it in the crevice.

"I understand, Your Highness" Liviya said meekly, quite proud how little anger was evident in her voice. She would do more if she could, but she couldn't afford to draw attention to herself. Then again, everyone in the palace thought poorly of her anyway. It would be expected that she have ill-manners. She tugged on her sleeve, adjusted her crown, and took a deep breath. "I wonder if they're not sending enough food."

Prince Daniel looked up from his tools. "I think you misunderstood what it meant when your father sent you here to be queen. All I need you to do is sit on the throne. You're not a priest, you're not a diplomat, and you're not my advisor. If you need something to keep you entertained, go sit with the noble ladies and sip tea."

Inside Liviya's skirts, her knees shook. She clenched her fists at her side. Her heart pounded fire into her veins. When she came here, she thought she would be escaping King Herrick's dungeons. No. She was still a prisoner, except this time she had been shackled with silver and gagged with gold.

Liviya returned to her room. Outside the door, the maids quarreled about whose turn it was to help her undress. She slammed it shut and turned the bolt. They didn't like her, but that was fine. She didn't travel here to make an alliance with the palace maids. In fact, she didn't need an alliance with any of the people. Even still, their dismissal hurt just as badly as Daniel's.

Liviya peeled off her dress and left it on a heap on her floor. In bed, the sleep came easily after the long day with Michael in the city. Nightmares haunted her. She dreamed of slipping into the canyon and falling forever, of poison oozing from Herrick's yellow skin and venom dripping from his fang-like smile. She dreamed of Michael, the dark-haired man on the street asking her to dance only to secure her chains. And lastly, she dreamed of the mice that infested the servants' shack and the sounds of tiny claws on the dirt floor. Something tickled her face. She jolted out of bed.

The room was empty. The silence screamed. Awake, her nightmares became reality as her thoughts turned to the girls at the home with barely more than the girls in Barlow, and Liviya, a princess, unable to help.

Liviya rose and wrapped herself in a robe. The wind outside rattled branches against her window. Below, the faint lights of the courtyard illuminated the goods that had been collected from the people. More wagons arrived from the farther cities.

Guards documented each of the items in a ledger, but their ledgers didn't mark the number of days the families would be left without food. They'd be hungry. At least in Barlow, she could have stolen to help them. Here, she could do nothing.

Liviya smoothed her nightgown as she considered a thought that was forming. Really, she wasn't any different than she was at home. She had simply changed her clothes. She would have stolen in Barlow. She could certainly steal in Saunder as well.

Liviya changed out of her night gown and into her plainest dress. She gently eased the window open and tested the edge of the lattice that climbed the side. It was sturdy. She climbed down and snuck around the corner of the palace.

The guards helped unload a wagon and tallied the goods. Liviya inched forward, keeping her feet silent on the courtyard stones. Just one bag, she told herself. No reason to be greedy and get herself caught. The man tossed a bag of coins into the pile and held up the lantern to inspect the ledger. Liviya snuck her hand from the shadows, grabbed the bag, and ran.

Down the road, Liviya paused to catch her breath. She dumped the bag into her hand and counted out fifty tilots. The guards had kept careful records. Someone would notice them missing. From what she knew about the prince, the entire kingdom would pay to replace them.

Michael and Daniel both knew about her anxiety toward the girls' home. If she delivered the coins there, they'd suspect her first. What would be immensely helpful was a larger crime to keep them distracted from a few tilots. The roads were empty and houses dark. Liviya would have to commit that crime herself. She felt along the ground until she found a sharp rock and carved the rebel sign into the sign post.

Liviya ran and ran, enjoying the night sky, the cool air, the adrenaline of running from guards. When she reached the girls' home, she dropped the money on the porch and left with three swift knocks on the door. She returned to the palace, sneaking past the patrolling guards. As she climbed the lattice, a stray branch caught her cheek and sliced it. In her room, she wiped away the warm blood, stuffed the dirty dress under her bed, and climbed under the covers. Outside the sun was just beginning to rise as Liviya fell asleep.

CHAPTER 15

$\mathcal{L}$iviya awoke to whispers about the vandalism. The rebel was still out there, the maids said to each other as they helped her dress. Despite the punishment for the window, he had struck again. He was daring. He was defiant. Liviya hid her yawns as they whispered amongst each other. The rebel was tired. There was no talk of the missing tilots or the mysterious aid to the girls' home. The plan had worked as perfectly as she had hoped. The scratch on her cheek was still fiery red. She dabbed some cream and powder on it before leaving for breakfast.

"Welcome, darling!" the king said when she arrived in the dining room. He tapped his cane against the leg of the chair next to him. "Please. Sit."

The king seemed to be the only one who was excited to see her, yet he was the one she wanted the most to avoid. Him and Michael.

Liviya adjusted her sleeve and sat. Chancey set the king's plate in front of him. It held carefully portioned helpings dished neatly on his plate. It was brightened with fresh garnishes. Food fit for a king.

Liviya's food was slopped onto her plate. The foods ran together. She had the burnt ends of a loaf of bread.

Chancey set a glass of water beside the plate. "This is water. They said to tell you that in case you didn't recognize it because it's clean."

In the kitchen doorway, several burst out laughing, among them, Sarah. Liviya had learned her name quickly. First, her face was memorable. She was beautiful. One of the eldest among the maids, she was the most vocal in her dislike of Liviya, and she was the one who teased Chancey the most cruelly.

The maids in the doorway danced with excitement, waiting for a reaction. Chancey waited for a reprimand, terrified, but more fearful of her peers than the princess. The king ate his meal without an awareness of the subtle scene before him. Liviya decided to speak her mind.

"You shouldn't let those girls pick on you." She pointed to her glass. "Next time they're mean, you throw this clean water in their faces."

The giggling girls fell silent immediately. They slunk back into the kitchen.

Liviya took a bit of food and savored the taste. "These sweet rolls are divine. Give my compliments to Mrs. Maude."

"I helped her make them," Chancey said, beaming. "I'll bring you another if you like." She skipped into the kitchen. The other maids stepped out of her way.

As breakfast neared its end, Prince Daniel arrived. He paused in the doorway a moment before entering. Michael followed behind. He ran his hand through his curly hair and sat down. His eyes lingered on Liviya's cheek for just a moment. The wound pulsed until Michael looked away.

"I've completed my challenge," the prince said. He pulled a pouch from his pocket and revealed a jewel that covered his entire hand. It was the same size and shape as the Heart of Saunder, and it was perfectly clear. He passed the jewel to the king. Liviya leaned to look closer. She had thought it to be impossible, but somehow, he had completed it.

The king held the jewel with both hands cupped together, studied it, and began to laugh. "You have offered me an imitation, and a poor one at that."

"This is the Heart of Saunder," Prince Daniel insisted, "and it's clear."

King Josiah held the jewel up to the light, still grinning. "Do you know the legend about this jewel?"

"I've heard it," the prince grumbled.

"Oh, I'm sure you've heard it. But do you know it?"

Prince Daniel sat down at the table. Sarah pushed Chancey toward him with his plate.

"I've never heard it," Liviya said. Michael and Daniel shot her an identical scowl.

King Josiah settled against his chair. "Centuries ago, our fathers were held in bondage under the rule of a terrible king. They were slaves, beaten and starved. Forced to work until the labor killed them. But it wasn't the guards or the gates that imprisoned them. Great mountains surrounded the land. The peaks were too high, the terrain too rocky, and food and water were scarce. Crossing the mountains was a sure death.

"There was only one way out. A river, long ago dried, had cut a route underneath the mountain, leaving a tunnel of perfect darkness. But this, too, was dangerous. Under the weight of the mountain, every time the earth breathed, the ceiling collapsed, crushing whatever stood beneath it. The people had no choice but to stay. One day, they chose freedom no matter the cost. They chose to travel the tunnel."

The king's words came in a choppy rhythm with long pauses where he needed to catch his breath. Some of the words came out as a mumble, others came loudly. Liviya listened to every word. The maids returned to the doorway.

"One by one, the people entered the tunnel, depending on their outstretched fingers to guide them. With every step they took, the tunnel shifted, spraying down sand and pebbles.

"The people continued walking. Ahead of them, light appeared. Freedom. Then the mountain groaned. Walls shaking, boulders came down. Awaiting death, the people fell to their knees. But one man stood. Raising his arms, he held the entire mountain. He urged the people to run. When the very last person was through, the man's strength left him. He dropped to the ground. The mountains above him fell. He was crushed."

The king paused and studied the prince. He was leaned back in his chair, arms crossed and face sullen.

"Years later, the people returned to the fallen mountain. They removed all of the rocks to find their hero's body and bury it with respect. The body had turned to dust. All that remained was the man's heart, perfectly preserved in stone. It is the Heart of Saunder, a combination of rare and precious elements combined under the weight carried to save a nation. The people took his heart and placed it upon the crown as a reminder that the weight of the people will always be carried by the king."

King Josiah furrowed his eyebrows. "Instead of the purity found in the Heart of Saunder, you have presented me with melted sand, an element so common that people sweep it from their houses into the street. This," he said, holding up the jewel, "is not the Heart of Saunder, and this will never adorn your crown."

Prince Daniel's scowl broke with a rude snort. "Then today I travel to the nearest mountain and begin removing stones."

"Oh, it doesn't have to be a mountain," the king said. "I've seen these jewels formed in battles. I've seen them formed at sea." The king shrugged. "I've even seen them formed in blizzards."

Michael stirred his food and seemed strangely focused on his plate. "It's a nice story. But it's just a story." He stood up. "I'd better check the stables."

King Josiah watched him leave then motioned to Liviya. "Help me up, darling."

Liviya hoisted the king to his feet like she had seen others do and helped him walk to his chair in the drawing room. Maybe it was because she walked with the king, but as she passed, the usually snickering maids were silent. Sarah looked away. Mrs. Maude waved her wooden spoon. Chancey grinned and followed behind them. Liviya's heart lifted. She had found a friend.

Mrs. Maude grumbled about it, but she let Michael take his
plate outside. Michael ate his breakfast in the refuge of the stables. The king's words made him uneasy, but he had other things to worry about. There had been another report of vandalism last night. Michael sent Geoffrey and a few guards to search while he finished helping the prince with the ruby.

The stable door creaked as it opened. Geoffrey walked in, chuckling. "Glass?"

Michael shrugged sheepishly. "I thought it might work." He pushed his plate toward Geoffrey.

"Daniel'll have your head." Geoffrey reached for a roll.

"Nah. He thinks it was his idea."

Geoffrey licked the glaze from his fingers. "Be careful about the words you tell him. You might have to take credit for them one day."

"I never tell him anything I wouldn't say myself." Michael cleared his throat. "What's new on the vandal?"

"Nothing," Geoffrey replied. "Probably just some kid angry about the prince collecting money from his family. It wasn't like the others. Besides, we've got bigger problems."

Michael chewed slowly, waiting for the details.

"The audit on the fines came up fifty tilots short."

"Count again," Michael said. "It's all there."

"They've counted a dozen times. Fifty tilots are missing."

"You think someone stole it?" Michael asked.

Geoffrey shrugged. "Might be. I also heard that Ms. Luther was out shopping for her girls with a purse full of money. Seems strange. We're missing money, she's got extra, and there's a carving on a signpost all in the same night. Might be it was the same man."

Michael wiped his face with a napkin. "Or woman."

Geoffrey raised his brow. "You think Ms. Luther did it?"

"No. No, I don't." He crumbled the napkin and tossed it into the garbage pail in the corner. "Don't tell Daniel it's missing yet. I'll go investigate."

CHANCEY FOLLOWED LIVIYA TO HER BEDROOM AFTER BREAKFAST. HER smock hung awkwardly on her shoulders, and she smiled with a mouth full of too-large teeth.

"You have beautiful hair," Liviya said.

Her dark curls sprang from out of her braid. Chancey licked her palms and tried to smooth it down. "They say it's unruly."

"They say I'm unruly as well. But it's a trait that has served me well." Liviya looked through her bottles of ointments and creams before selecting one. She scooped a dollop with two fingers. "May I?"

Liviya untied her braid. She combed it through Chancey's thick hair until the frizz became tight curls. As she stepped back for a better look, she noted more delight and considerably less fear. She pinned a few wayward curls out of Chancey's eyes.

"You remind me of one of the maids back home. Her name was Bicka." Liviya felt her own smile slip. She missed her. She missed all of them.

Her thoughts were interrupted by Michael throwing open the door. Mrs. Maude followed, as well as a handful of other maids and the guards who stood at her door.

"Michael, this is wildly inappropriate!" Mrs. Maude said, huffing from behind.

Michael ignored her. He reached his hand and gently turned Liviya's face. "What happened to your cheek?"

"I was sipping tea," she said dryly. "My cup broke."

Michael was not amused. "Someone robbed Prince Daniel last night."

"Oh dear," Liviya said, bringing a hand to her forehead. "I thought all the liars and cheats lived in Barlow."

Michael ran his tongue along his teeth. "Coincidentally, the girls received some anonymous aid in the form of fifty tilots. That's a week's worth of food, you may remember."

"Now Michael, you don't really think she did it, do you?" Mrs. Maude asked.

One look from Michael silenced her.

"Did she leave this room last night?" Michael asked the guards.

The guards shook their heads.

"If you are lying to me, I'll split you open and hang you with your own entrails."

The guards shook their heads even faster. "This door didn't open until the maids entered to help her dress, 'bout half hour before breakfast," one said.

Michael pushed the rest of the way into the room. Liviya was slightly embarrassed at the unmade bed and nightgown hanging on the back of the chair. Then she remembered it was the maids' job and not hers.

Michael pushed open the window. He looked down to the ground, at the lattice along the wall, back to the princess, then back to the window. "Ten lashings to the person who stole it. What do you think of that?"

"I'm thrilled," Liviya replied. "Days ago I was called a murderer and threatened with death. Now I'm just a thief and threatened with a lashing. I think the people are starting to like me. Tomorrow, I just may very well be queen."

Someone snickered. Michael was not amused. "Station two guards below that window. Keep a close eye on her."

Michael, Mrs. Maude, and most of the maids left, but Sarah lingered for just a moment. She looked like she had a lot of questions, and a lot of suspicions. "Have a good day, Your Highness," she said with a bow. "If you need help with anything, you just let me know. Help with dressing, or hair, or, you know, whatever."

"Thank you. I'll remember that. And Sarah," Liviya called as she left, "if you need anything, you let me know as well."

CHAPTER 16

*M*ichael's questions in Liviya's bedroom was the last she heard of the missing tilots and the mysterious delivery to the girls' home. Everyone else was either talking about the vandal or the ball. Somewhere in all the chaos of questions and searches, the king decided that Liviya hadn't been properly introduced to the people. Thus, a ball was planned.

Liviya had spent the entire week trying to convince the king not to throw the ball. He refuted all of her excuses. She was terrified. It was one thing to tell a lie to the handful of people in the palace. It was quite another to parade it about in front of an entire kingdom. In a crowd of thousands, someone would be watching closely enough to see through her charade.

When the maids finished helping her dress, Liviya stood in front of the mirror and studied her reflection. She pulled on her long sleeves, ensuring her scar was covered. She practiced some lies so they'd be easy to speak. With a smile, she straightened her crown and hoped the people would believe her.

Chancey sank into a chair and sighed. "I wish I could go to the ball."

Chancey's duties would keep her to the kitchen tonight. She had complained about it nearly as much as Liviya had about the ball.

"Next time, I'll make sure you're invited," Liviya said. She rummaged through her drawers and pulled out a pink ribbon. She motioned for Chancey to turn and tied it around her head. "There. Just in case a prince asks you to dance tonight."

Chancey beamed. For a moment, Liviya forgot her fears.

A knock sounded at the door. Prince Daniel waited outside. Some would consider him handsome, but Liviya didn't. He was a bit too fancy, a bit too polished. Perhaps if she had been raised among men like that, she would find him more attractive. Instead, she had been raised among working men. Men like Michael.

Prince Daniel's hair gleamed and was tied back with a ribbon. A polished sword waited at his side. Liviya studied their reflections in the mirror. Next to him, she looked plain and out of place. It was obvious to the mirror that only one was genuinely noble; the other was an imposter. Thankfully Prince Daniel didn't seem to notice. He herded Liviya down the corridor and through the great doors leading to the ballroom.

In the ballroom, three identical chandeliers hung from the ceiling. The crystals cast dancing rainbows across the walls. The room stood two floors high with a mural of the heavens on the ceiling. A grand staircase rose in the center, leading to a balcony. Inside, hundreds of people waited. Liviya tugged on her sleeve once more. As they entered the ballroom, the music stopped.

"My people," Prince Daniel called, "I present to you Princess Liviya of Barlow."

The crowd applauded politely. Then the whispers began. *Barlow. Prince Nathan. Murder.* Any confidence that Liviya had pretended to possess disappeared. She was a peasant dressed as a princess and no gown or crown could ever change that. Nobody voiced any accusations, but Liviya knew. She would always know that she was nothing.

The music began again. Prince Daniel folded one arm at his waist and bowed. "May I have the pleasure of this dance?"

The prince and his people waited for Liviya's reply. She wilted under their stares. Above all else, this was why she had dreaded the ball the most. She couldn't dance. But she could lie.

"I'm unfamiliar with the custom here, but in my land, the first dance is reserved for the king."

Prince Daniel's mouth hung open for just a moment before he spoke. "He can't dance. You'll wait all night."

Liviya turned her lips down into what she hoped appeared to be a sincere frown. "How unfortunate."

Recovering enough to smile, Prince Daniel extended his hand toward a beautiful woman who lingered near his elbow. "Victoria, may I have the pleasure of this dance?"

Victoria obliged with a smile as bright as the diamonds in her hair. Prince Daniel pulled her into his arms, and they twirled away. Victoria was graceful. Wealthy. Beautiful. Watching them dance, Liviya quickly realized that Victoria should have been the princess. She had everything. Liviya had only lies.

From his throne on the balcony, the king tapped his cane against the chair next to him. Liviya walked up the stairs and sat down. The jealousy was bitter. Prince Daniel barely noticed her when she was beside him and didn't miss her at all when she wasn't. She reminded herself that the choice was hers. She had chosen not to dance. While she understood that Prince Daniel would likely dance without her, she would have appreciated his company, even if it was just a moment or two. If she couldn't have his company, at least some disappointment from him would have been nice. Instead, she got nothing when she had given everything to be there.

Liviya scanned the room, the nameless faces melting into a blur of colorful gowns. Michael, she noticed, wasn't there. Whatever excuse he had used, she'd have to try next time.

The king didn't speak, but patted Liviya's arm. What a strange feeling it was to be so alone in a room so crowded, so overlooked when everyone stared. For Barlow, she told herself. Even if her time in Saunder only bought her people a loaf of bread, then it was worth it. Liviya blinked quickly. The sacrifice was worth it. She just wished sacrifices didn't have to be so lonely.

~

MICHAEL SPENT THE DAY AVOIDING THE BALL, AND MORE IMPORTANTLY, avoiding the king. Night was falling. The ballroom was full. Nobody had even noticed he was gone. He kept himself busy in the stables where he repaired some of the tack. Outside, music danced along the evening air. The whispers traveled with it. Even in the stables, Michael had heard the rumors. The princess wasn't dancing. What a scene that must have caused. He was almost sorry to have missed it.

Michael looked around the stables, but no matter how hard he looked, he couldn't find any more work to do. At least not any work that couldn't wait until the next day. He dusted off his hands. With seemingly no other choice, he returned to the palace.

"Wipe yer boots!" Mrs. Maude hollered from the kitchen. Michael scraped his boots along the coarse mat before coming inside. He peeled off his dirty shirt in his room and looked for a clean one, smelling it first to be sure it didn't stink of horses. When he was dressed, he wandered into the kitchen.

Mrs. Maude handed him a crust of bread. "The feast is in the ball-room. You go sit with them if you want to eat proper."

"This is plenty for me," Michael replied with a full mouth. He'd have to be starving before he spent the night eating with the barons.

Chancey bounced into the kitchen with a bright smile. She pointed to a pink ribbon in her hair. "Look what the princess gave me."

Michael smiled. "You look beautiful, Your Highness." He bowed and held out his arm. "May I have the honor of this dance?"

He led her around the kitchen, stepping carefully to miss the counter, the sack of flour, and a stack of pans on the floor. Mrs. Maude hummed along and tapped her toe in front of her kettle.

When they had made a lap around the kitchen, Chancey stopped. "How come the princess won't dance?"

"She's waiting for the king," Michael replied, relaying the gossip the stable hands had passed.

"No one else is waiting for the king."

"That's because it's just a rule in Barlow," Michael said.

Chancey looked down, then back up. "The prince is almost king."

Michael shrugged. "I'm sure he told her that."

"Maybe if you help the king stand, they can dance. Then she doesn't have to sit there all night."

"I'm not going to help him stand," Michael replied. "It's too hard for him, and it's not necessary. She can dance when she wants with whomever she wants." There was no rule governing dance partners. In theory, Liviya could dance with Michael if she wanted. Not that he'd ever ask her.

"It's such a strange rule," Chancey said.

With a groan, Michael sat down and buried his face in his hands.

"Isn't the king of Barlow her father? Does she dance with him first at all their balls?"

Thankfully, Mrs. Maude intervened. She leaned down and looked directly in Chancey's eyes. "Chancey, honey, sometimes people say things that aren't entirely true. She doesn't have to dance with the king first. She just said that 'cause it's a little easier than askin' for help."

"Help with what?" Chancey asked.

Mrs. Maude put a hand on her hip. "Girls ain't born knowing how to dance, princesses or not. If she ain't ever learned, she ain't gonna know how. I'd lie too if I was her."

Michael lifted his head from his hand. Did Liviya not know how to dance? He stood up and opened the door that led from the kitchen to the ballroom.

In the crowd, he found Liviya immediately. She was dressed in the same style as the others, but something about her was so different, something more than being from a different kingdom. She sat beside the king, looking as stunning as the first time he saw her. But her toe tapped to a beat far faster than the music. She couldn't dance, not because etiquette refused it, but because she didn't know how. Liviya, he saw, was terrified.

Michael was dumbfounded. She was more uncomfortable in the ballroom than he'd ever been, and he had been raised in an orphanage.

"You should help her," Chancey said, appearing at his side.

Michael found himself nodding without really knowing what he intended to do.

Mrs. Maude shooed Chancey back to work. Michael sat down and finished his bread. Mrs. Maude remained at the pot, stirring slowly. Her body language suggested she was listening closely, waiting for Michael to speak.

"I suppose I better go get myself some real supper in the ballroom."

"Got a real nice feast out there for ya. I think you'll enjoy it," Mrs. Maude replied.

Michael appreciated that she tried to hide how pleased she was. He cleared his throat, straightened his coat, and found himself walking into the very ballroom he had spent an entire evening avoiding.

The king looked up as Michael approached. "Good heavens, Michael has arrived. Late, but on his own accord. I never thought it'd be." The king nudged Liviya. "Michael doesn't like fancy people."

"I don't see why not," Liviya said. "This party has been thrilling." Her voice was flat.

Michael rubbed at his nose to hide his smile. He pulled a chair to Liviya's side. "No one's throwing rocks, Your Highness."

Liviya glared her response.

"If you want to dance—"

"Nope," Liviya replied. "Custom requires I dance with the king first."

"So I heard," Michael replied. "What if I were king? Would you dance with me then or would you find another excuse to hide that you don't know how?"

"If you were king, I'd walk right back to Barlow and never return," Liviya spat.

"If I were king, I never would have brought you here," Michael replied. "And if I were king—" he let his voice trail off because this was a dangerous conversation to have, because King Josiah was listening closely, and because he found he had far too many ideas of what he would do if he were king. He cleared his throat. "Were you too good for all of the men in Barlow or did none of them ever ask you?"

Liviya turned away. "There just wasn't much to celebrate back home."

In that moment, Michael saw a glimpse of pain in her eyes, and he felt the sting of regret.

"I'm sorry, Highness." He scratched his head. "I just came out here to say that you look beautiful today."

If Daniel hadn't told her that, then he was a fool.

Liviya twisted her wrist with her other hand. Michael followed her gaze to the prince who danced with Victoria. In Liviya's face, he read all the emotions that he was all too familiar with: inadequacy, discomfort, fear. And jealousy. Michael was learning a lot about jealousy lately.

Michael offered his hand. "I'll teach you the steps."

Liviya unfurled a fan and waved it across her face. "No, thank you."

"Another time then," Michael said.

"Perhaps," Liviya replied.

Michael sat still to enjoy the moment. That was more progress than he had ever dared hope for. He stayed silent with a single thought: If he were king, if only for an hour, he'd dance with Liviya.

Liviya stayed in her seat on the balcony between Michael and King Josiah. The crowd felt far less cruel with Michael's company. Michael told her about the people as they danced, naming the lords and barons and ladies. He told her about the land and each city —the mountainous peaks in the east and the fiery red sand of the south. He told her about their universities and libraries and the ancient temples built centuries ago. He pointed out the guards and fellow captains, recounting their heroic battles, which Liviya suspected were highly exaggerated.

Soon she began to remember the names and the faces. She almost enjoyed watching the people dance. Maybe next time she would dance among them. When the announcement came for dinner, she was surprisingly disappointed.

Michael helped King Josiah stand and eased him down the stairs. Liviya followed close behind. From the center of the ballroom, Prince Daniel staggered to the table, knocking the side as he sat down.

The table was set with gold-rimmed china and crystal goblets. Each setting had several pieces of silver cutlery. Liviya shuddered sympathetically for whomever would polish all of it after the meal.

The food was delicious. The spread continued into the night as the maids brought out multiple courses. The king sat at the head of the table. Maids filled and cleared his plates with the rest of the group, but he didn't eat. He kept his head ducked and sometimes moaned. The prince sat on one side of him, Michael on the other. Liviya sat next to Daniel.

All around her, the men talked about politics and taxes and courts and customs, conversations Liviya didn't care to follow. She rubbed her forearm, just to be certain the scar hadn't raised and become visible beneath her satin sleeves. It always seemed people were staring there. Soon enough the topic switched to the graffiti spreading throughout the kingdom. Her weak scratch in the pole from the previous week was long forgotten as people discussed the others—the burning sign on the mountain side, the carving on the prince's stables. Someone had even scaled the gates at the entrance to the city and replaced the land's flag with a crudely quilted flag displaying the rebel sign. Everywhere else, people talked in whispers and exchanged codes. Liviya looked the length of the table, wondering if any among them had been the cause of the graffiti. Any besides her, that is. She met eyes with Baron Van Cleef. He offered her a cheery smile over his goblet.

"The people are like a defiant child, and I their father," the prince said with slurred words. "A smart snap with a whip will put them in line. They're simply testing boundaries."

"Is that how your father would have raised you?" Baron Van Cleef asked. "With a smart snap of a whip?"

The table grew silent. Liviya had been in Saunder long enough to develop respect for the late Prince Nathan. Prince Daniel's comment made her just as defensive as the others. He was a good and kind man. He never would have whipped his child.

"Maybe he should have," the prince said. "A little more aggression on his part could have spared his life from the miscreants in Barlow."

Michael looked at Liviya and gave a subtle shake of his head. Liviya rolled her eyes. He was probably afraid she'd lash out. She wasn't that volatile.

"Just keep adding fines," another baron suggested. "They'll learn soon enough."

"They're already out of money," someone replied. "The amount of tilots brought in for the window was far below the projected total. Soon they'll be fined from the thatch on their roofs and the doors on the huts. Then what will they pay?"

Michael shot her another look that seemed to beg her to stay silent. Liviya took a bite of food and kept her expression muted. She was simply enjoying the meal. Their conversation didn't vex her.

"Let them pay in labor," Lord Drake said. "When the families run out of money, they can send their children to the palace to work until the fine is paid."

That comment was harder to ignore. Liviya tried to swallow, but her throat refused to accept the food. She pressed a napkin against her lips to keep from spitting it back onto her plate.

After a long look at Liviya, Geoffrey spoke for the first time that evening. "How would we keep track of which children are free and which belonged to the prince?"

"I suppose we'd have to mark them somehow," Daniel replied.

Liviya forced the food down her throat. "I have an idea. Burn a mark in their arms." Her words were sharp.

"Your Highness," Michael said nervously.

Liviya ignored him. "But before you begin, there are a few disadvantages you may want to be aware of. First, it's a substantial injury that takes weeks to heal, leaving you without laborers during that time. Second, the burns are often subject to disease and infection, causing a high mortality rate. What begins as simple slavery soon becomes murder. Third, the children's screams are enough to raise every demon from the dead, and those demons will haunt you till you die."

The entire crowd was stunned, forks hovering in air, mouths open wide. Michael stood up, his chair screeching as it moved back.

"Your Highness, have you seen the view from this balcony? It's spectacular. You may even catch a glimpse of Barlow."

He came around and gently pulled Liviya away from the crowd. He said something to those still sitting that made them chuckle, probably some joke at her expense. She couldn't hear it past the angry ringing in her ears.

When they reached the balcony, Michael faced her. "You are the most ill-tempered, quick-tongued, wild mess of a princess I've ever met." He ran his hands through his hair. "You can't speak to the prince like that. Have you no decency?"

Liviya lifted her chin. "I know I lack tact. I've been rapped for that every day of my life. But the only indecent response to that conversation was silence." She patted his chest. "Enjoy the ball, Captain. I'm leaving." She stormed away from the ballroom, hoping she'd never have to return.

That night, Liviya awoke to a strange sound in her room. She peeled open her eyes and froze until she could identify it. It was sniffling. When her eyes adjusted to the dark, she saw Sarah in the corner, chewing on her fingernail.

"Sorry to bother you, Princess," she whispered in a hoarse voice.

Liviya rubbed her eyes. "No, it's ok." She sat up in bed, head spinning as it tried to orient itself in the dark room. With no moon, the sky was dark. The air held the chill of midnight. She looked at Sarah. "What are you doing?"

Sarah pulled her dress collar over her eyes and tried to muffle her sobs. "I need help."

Liviya scrambled out of bed to Sarah's side and pulled her into a hug. "What happened? Are you hurt?"

Sarah sniffed. When she tried to speak, her voice jumped with waiting sobs. "My brother got himself in trouble. Just wrote a little bit of graffiti, is all. He didn't mean no harm by it or nothing, was just being a boy. My daddy took it down and thumped him good. But our bully neighbor saw him and says we've gotta pay him big or he'll report it to the guards." The words came out quickly. More tears trailed closely behind. "Can you help us?"

Liviya wrapped her in a hug, letting Sarah's tears drip onto her nightgown. There was nothing she could do. The disappointment was crushing. Here she was, still lacking the money she needed to help those who shouldn't have to pay.

"How much does he want?"

Sarah wiped her eyes. "Twenty tilots."

It was like a knife to her gut. The money would have to be stolen, but there were guards everywhere. Ever since the last tilots were missing, they had kept an especially close eye on Liviya. They'd report it immediately if she left her room. She was surprised they let Sarah in at such an hour. Then again, people rarely looked twice at maids.

"Sarah," Liviya whispered, looking around the dark room for anyone who might overhear. "Perhaps I could borrow your clothes. It's dark enough nobody will see me clearly, and they'll just think that you're leaving. I'll get the money."

A final tear slipped down Sarah's cheek. "What if you're caught?"

"I never get caught," Liviya replied. "Give me your dress."

Dressed as a maid, Liviya opened her bedroom door and stepped into the corridors, leaving Sarah in the room. The guards at Liviya's door barely glanced her direction, one of the small perks of being insignificant. Soon enough, she was outside.

Liviya's body warmed quickly as she jogged across the palace grounds. She stopped in the stables and took a heavy herder's coat. It would offer warmth and a little disguise. She walked along the wall surrounding the palace grounds, dropping to her hands and knees to search along the bottom until she found a place where weakened rocks formed a hole. The dry bushes along the bottom left twigs in her hair. The dew left her covered in mud. Once through, she wiped her palms and looked around.

The world was different on the other side of the wall. Overgrown weeds and bare fields replaced the perfectly groomed gardens. The cobblestone roads became rutted routes of dirt. Scraggly bushes lined the roadside. Liviya stayed behind them and pulled the coat up around her cheeks.

Liviya stole across the village, hiding behind whatever offered her cover—leaning cabins, a large stump whose trunk had long since been cut down for fuel, a rickety wagon next to a corral that housed a sick-looking donkey. There was no money here, but she knew where to look.

It wasn't hard to pick a victim. Lord Drake's callous comments from the banquet still made her heart burn. He wouldn't miss the money, and he could use a lesson. His estate towered over the village from the top of the next hill, second only to the palace in grandeur. It, too, was surrounded by a fence, but that wouldn't be a problem for Liviya.

As she neared, she slowed down, hiding behind boulders and bushes until she was sure no one saw her. Liviya climbed the fence and crept across the grounds toward the mansion's back door. Slowly, she opened it and stepped inside.

The rooms were huge with wide windows and wall-length shelves full of books and trinkets that were proof of generations of money. Anything on there would be worth far more than twenty tilots, but someone would notice if they went missing. It would be best to steal coins. If she couldn't find any, she'd take something common and easy to hide. In the dark corridors, she fumbled around for a door and pushed it open. It was the kitchen. Polished silver waited in a tray. Perfect. Liviya tip-toed across the room and slipped a silver spoon into the pocket of Sarah's dress.

Heart pounding, she crept back into the corridor. In the darkness, Liviya reached out for the wall to lead her out, but she bumped a table. A vase crashed to the floor, shattering to pieces. She ran before waiting to see if anyone woke up. Halfway to the door, she heard the shouts, and shortly after that, pounding feet behind her.

Once outside, Liviya raced across the field and hurdled the fence, pausing just long enough to turn around and see if she had escaped. She hadn't. Lord Drake's guards crossed the fence just as easily. Liviya splashed through the stream separating two fields and weaved through the weeds. As she bounded, the hood fell from her head. When she reached the woods, the guards were still behind her.

Liviya raced down the road toward the village. The guards multiplied with every step she took. The first rays of light lit the street. A few villagers left their houses. A woman walked toward her carrying water. She looked surprised when she saw Liviya running and even more surprised when she saw the guards behind her.

"More guards down that way," she said as Liviya flew past.

Skidding as she slowed, Liviya veered to the left. The guards shouted orders. More appeared.

"Stop him!"

"Block the road!"

A short distance ahead, a boulder rose from the ground. Liviya ran and crouched behind it, sucking in big gulps of air. Her legs burned. She wouldn't be able to run much longer. Liviya dug her fingernails into her palms. She was powerless as a princess and a failure as a thief. Guards filled the streets, stopping the people and shouting questions. Their answers would lead them to Liviya. She never should have left the palace.

"Psst."

Liviya lifted her head above the boulder. An old man motioned to her from his house. She waited for the guards to pass, then crept toward him.

The man's house was bare. He opened the floor boards and hurried her into the cellar. It was dark and smelled of old potatoes, but it was a welcoming sight. The man shut the door above her and sat in a rocking chair. It was silent for only a moment until a strong knock threw open his door.

"We're chasing a thief. He came this way," a gruff voice said. At least two sets of feet moved around the man's house.

"'I 'aven't seen 'im," the man said. His rocking chair squeaked rhythmically.

"Five hundred tilots for catching him," the guard said.

"Hefty reward," the man replied. "I'll keep watch."

The guards took a few more steps above Liviya. She held her

breath until their footsteps moved toward the door. They shut the door behind them and shouted their update to the other guards outside. The man remained in his chair and continued rocking. Liviya didn't know how much time had passed while she was down there, but her breathing settled. Finally, the old man opened the door.

Liviya crawled out of the cellar and shook the cramps from her legs. She pulled the hood back over her head and kept her arm well within her deep sleeve, hoping to hide the fact that she was a princess and a maid.

"You got yourself in a mite of trouble, didn't ya, Princess?"

Heat flared into Liviya's cheeks. He knew exactly who she was. It was embarrassing for her and dangerous for everyone who saw her.

The man leaned on a crutch with one of his pant legs pinned below his knee. "Lost my leg," he said, even though Liviya had tried not to stare. He extended a calloused hand. "My name's Humphrey. It's a pleasure to help you. A real pleasure. I got some taters if you're hungry." He set a plate on the table.

Liviya was hungry, but there wasn't enough food for both of them. She wouldn't take food from a poor man. Not when she could return to the palace to eat. Assuming she made it back there alive.

"Please," Humphrey said. He pushed the plate toward her. Something about his plea made it impossible to refuse.

Liviya sat down and cut the potato on her plate. The small potatoes brought back memories of Barlow, Bicka, and all the nights with nothing else to eat.

The guards were gone now, but the entire village was awake. They talked excitedly in small groups. They were talking about her. Liviya ducked her head, hiding deeper in her hood.

"Make off with anything good?"

Liviya took the spoon from her pocket and set it on the table.

Humphrey slapped his good thigh. "You know, if you're tryin' to fill that canyon, a shovel would be much faster."

"Just trying to help a friend," Liviya muttered. She wouldn't waste time and energy on her challenge. She knew very well it was just a ploy from King Herrick to keep her from ever truly ruling.

Humphrey raised his eyebrows. "You don't think it can be done."

"Of course it can't. The river cuts it bigger every day."

"Sometimes if you want to make something stop, you gotta know how it started. You ever heard the legend of that canyon?"

Liviya shook her head and took another bite of potato.

Humphrey poured her some water from a chipped pitcher. "Legend tells that Saunder and Barlow combined was once ruled by a single king. He had two sons, as different as dirt and water, yet both would make a right solid king.

"Now, the king was a fair man. He split the kingdom between his boys. The border ran right through a man's farm where he lived with his beautiful daughter. Each prince fell in love with the girl and sought her hand. But like they do, the boys fought. The girl stood between them and was struck. It was only as she lay dying that the brothers set down their swords. They buried her on the border of their countries.

"Both blamed the other for her death, and neither could forgive. Every year, her grave grew deeper, separating the brothers more until it divided their entire lands and carved a hole into the earth." Humphrey wagged his finger at her. "Hate formed that canyon, Princess. Love will make it heal."

Liviya finished her potato and traced her fork along the plate while she pondered the legend, the brothers who battled, and the girl who died. It was an interesting story, but of no use to her. Even if she made it back to the palace, even if she did manage to fill the divide, she still had a scar. She'd never be queen.

"Best get you home before they miss you. You trade me coats." Humphrey pulled his coat from a hook. "They won't recognize you in this one, and I could use a better one." He chuckled heartily. Despite all the chaos, Liviya smiled.

The guards in the village slowly thinned. A final guard jogged past. Outside, the road was empty for a long time. Humphrey stood up and hobbled to his door, pushing it open.

"Go!" Humphrey whispered. "And thank you." It was a strange

reply, since he was the one who had helped her, but Liviya accepted it with a smile and ran.

Back at the palace, the grounds were alive with workers. Some were attending their chores. Many others were talking. Word of the thief had crossed the palace wall. Liviya remained crouched in the bushes. She had been gone much longer than she had intended. It would be difficult to get back inside.

Already someone approached. She ducked her head hoping she wouldn't be seen. It was Jacob, the stable hand who was often tagging along behind Michael. It was almost as bad as being found by Michael himself. Jacob hadn't seen her yet, but did sense something strange. He looked closer until he found Liviya hiding in the bushes. Despite the coat and the cover of the leaves, he recognized her. He gaped. "Princess?"

Jacob didn't ask for an explanation. "Come this way. It's clear." He led Liviya to the palace's back door, expertly avoiding everyone on the grounds.

"Wipe yer boots!" Mrs. Maude hollered as he pushed open the door. When she saw them, her mouth fell open. "Oh my."

MRS. MAUDE AND THE GROUP OF MAIDS THAT HAD GATHERED STARED AT Liviya. When she saw herself in the mirror, she stared, too. She was soaking wet. Her torn dress clung to her body. Blood dripped from her knuckles. She wasn't even sure when she had scraped them. Mud streaked her face and matted her hair. She was filthy, but still within recognition, and many people had seen her. All around the palace, the word of the thief was spreading. Soon it would become obvious that the princess was the thief.

"Get a bath going," Mrs. Maude ordered a maid. She looked around. "And where in the blazes is Sarah?"

"We switched places. That's how I got out. The guards think I'm still in my room." Liviya grimaced. It'd be impossible to return to her room without the guards seeing. It would be even more difficult to explain how she got out. This problem was well beyond their ability to solve. Liviya regretted dragging them into it.

"I'll go get Michael," another maid offered.

"Not Michael!" Liviya and Mrs. Maude said at the same time. Michael didn't need another reason to send her back home to Barlow.

"Go get the king," Mrs. Maude whispered. The maid nodded and ran down the hall, skirt flying behind her.

Mrs. Maude looked at the group gathered around her. "Now you all get back to work and give the princess some privacy. She don't sit and stare at you!" The maids slunk away. If rumors spread half as quickly here as they did in Barlow, Liviya would find herself arrested in a matter of minutes.

One of the maids curtsied. "I hope you had a good walk. The grounds sure are beautiful at sunrise."

"A girl just needs a moment's peace is all. Ain't my business how she goes about getting it," said another.

"And if Daniel didn't take all our money, nobody'd have to steal!" Chancey said. The other maids shushed her, but even Mrs. Maude smiled.

When they were alone, Mrs. Maude sat Liviya in a chair and began picking twigs from her hair. After Liviya's quick bath, Mrs. Maude gently combed the tangles.

Minutes later, Liviya sensed the king before she saw him. Something about his presence changed the air in the room. Behind them, he hung on Geoffrey's arm.

"Ah, Princess, what a delight to see you, as always."

Liviya smiled sheepishly.

"How bad is it?" he asked Mrs. Maude.

"All's clear from within the palace," Mrs. Maude replied. "Those girls ain't gonna say a word. Lucky for the princess, they've all taken a liking to her."

"And there's no mention of anything out of the grounds either," Geoffrey replied. "I'd dare say that the people inside the palace are just as loyal as the ones outside of it."

"Yet you dragged me down here," King Josiah said.

"Well," Mrs. Maude began, focusing on a particularly difficult tangle. "Michael stationed those bully guards at her room and they don't know she left. We're hurtin' to find a way to get her back without them asking us all sortsa nosy questions and gettin' word to Michael."

King Josiah looked around the room. "Yes, this seems like information Michael isn't quite ready to hear. He's making progress though, no?"

"Hard to say," Mrs. Maude replied. "He's so blasted stubborn."

The king looked to Geoffrey who shrugged. "He's making progress. Worried it's not going to be fast enough though."

"Do what you can to expedite this process," the king said. "I'm not going to live forever." He held a crooked arm toward Liviya. "May I escort you to your room?"

Without much of a choice, and without really knowing what they were talking about, Liviya left, holding on to one of the king's arms while Geoffrey held the other. While they walked, she wondered how much he knew. Liviya rubbed her forearm. He couldn't know that. She wouldn't still be here if he did.

The guards stood at perfect attention on each side of Liviya's door. They both blanched when they saw Liviya. One of them threw her door open and peeked inside. He stepped back out, eyes wide. Sarah came out behind him. She looked at Liviya hopefully, who nodded just a bit. She had succeeded. She had also made a huge mess, but Sarah's brother would be safe. It was a victory worth celebrating.

"As you may remember," the king said sternly, "I came for Liviya at sunrise. We went to the library and spent several hours working on her challenge. We are just now returning. You'll report this to Michael along with whatever it takes to make him believe it."

One guard nodded. The other furrowed his brow.

"I'm certain you remember this," Geoffrey said. "If you were sleeping on your watch, I'll have you dismissed from your post."

"We weren't sleeping, not at all, sir," the shorter of the two said. "In fact, I remember now. Right after sunrise."

The king looked at the other guard. "And do you remember as well?"

The guard shook his head. "I can't do it, Your Majesty. I can't lie to my captain. Not when he's only ever been honest to me."

"I ask you again, soldier," Geoffrey said, "Do you remember him coming for the princess?"

The man licked his lips and looked down to his boots.

"I'll do all the talking, Your Majesty," the shorter one said. "He won't have to say anything at all."

"Very good," the king said. "Under no circumstances will anyone speak otherwise." He looked to Liviya. "*Under no circumstances.*"

Liviya nodded. She would never say a word.

The king offered a small salute. Geoffrey helped him turn.

The guards pushed the door open the rest of the way and held out an arm for Liviya to get inside.

"Welcome back, Princess."

Liviya couldn't even muster a small smile. That was too close. She had nearly been caught—no, she had been caught. She was only lucky to have been caught by friends. That was stupid. She'd never sneak out again.

CHAPTER 18

*P*rince Daniel ordered the guards to interview every person in the village that morning. It took hours of painstaking labor. Still, they had learned nothing about the thief. Not a height, not a hair color, not a location. The people had refused rewards and withstood threats. Prince Daniel grew impatient.

Michael took off his captain's coat, opting instead for his white shirt with rolled sleeves. It was what he typically wore when he helped people mend their plows or harvest their crops or a myriad of other tasks he commonly performed alongside his neighbors. Today he wouldn't be talking to people as their captain, but as their friend. He would find the group of rebels. Today would be its last.

Michael started within the palace. Unflattering stories about the prince spread quickly to the people. Someone inside was sharing them. Whoever knew the prince's secrets probably had knowledge of the thief as well.

Michael found Jacob first. Inside the stables, he whistled as he oiled the saddles. Michael rustled his hair. "You fully recuperated from that blizzard?"

"I'm back fully strong. And you?"

"I work when I want and claim to ache when I don't," Michael said. "Best type of recuperated."

They shared a hearty laugh. When it died, Michael fiddled with some of the tack and pretended not to be eager to discuss the thief. "Sure was bold of someone to rob Lord Drake."

"Still can't believe it," Jacob said.

"Wonder who would be so stupid?" Michael asked

"Don't know." Jacob swirled the rag in circles against the saddle with his thumb.

"Five hundred tilots for information leading to the man's arrest."

Jacob dropped the rag. "Five hundred tilots? No, sir. I'd be the thief's next target, and your guards would let him escape again."

"Nobody escapes my guards," Michael snapped. "Somebody helped him."

"That's illegal. Now you've got two criminals."

"I've got dozens of criminals. Anybody who knows and doesn't speak is subject to the same punishment."

"Then I'm relieved I don't know nothin'." Jacob shifted his eyes to the ground and chewed on his lip.

"You listen to me, Jacob," Michael began. He was mildly annoyed to use a lesson he learned from Liviya, but he was certain it would work. "Sometimes there are tough choices to make and you don't know what to do, but let me tell you something. The only wrong choice is silence." Michael pointed a finger gently into Jacob's chest. "You're a brave lad. You listen to your heart and you do the right thing."

Michael watched as Jacob battled loyalties internally. He would make the right decision. Michael was sure of it.

"I don't know nothing," Jacob said.

Michael tilted his head. Usually when Jacob spoke, he ended his sentences with captain and sir. There in the stables, he couldn't even look Michael in the eye.

"Might be you've forgotten," Michael said, not wanting to push him too hard. "When you've remembered, come tell me."

Jacob tapped his temple. "I'll be thinkin'."

Michael found Chancey next. She walked down the hall toward the kitchen with a tray of dirty dishes. Michael tugged gently on her braid. "You hear any talk about the thief down in the kitchens?"

Chancey peered above the stack of dirty dishes. "Nobody tells me anything. I'm the lowest runt in this palace."

"Now you know that's not true," Michael said, dropping his eyebrows into a stern line. "You're my favorite girl here. And the princess likes you, too." Michael had once been Chancey's favorite, but he had been shoved aside within days of the princess arriving in the palace. Liviya seemed to understand Chancey and her heartache much better than Michael ever could.

"Listen," Michael said, "you tell me everything you know and I'll tell the princess to get you one of them shiny pins like I've got on my coat. It means you're brave. A hero."

Chancey, the girl who got excited about ribbons, bits of bread with extra spread, and even the mildest of praise, rolled her eyes. "You're in my way."

Michael stepped aside, but took the tray from her hands. He was walking to the kitchen anyway; he might as well lighten Chancey's load just a little. Besides, she might decide to remember something.

Michael walked into the kitchen with Chancey following closely behind. He took a deep breath. "Smells delicious in here."

Mrs. Maude leaned over a boiling pot. "Hello, Michael."

"How's Mr. Maude's back doing?"

"It hurts him, but he's alive."

"I bet you're glad he was discharged from the army," Michael said.

Mrs. Maude stood up straight. She faced Michael and shook her spoon in his face. "I was up before the sun, and I been slavin' over these pots all mornin'. Don't be kissin' me for gossip. I ain't heard any."

Frustration growing, Michael continued his rounds of the palace grounds. Nobody said anything, but they all knew something. The maids were silent, the stable boys whispered. People seemed to wander about, not knowing where to go or what to do, just knowing they wanted to look busy. The air in the palace felt stuffy and every conversation sounded stilted. Except for Liviya, who bounded down the stairs with a smile, nearly plowing into Michael.

"Good morning, Michael," she chirped. In a palace full of people who looked guilty, Liviya looked innocent. That made Michael very suspicious. Could Liviya have robbed Lord Drake? She didn't like him. She made that clear at the ball. But why would she need a silver spoon, the only item reported missing? And how would she have gotten out of the palace? Unless the rebellion had worked its way into the ranks of the army and the guards let her escape.

Michael scaled the stairs to Liviya's room. He met the guards in the hall. They did not look surprised to see him.

"Did the princess leave this room last night?"

"The king came for her first thing this morning," the first guard replied.

"You're certain? Was there anything unusual at all? Anything different than other nights?"

"No, sir," the guard said again.

Michael fixed his gaze deeper. "I've heard nothing but lies all morning. Tell me what you know."

The guard shrugged. "All I know is what I saw. The king came about sunrise. They came back a few hours later."

The other guard stared straight ahead. His name caught on Michael's tongue. Michael shuffled through several names trying to remember it. Gilbert. His brother had been injured in a skirmish just last spring. Michael had been the one to tell his family that he wouldn't survive. He died shortly after. Michael had helped him bury the body.

"Gilbert, I need your help. Please."

Gilbert chewed on the inside of his cheek. Michael had nearly given up when he finally spoke. "The first time I saw the princess this morning. She was with the king."

Michael sighed. More useless lies.

"There is one thing," Gilbert said. "A maid came by last night. Sounded like she was upset in there."

Finally, a clue. But it wasn't enough to figure out how this placed

Liviya in Lord Drake's house last night or how she would have gotten back into the palace.

"Which maid was it?" Michael asked.

"I don't know the difference between them," Gilbert said.

"She was real pretty," the other guard said. "Long blonde hair."

"Thank you, gentlemen," Michael said, bowing slightly. "You've done well."

The guards stood straighter and looked as pleased as professionalism would allow. Michael nodded his approval and continued his search. He found Sarah in the kitchen. She jumped when Michael addressed her.

"Blast it, Michael, you scared me." Scowling, she focused more intently on the needle in her hand and dress spread on her lap.

"The guards say you attended to the princess last night."

"What's it to you?" Sarah asked.

"The guards said she was upset."

"I didn't do or say nothin', if that's what you're saying. I just took in fresh towels and a pitcher of water." She stared at the hem line. Her eyes moved back and forth quickly, like she was reading the answers to questions Michael hadn't asked yet.

"Huh," Michael said. "You have any idea where she was this morning? She missed breakfast."

"She was attending to private matters," Sarah replied.

"What private matters?"

"I didn't ask." She clipped the thread with her teeth. "It would have made them not private."

Michael studied her. She knew more than she was saying, but Michael couldn't force the information out of her.

"Keep an eye on her, will you?" Michael said. "The princess has some wild in her."

Sarah puffed up her cheeks and blew out the air slowly. "I'll certainly try."

Michael returned to the drawing room and sat down. Geoffrey entered and sat across from him. A gleam lit his eye.

"What do you know?" Michael grumbled.

"All I know is that these people love their thief a lot more than they love you."

"Calling him a thief is generous. All he took was a spoon."

Geoffrey nodded his concession. "But he gave the people something they were wanting. They got themselves a mascot now. A leader. Someone to follow."

Geoffrey was right. This was different than the others. This was a targeted attack.

Michael sat in silence until it broke with the sound of Prince Daniel's boots. "Where is he?"

Michael inhaled slowly. "Nobody saw him, Your Highness."

Daniel roared, "Nobody saw him? That thief ran circles around my village followed by dozens of guards, and nobody saw him?" He beat his fists against the table. "I want him found, and I want anyone involved in his hiding or escape whipped."

Michael grimaced. "I don't know who saw him and who's lying."

Prince Daniel looked up with a fiery gaze. "Then whip them all."

For days Liviya had feared what would happen if someone had reported her name. What she should have feared is what would happen if nobody did. Prince Daniel had arrested the entire village and gathered them to be publicly tried. Liviya sat between the king and the prince on the balcony overlooking the courtyard. Below, guards erected the lashing beam that would stand until someone spoke or everyone bled. Liviya was certain Prince Daniel would show no mercy.

Michael read the first name from the list. "Jameson of Teel, you are accused of withholding information from the king's guards. The punishment is ten lashes. Do you wish to speak now?"

A man came to the front, a poor man, like everyone else in the village. His coat was tattered and stained, but he looked determined. "Got no words to say."

Michael shrugged regrettably and motioned to the hooded guard.

He flexed his muscles and uncurled the whip. Liviya looked away. The king dropped his gaze to his knees. The whip landed against the man's back with ten loud cracks that echoed across the crowd. When it was done, the man faced the crowd. He raised his fist into the air. The people cheered. Liviya's stomach flipped.

Michael looked back to his list. "Matthew of Teel, you are also accused of withholding information from the king's guards. Do you wish to speak now?"

The man shook his head.

Prince Daniel gave the order. As the whip fell, the crowd chanted. *One. Two. Three. Four.* When they reached ten, they cheered again so loudly that nobody heard the next name. A man from the crowd came forward voluntarily.

"I withheld information, but I ain't ready to speak."

Michael pointed him to the guards.

The celebrations grew louder. Next, several volunteers came forward and formed a line at the lashing beam.

Michael looked to the prince, seeming to ask the same question Liviya wondered. Did Prince Daniel really intend to whip them all? These people wouldn't break. Prince Daniel motioned to the guard. In a quick succession, four men received their lashes.

Humphrey hobbled forward next. He had saved her life. Liviya wouldn't let him be punished. She had to speak. King Josiah placed a firm hand on her knee. Liviya swallowed her words. She hid her eyes, but it was impossible to drown out the sounds.

As the morning sun lifted, the punishments continued to fall until, finally, all the men from the village had received their lashings.

The people cheered again, even louder than before. Michael crumpled his list and threw it behind him. He looked exhausted, like reading those names had required every bit of his energy. Liviya exhaled. The people had won. She had thought that Prince Daniel would be angry, but he just watched. He almost looked amused.

When the applause finally died. Prince Daniel stood up. "Now whip the others."

Jane passed their daughter to Dmitri and came forward.

"No," Prince Daniel said. "Whip the children." He pointed into the crowd. "Start there."

A hush fell over the crowd. Prince Daniel pointed to a boy about eight. His mother muffled a sob.

Liviya held a hand against her mouth to keep the vomit down. Michael hesitated for a few counts, too long for the prince.

"Whip him," the prince ordered.

Michael frowned. "He's too young to have seen anything."

Prince Daniel didn't bother to reply.

Michael rubbed both hands across his stubbled face.

The boy's parents communicated a thousand things through a single stare, then in agreement, the father, back bruised, struggled to kneel in front of his son. He adjusted the boy's shirt and uttered some words of encouragement with a grave, but optimistic, smile.

The boy nodded, then with the confidence of someone who knew he was doing something important, he began to walk forward. The people parted. A low murmur of praise rose above the crowd.

Liviya looked to the king. He'd stop this. He'd either let her confess or command Prince Daniel to stop. But he seemed rather oblivious to the scene. His subtle distress from earlier was replaced with a keen interest in Michael.

Michael turned to the crowd. "Any who remains silent defies the laws of their future king. Someone speak!"

Liviya stood up. She needed to stop this. A voice rose from the crowd first. "I'll speak."

The crowd parted. Humphrey came forward, leaning more heavily on his crutch than usual. "I'll speak, but I've only got one thing to say." He hobbled to the front of the crowd and faced Michael. "You accuse us of defying our future king." He pointed at Prince Daniel. "That man is not my king. Not now, not ever."

The cheers erupted again, and this time, they didn't subside. Prince Daniel leapt to his feet. "Seize him!"

The guards came forward and grabbed Humphrey underneath his elbows. They pulled him back to the beam. In seemingly slow-motion, his crutch fell to the ground.

The cheers became near violent outbursts. With ten more loud cracks, the whip fell against Humphrey's back. The guards struggled to contain the angry crowd who pushed against their swords. Prince Daniel descended the balcony stairs. He stood in front of Humphrey who hung weakly from the beams, only standing because he was tied. "Who was the thief?"

Humphrey shook his head.

"Who is your king?"

Humphrey spat at the prince's feet.

Prince Daniel turned his finger in a circle and stood back a few feet as the guard lashed him again. The lashes came again with furious cracks that echoed across the courtyard. This time, they cut through the skin. Blood trickled down Humphrey's back. The ropes dug into his arms as he struggled to stand.

"Say it," Prince Daniel said.

Liviya was quite sure Daniel had forgotten about the thief and only wanted Humphrey to call him king. Humphrey moaned and struggled to pull himself up. Legs failing, he collapsed further.

"Again," Daniel said.

The whip fell again. Crack. Scream. Crack. Scream. Crack. Scream. The people roared, charging against the guards.

Now Humphrey lay on the floor in a bloody heap, shoulders straining against the pull of the ropes.

"Say it," Prince Daniel ordered.

Blood in Humphrey's mouth made his refusal only a gurgle. He was going to die. Prince Daniel was going to kill him in front of an entire village, and he hadn't done a single thing wrong.

"Again," the prince said.

Liviya's panic erupted in complete hysteria. She screamed pleas to anyone near, the prince, the king, Michael. She pleaded with Humphrey to take back his words. She screamed that she was the thief. Nobody heard her over the clamor of the crowd. The king watched without a word. The guard raised the whip.

Michael held up a hand. "Let him go."

The silence fell immediately.

Prince Daniel turned to Michael, face twisted. "Let him go?"

"Let him go," Michael repeated.

The guard dropped the whip. Others rushed forward to untie Humphrey's arms. He crumpled to the stone.

Liviya sank into her chair, shaking. She hid her hands in her face. The sound of rushing blood made her dizzy and muddled the sounds of the crowd. This was her fault. She had been stupid and reckless. She focused on even breaths, telling herself it was done. The words didn't relieve her. Her stomach churned. Knocking into the chairs as she ran down the stairs, she knelt into the bushes and vomited. Each heave threw her body forward as the bile erupted from her mouth. She was shaking and sweating, and all she could think was those people had been punished because of her. And they would be punished again.

MICHAEL WALKED INTO THE PALACE. PRINCE DANIEL FOLLOWED A FEW steps behind. He slammed the door. The windows rattled. "I gave you orders!"

It was the first time Michael had intentionally disobeyed the prince. In his loyalty to the prince, he couldn't allow him to do something that would be harmful, even if that meant defying him in front of an entire village. In the process of searching for a traitor, the prince had made one.

"That man's life would have cost you your crown." Michael pulled the curtain back from the window, revealing the crowd below. The fury had simmered somewhat, but it would reignite without much provocation. "Forget the graffiti. Forget the thief. Forget the people who let him run. Focus on your challenge. That's the only thing preventing you from receiving your crown."

Prince Daniel pulled the ruby from his pocket and launched it across the room. It hit a mirror, showering glass against the floor. "I can't make the worthless thing clear!"

Michael crouched down and reached out, gently touching the ruby before he took hold of it. He always feared that it was hot, or worse, that it would change color under his touch. The deep red color remained. The ruby was supposed to be red. Prince Daniel was supposed to be king. Why did so many want to change what shouldn't be changed?

Michael held it up to the light. It really was remarkable, deep red without a single blemish. He exhaled deeply, trying to think of anything that would help his prince. "What if you purged it of its color? Maybe a fire."

Prince Daniel rubbed his jaw. The anger melted to thoughtfulness. Slowly, a smile formed. Then Prince Daniel rubbed his hands together. "A fire!"

"Perhaps the potter," Michael suggested, eager to offer a place where the heat and flames would be contained under the care of an expert.

Prince Daniel left, muttering plans to himself. Michael felt uneasy. The prince was planning something, probably something stupid.

With a sigh, Michael returned to the courtyard. Nearby, Liviya vomited into the bushes. Sarah stood beside her, holding her hair. Chancey waited with a towel. When Liviya finished, Michael helped her stand.

Shaking, she wiped her mouth on her sleeve. "I'm so sorry."

"It's quite all right," Michael said. "Go fetch some water."

Liviya folded into a curtsy. "Yes, Your Majesty."

Michael cocked his head. For what seemed several minutes, he was confused. Clearly, he was talking to the maid. But Liviya had responded instead. He saw the terror on Sarah's face, the confusion on Chancey's, and the disbelief on Liviya's. It was the look of someone who had made the biggest mistake of her life. Then Michael understood. He reached for Liviya's arm and pulled up her sleeve. Embedded into her skin was the raised, purple P. *Purchased.* Liviya was King Herrick's slave.

Michael, speechless, stared into Liviya's eyes. She stared back, resolute. She'd die. She had known her fate for weeks, and she wasn't scared at all.

CHAPTER 19

*L*iviya wasn't gone, not yet. She was locked in her room under the watch of Michael's most trusted guards while he tried to decide what to do. Prince Daniel hadn't asked about Liviya. He probably didn't even know she was missing, though Michael keenly felt her absence. The entire kingdom did. She might have only been a maid, but she had become a dear friend to many people. Her presence brought a light into the palace that was sorely needed.

Michael sat with Geoffrey in the potter's shop in the city. The ruby, still hot from the oven, sat at the table. Each second it cooled, it turned a brighter, more brilliant red. It was another failed attempt to make it clear. Michael was exhausting his ideas.

"Liviya lied," Michael said. He had been keeping the secret himself, but he needed advice.

"Well, I'll be." Geoffrey smiled. "You know, I was always suspicious she didn't hate you near as much as she claimed."

Michael startled. "Not about that. About the alliance."

"Oh," Geoffrey said slowly. He prodded the ruby with the tongs. "You mean all that talk about wanting to run away but coming to save her people instead? That was all a lie?"

The words left Michael again, and he fumbled to explain the problem. "I saw a scar on her arm. She's just a maid."

He waited for Geoffrey's reaction, the same anger and betrayal that Michael had felt, the shock of her lie, the vindication of being right about the alliance. But there was no reaction at all. He had already known.

"How did you know?" Michael asked.

"Just suspected, is all," Geoffrey replied. "Are you a reader of history? It often repeats itself, you know."

Michael hadn't read the history. There were far more pressing matters. "I can't tell Daniel." Michael studied the exaggerated roundness of his face reflected by the ruby. "The people love her. If Daniel hurts her, they'll hate him even more." There it was, his biggest fear spoken aloud. It wasn't the fake alliance, the lying maid-turned-princess, the scar on her arm. It was how Prince Daniel would react. He'd kill her.

Geoffrey nodded. He knew this every bit as well as Michael did.

"So what are you going to do?" Geoffrey asked.

"Well, she can't go home. Otherwise the alliance is nulled. Prince Daniel would have to defeat a different enemy." The prince's previous idea had been a war. Michael didn't want that either. "But she can't stay," Michael added, fearful Geoffrey would suggest that.

"Of course not," Geoffrey agreed. "If she became queen, what's to stop, say, someone like you from becoming king?"

Michael rubbed his nose and stole a glance at Geoffrey, trying to decide how much Geoffrey knew about Michael's personal conversations with the king. His expression didn't offer any clues.

"Besides, she was a terrible liar," Geoffrey added. "Someone would find out her history eventually. She was much too friendly with the maids, didn't know a darn thing about being fancy, and she was always causing trouble, what with robbing Lord Drake and such."

Michael punched the air. "I knew it was her!" He growled and shook his head. "She almost got herself killed."

Geoffrey shrugged. "There was a problem, she stepped up and solved it as best she could. I don't fault her for trying." His voice became softer. Almost reverent. "I sure was shocked to see every single person take a beating for her. Thought at least one would be bought or bled out. They're a loyal bunch, aren't they?"

Michael shook his head. "Loyalty is awfully subjective. Prince Daniel is sure his rebels live in that village."

It was silent for a long minute. Geoffrey turned his gaze to the ruby and prodded it again with the tongs. He almost looked bored. "It's a good thing she won't be queen. You're about her only enemy. The people would have helped make her queen, even if it meant defeating you."

"That's probably true." Michael stood up and dusted off his pants. He didn't have to make a decision today. An answer would come. Until then, he'd just think on it.

The ruby waited on the table, still red as blood. Michael put it in a pouch and returned the tools to their shelves. As Geoffrey pushed the door open, something outside caught Michael's eye. "What in the blazes?"

LIVIYA SAT IN HER ROOM FOR TWO DAYS, ALONE EXCEPT THE GUARDS. She wasn't sure how long it took most people to determine punishments for treason, but she was pretty sure it wasn't supposed to take two days. Yet, she sat there, waiting and waiting.

The guards didn't move. They barely blinked. Their weapons were poised and ready for any escape attempt. Liviya had lied too many times. There wasn't a single second that she wasn't watched. That made escaping difficult. Instead, she sat and sat and sat.

Liviya leaned onto the back two legs of the chair and picked at her fingernails, pretending to be painfully bored, when really her mind was racing. She needed just a moment with the guards distracted. Anything would do it, a clatter from the hall or a shout from below the window. If they only briefly turned their heads, she could run out the door and be gone. But there was nothing.

Sighing, Liviya turned to the window and calculated how long she had been in Saunder. Only a few weeks., but it was longer than she would have guessed she would survive. King Herrick was probably surprised as well. She had made a few friends, made a few messes, eaten some good meals, and attended a ball. Overall, it had been a good experience. She was sad to see it end. And though she pretended otherwise, she was quite scared to die.

Outside, the sun began its descent. It sat above the mountain in a perfect circle of brilliant red, like blood. Liviya had watched the sunset many times from her window, but she had never seen this before. "What a peculiar sunset," Liviya said, mostly to herself.

One guard kept his gaze on Liviya. He nudged the other, who turned to look.

"I've seen that before," he said thoughtfully. "It was during a fire. The light looked different when it was shining through the smoke."

Then the smell of smoke reached Liviya's nose, like it hadn't been there until it was invited.

"Fire! The village is on fire!" someone screamed outside.

The guards and Liviya raced to the window. She stood on her toes to peer over their shoulders.

In seconds that moved like hours, a crowd appeared. Their voices swelled in a chorus of panic. In the distance, a plume of smoke rose into the sky, thick and dark like an impending storm. All Liviya could do was stare.

Just outside the palace walls, flames crawled into the sky, spitting sparks and curses. Men gathered tools from the sheds and loaded them into wagons. Liviya watched them race into the village and knew it was too late. The fire was too big, too hot. It would stop burning only when it ran out of fuel. No number of men could stop it. It was terrifying, it was tragic, and, Liviya realized, it was distracting.

"Heaven help us," a guard whispered. They both continued to stare out the window. Liviya took a single step backward. Then another. When she had reached the door, she turned the knob. Then she ran.

∾

MICHAEL AND GEOFFREY RACED BACK TO THE PALACE. LIVIYA'S GUARDS met them at the bottom of the steps.

"She's gone, Captain," one said, hanging his head.

Michael pressed his eyes closed. Liviya was gone. He should have been happy. She was safe, and Michael didn't have to lie to Daniel to make it happen. Instead, his whole core felt empty, like his heart had stopped beating.

"Go find her," Geoffrey told him gently. "She can't be far."

Michael scanned the horizon. He could find her easily; he was sure of it. He knew every inch of his land. But what would he do when he found her? Offer her a ride home? Ask her to stay? Say goodbye and watch her leave? No. There was nothing to say, nothing to do. Michael turned his gaze back to the smoke, slicing across the sky like the cut of an angry knife. "These people need help."

The guards fell in line behind him, eager to follow him to the fight. But he was no hero. He would rather walk into flames and risk his life than walk across a field and risk his heart. He was a coward. The realization was humbling, and it was painful.

CHAPTER 20

Run for the mountains, Liviya told herself as soon as she was out of the palace. It was the best place to hide and would offer protection until she returned home. *Run for the mountains*. Even as she said the words aloud, her feet moved her toward the village. People were dying, and she owed each one of them her life. Besides, nobody would look for her there. She'd help as best she could. Then she'd return home.

Liviya rummaged around the stables for some supplies, filled a canteen of water, and crawled under the wall.

The smoke was thick in the village. Liviya's eyes watered. Her lungs burned. She pulled her shawl over her nose. Still, she coughed on inhaled sediment. Flames roared into the night sky, stretching their fiery fingers toward the stars. The village was already burnt. Mounds of ash sat where homes once were, glowing orange with hot embers. Despite the losses, the people still fought. Every horse and every plow and every man and woman with a shovel overturned the dirt. Under the light of the flames, their sweaty backs and faces glistened. The hungry fire wanted the forest. The trees would pass the sparks among their leaves until they reached the palace.

Liviya tore her gaze from the flames. She didn't come here to fight fire. People were hurt. On the outside of the village, behind the meager protection of tilled ground, dozens of bodies lay on worn blankets. Wails and screams rose above the roaring flames. As best as they were able, two women attended to the injured. Liviya ran to them, her stolen canteen of water thumping against her back. A knot formed in Liviya's throat as she imagined the people, backs still welted, struggling to escape.

Hour after hour, people beat the flames, and hour after hour, Liviya helped those who were injured. The line of needy grew throughout the night. Many were moved to the pile of lifeless bodies. Liviya worked without stopping. There was no time to mourn them. Others waited.

Liviya wrapped a crying child in a blanket, praying his parents were alive. She stepped to the next in line when someone grabbed her hand. Ash colored the man's face and streaked his silver hair. She wouldn't have recognized him except for the pant leg pinned under his knee. Liviya dropped to her knees beside him, her shadow shielding him from the light of the flames.

"Are you all right?"

Humphrey coughed and smiled weakly. "There's a legend about the canyon, you know."

"I know," Liviya said. "You told me."

"Hate caused that divide. Love will bring it back together." His voice was raspy.

Though Liviya had stitched wounds and cut off burnt flesh, she began to panic. "Breathe," she ordered. "Breathe slowly."

"I'm sorry I couldn't do more." He wheezed a shaky breath. He was dying. Liviya didn't know how to give the help she owed. Easing him onto a blanket, Liviya stroked his hair. She sang a lullaby, forcing the words through her tight throat. Humphrey's gaze softened, his tense body grew limp, and his wide eyes slowly closed.

"No. No." Liviya's head swirled. This man had saved her life. He had kept her secret and been punished to protect her. Liviya dropped her face to her hands. Sobs shook her body, but no tears fell. They had been licked away by the flames. She had never experienced death in this way, but somehow the tragedy was all too familiar. Inside, something told her that King Herrick had started that fire.

MICHAEL DIDN'T SLEEP THAT NIGHT, BECAUSE NIGHT NEVER FELL. As the morning sun rose, the flames died, but the world remained gray, covered in a cloud that Michael feared would never pass.

All through the night, Michael fought the fire. It took hours of labor from dozens of men and women to protect the palace from the flames. The people worked without rest, without water. They worked without breathing.

It was well into the morning, flames long since gone, when Prince Daniel arrived. Michael stood in a line with the other shadows, people silent and blackened by ash. They huddled together. Some cried. Most were still. In the distance, a few men dragged dead bodies to a crude pile until they could be buried beneath the very ash that killed them.

Prince Daniel stepped down from his carriage. The horses were brushed, coats shining. The slick sides of the carriage glistened. Prince Daniel was clean and well-dressed. Michael twisted in his coat, knowing full well that the coat wasn't the cause of his discomfort.

Holding his arms above his head, the prince waved to the people. "Come. Gather."

The people inched forward as best as their injuries, exhaustion, and shock would allow. Prince Daniel waited within arm's reach of his wagon and addressed the crowd. He was a wonderful orator, that was certain. Soothing words fell from his lips like sounds of nature.

The people applauded, except Geoffrey. He stood next to Michael with his arms folded across his chest, expression stern.

"That's not a king," Geoffrey said. "That's a boy in a silly coat. A king would have fought with his people."

Michael stepped sideways. He didn't agree with Geoffrey's words, but he had been struggling with the same questions. Where had Daniel been all night when everyone else in the kingdom fought side by side?

Prince Daniel climbed back in the wagon with a proud grin.

Confused and exhausted, Michael couldn't return even a polite smile. "I'm going to stay. They'll need help digging graves."

MICHAEL WALKED ACROSS THE BURNT VILLAGE TO WHERE GEOFFREY AND others had resumed digging. He patted Geoffrey on the shoulder and passed him some water.

"Seventeen." Geoffrey sank to the ground. Exhaustion cut creases across his forehead. His hands were black and clothes ruined. He chugged the water. When it was gone, Geoffrey grabbed his shovel and dug alongside Michael.

Michael drove the shovel into the ground and threw the dirt next to his hole. Again and again he pierced the earth. The emotions from every recent disaster combined into a furious rage. He was powerless against the flames. The rebels were completely hidden to him. Prince Daniel lost more favor with his people every day. The king wanted Michael to take the crown. And Liviya. Liviya. He wished that he had never met her. No. He wished he had never seen that scar.

Michael dug until blisters tore open his palms. He was aware he was bleeding, but didn't feel the pain. The graves were shallow, barely more than a trench in the dirt to cover the bodies. Michael wiped the sweat off his face with his forearm, knowing that it colored his face black with ash. He pressed the shovel into the ground again, hopping on the blade when it stuck. He pulled back on the handle, and it broke. Splintered wood sliced across his palm.

Michael howled and hurled the broken shovel across the burnt village.

"Better get that looked at," Geoffrey said. "They're cleaning people up over there." He offered Michael a dirty handkerchief. Kicking debris as he passed, Michael walked to the outskirts of city.

Dozens of injured people gathered under a tent in a makeshift hospital. Michael joined the crowd. He bowed his head and closed his eyes, taking advantage of a small moment to rest. Someone placed a gentle hand on his shoulder and placed a cup of water in his clasped hands.

"Are you all right?" she asked.

"I'm fine, thank you, miss." Michael lifted his head. The girl wore pants and a heavy coat caked in ash. A shawl that probably once covered her face hung around her shoulders. Her face was filthy, but she was beautiful. Amidst the devastation, he recognized her immediately. "Princess?"

Liviya stumbled back a step. It looked like she might run. Then she caught sight of Michael's hand. Thankfully, the handkerchief was stained with blood. True to one of her only weaknesses, Liviya's compassion won over her concern for her life. She took the bloody handkerchief from his hand and poured water onto his wound. It burned like the devil.

"I thought you were running away," Michael said through clenched teeth.

Liviya's hand shook. She breathed deeply to hold her voice steady. "I thought about it. But the people needed help."

Michael grimaced, feeling even more discouraged about Daniel. Even Liviya had come to help the people fight. Geoffrey would probably consider her closer to the crown than Daniel based on her service alone.

Liviya knelt in front of him. Ash dotted her cheeks like freckles. Courage shone through her eyes. She was fearless, yet she had none of the coarseness of a soldier. Her hands were gentle. Her body swayed slowly as she nursed Michael's hand, like every movement was a beat from a lullaby bringing peace to a nightmare.

Michael wiped his mouth, remembering his searches for the thief who had been in front of him all along. The frustration of all the lies was humorous now. Of course the people chose her over him.

"You robbed Lord Drake," Michael said.

At least Liviya had the decency to look chagrined. "I didn't want everyone to get punished. I tried to speak up, but the king didn't let me say one word."

"The king knew?" Michael groaned and dropped his head back.

Whose loyalty hadn't she won? As soon as the question was asked, the answer came. She hadn't won Michael's loyalty. Geoffrey was right. Michael was her enemy. Everyone in Barlow and Saunder served her like the queen she should be. Michael was upset about her past as a peasant.

In the humble hospital, dozens of people had received her care. Even dressed like a peasant, the people knew who she was and exhibited a loyalty equal to what they showed King Josiah.

Michael didn't know why King Herrick chose to send her, but he saw very clearly why King Josiah chose to keep her. She was simply perfection. It might have been true that her blood wasn't royal, but it was pumped through her body from a heart of gold. That was more valuable than unending royal ancestors. It was more valuable than treasuries of jewels. This girl was good. She was born to be queen.

If it weren't for King Herrick's branding, she would have been. Without seeing it, Michael never would have suspected she was anything other than a queen, a goddess, even.

Liviya pulled the towel away from Michael's hand and inspected the bleeding. "You should get some salve on this so it doesn't scar."

Michael slowly extended his fingers, testing the pain. "What salve gets rid of scars?"

"Ask a physician," Liviya said impatiently. "I don't know which ones."

Michael turned his scarred hands over in his lap. Everyone had scars. Physical or otherwise. If Liviya's only scar was on her arm, well, that was a lot better than a scar in a heart or a scar in a soul.

Liviya's arm was covered with a long sleeve, as always. "Have you, uh, have you ever tried to get rid of your scar?"

Liviya rolled her eyes. "I barely had food, Michael."

Michael turned his gaze to the cut on his hand, grateful for the distraction it offered as he carefully formed his next thought. The people closest, sensing the privacy of the conversation, eased away and returned to their work. When they were alone, Michael spoke. "Suppose you stayed."

"The palace has plenty of people to polish silver."

Michael met her eyes. "Suppose you stayed and became queen."

"No." Liviya fastened the bandage around his hand. "Try to keep it clean. I've got others to help now."

"You'd live in a palace, be married to the prince."

Liviya wrinkled her nose. Michael shifted thoughts quickly.

"The alliance would be real. Your land would have water."

Shaking her head, Liviya pulled away. "You can send as much water as you want, but Herrick will never give it to my people."

"Liviya," Michael called as she walked away. It was the first time he had used her name since the day he met her. He loved the way it sounded, the way it felt in his mouth. "I'll kill Herrick."

Liviya paused and turned. She bit her lip. "When?"

"As soon as you're queen. We'll take your people food, too. I'll send my guards. Hundreds of them. They'll put the food right in the people's hands."

With a frown, Liviya shook her head. "I can't lie forever."

Michael stood up and followed after her. "Just complete the requirements. Then you'll be queen. No lies."

Liviya pulled up her sleeve, revealing the thick scar. "Have you forgotten?"

"Please," Michael whispered. "I'll help you."

Liviya cocked her head like she was listening for something, a sign of danger, perhaps. Michael held his breath. He was afraid to speak, afraid the wrong words would crush the fragile dream.

Finally, Liviya spoke. "Promise?"

Michael held out his bandaged hand. "I swear on my life."

Liviya placed her hand in his and gave it three solid pumps. They stood in the ash under the moonlight, hand in hand.

Michael studied her face and saw the signs of exhaustion. Like most others, Liviya had probably been there all night. "You should rest." Michael motioned to the palace behind them. "May I?"

Arm in arm, Michael led Liviya through the burnt village and toward the front gates of the palace. Like the first time they entered the kingdom, Michael wondered what it would be like to lead her to a palace that was his. Unlike the first time, as they passed, every person bowed.

THAT NIGHT, MICHAEL SAT IN THE SERVANTS' QUARTERS WITH A SMALL group of people, people he considered the elect of the kingdom. Liviya was asleep in her room, a fact that Michael had verified with his own eyes.

Each of the people knew at least one of Liviya's secrets. Several, like Mrs. Maude, knew that Liviya had robbed Lord Drake. Others, like Chancey and Sarah, had seen her scar. Geoffrey seemed to know everything. Michael was sure that a few people among them knew secrets even he didn't know.

Michael stood in front of the group and tacked a few pictures to the wall. "I've been researching the canyon." He used a stick to point to one of the pictures. "All information I found indicated, as we knew, that the canyon was there well before any people of Saunder came to the area. Ancient inhabitants have varying views on how the canyon formed. Some claim it was thousands of years' worth of erosion. Others say a flood that tore through the area, digging into the ground in a matter of hours. It's possible it was a mix of both. Either way, filling it is not an option. We risk damming the river. Without water, we're no different than Barlow."

He moved to another picture. "I've consulted with some experts about covering the canyon. While it wouldn't technically be filled, the divide would be sealed, but I haven't received a report on possible consequences of that. I'd also like to discuss the specifics with the king. It's possible we don't need to fill it entirely or we could find a way to fill it temporarily to spare our water."

Michael moved to the next picture.

"Hold up, Professor," Geoffrey said.

Geoffrey stood up and took Michael's spot. Michael slumped into Geoffrey's chair. The challenges were frustrating. Michael didn't want the kingdom, he reminded himself. Still, he would have liked to have been able to solve both challenges, or at least help Liviya and Daniel with theirs. Michael brushed his frustration aside. Geoffrey was quite a bit older and worked with the king far longer than Michael had. That gave him a distinct advantage in solving the riddles. Geoffrey stood at the front of the room, his stance commanding the attention of everyone there. If Prince Daniel didn't become king, Geoffrey would sure make a good one. Much better than Michael.

"Like Michael, I did some research," Geoffrey said. "Unlike Michael, rather than researching the canyon, I researched the actual challenge." He placed a worn, leather-bound book on the table in front of them. "This is the king's personal history." Geoffrey ran his thumb along the book's edge. "The first recorded use of this challenge came just over twenty years ago. Prince Nathan, about to become king, was working on his requirements. He had fallen in love and brought the girl to his father for his blessing in marriage. Interestingly, he had fallen in love with a palace maid."

That was interesting. How peculiar to have two palace maids be presented to become queen of the same land.

"King Josiah was furious," Geoffrey said. "Prince Nathan argued that she could be queen, that if she completed the requirements then she could rule. King Josiah issued the challenge that she fill the canyon, knowing that it would never be completed."

Michael ran his fingers through his hair. "Then he means to prevent it from happening again."

"Slow down," Geoffrey replied, extending his hand. "What's interesting to note is that it was not King Josiah who gave Liviya her challenge. King Herrick did. When Liviya arrived," Geoffrey continued, "King Josiah respected Herrick's wishes and confirmed her challenge. There was a slight difference, though. 'Fill the canyon,' the king said. 'The division between the lands.'"

Geoffrey looked rather pleased with himself. Michael furrowed his brow, still trying to understand. As he glanced around, he was glad to see others looked just as confused as he was.

Geoffrey sighed, and continued. "There is a literal and figurative division between Barlow and Saunder. We witnessed this in the mob that assembled when Liviya first arrived. Yet weeks later, an entire village withstood a beating in order to defend her. Where in that trial in the courtyard was there evidence of a division between our lands? There was none. Every person who protected Liviya that day threw a scoop of dirt into the canyon that divides our lands."

Geoffrey paced in front of the small group. "Our countries have been at war for a long time. But the war is coming to an end. When Liviya becomes queen, the alliance will be sealed. Both lands will serve her. The divide will be filled."

Michael stroked his chin as he thought. It was actually a pretty good idea, one that he hadn't ever considered. There was only a small problem. "Do you think the people will support it?"

Geoffrey squinted. "There isn't a king is this world that has the support of everyone he serves."

Nobody except King Josiah. Everyone loved him. They always had. The book on the table caught Michael's eye. Maybe Geoffrey was right. Maybe no king truly had the support of everyone, not even King Josiah. Michael cleared his throat and looked away. He wasn't interested in the king's history. It was long ago, and frankly, it was none of Michael's business.

"So we fill the divide between our lands. That division is a lot easier than the canyon," Michael said, bringing his thoughts back to the task. "How do we do it?"

Mrs. Maude answered first. "Liviya's doin' right fine. You just let her keep doin' what feels right to her." Mrs. Maude wiped a tear from her cheek. "And each of you make sure you lovin' her as much as she loves you. That girl's bout the most homesick thing I ever seen, but we gotta keep her here."

The room was silent for a moment. Soon Michael found everyone looking at him. He pondered Liviya and all that he was learning about her. She was making an incredible sacrifice to benefit her people. He knew exactly how difficult it was to make; he had been unwilling to do it himself. The king's words from weeks earlier haunted Michael. Indeed, he was a coward.

CHAPTER 21

When Liviya went downstairs for breakfast the next morning, she got the sense that everyone else had been awake for a long time. They all seemed to be waiting for her.

Mrs. Maude saw her first. She rose and wrapped Liviya in a tight hug, like all the sadness would leave if she just squeezed hard enough. "Glad to see you, honey," she whispered. "And I'm glad you's stayin'."

Over Mrs. Maude's shoulder, Liviya caught Michael's eye. He looked tired, and he needed a shave. Despite that, he looked calm, hands folded on the table, half a smile on his face. Mrs. Maude thumped Liviya's back a few times before releasing her. Eyes dry but heart breaking, Liviya sat down. Sarah was quick with a heaping plate of food. Liviya opted for the water first and drained it, wetting her smoke-dusted throat.

She had barely sat down before each of them began talking at once. She struggled to follow the excited voices until Michael stood up. Everyone fell silent as he gave a brief explanation about the canyon, the figurative divide, and peace between the kingdoms.

"No," Liviya said when he was done.

Michael cocked his head, confused. "Your Highness, it's the only way."

"Then I'll fill the real canyon," Liviya said. "But I'm not committing to peace with Barlow. I want Herrick dead." She'd hike across the border and stab him herself if she had to. "You promised," she reminded.

"And I'll keep that promise," Michael replied. "Peace for all but Herrick. That's close enough for me."

"And my enemy?" Liviya asked. While she sometimes claimed she'd kill Herrick, she wasn't entirely sure she could do it.

"You've already done it, Your Highness." Michael bowed.

Liviya looked away, wondering if it ever got any less uncomfortable to have people bow before her. Liviya would be queen, Herrick would die. Michael was a friend. She should have been happy. Instead, Liviya stared at her toes wiggling in her shoes.

"What's the matter?" Mrs. Maude asked.

"I guess I was hoping for something more adventurous." So far, her experience as a princess had been quite dull. Her biggest adventures came from things she had already been doing at home. Like thieving.

"Oh, honey, you can still have an adventure. Michael will help you." Mrs. Maude nodded, answering for him. "Won't you, Michael?"

Michael lifted his hands and held his breath as he searched for an answer. "Have you ever considered archery?"

Liviya threw her fists into the air. Archery was far better than anything she could have imagined. Overnight, life as a princess became infinitely better. She would be doing archery. She was also surprisingly ecstatic to be doing archery with Michael. She had missed the Michael she met on the streets in Barlow. It was nice to longer be at odds with him.

Everyone chatted for a few minutes, talking about more pleasant things than the fire, the death toll, and the dangerous plan to make Liviya queen. Soon, Mrs. Maude ushered Chancey and Sarah back to the kitchen. Geoffrey asked for Jacob's help out in the stables, leaving Michael and Liviya alone.

When Liviya was through eating, she pulled up her sleeve. Michael has seen the scar twice before, but just glances. This time he took her arm in his hands and inspected it closely. Liviya had lived with it for so long that she barely noticed it now. As Michael studied it, she saw it with new eyes. It was ugly. She had never thought about removing the scar. Now that it was possible, she wanted it gone. Even if she didn't become queen, she didn't want to be Herrick's property any longer.

"How long did it hurt?" Michael asked.

"Months." The nightmares still occurred. In her dreams, she was never being burnt; she was watching the hot iron being pressed against the flesh of children. Every night, she woke up to the screams of strangers miles away.

Michael gently stroked her arm. Behind his eyes, his mind seemed to be racing with thoughts he didn't voice. Liviya couldn't guess any of them. He dipped two fingers into the yellow cream and spread it onto her forearm, massaging it across the entire scar. When her arm was covered, he wound a gray bandage along the length of her arm. His face shone, like he thought the decade-old scar would dissolve in minutes. Liviya suppressed a shudder, offering a grin instead.

They sat across from each other, nearly touching, neither speaking. Liviya looked away first.

Michael cleared his throat and stood up. "Thank you. For staying. And for everything." He seemed to linger, not sure if he should leave or if there was reason to stay. After a moment, he turned for the door.

"Michael," Liviya called. Something had been on her mind. She wanted to talk about it.

Michael turned around. His eyes were inviting, making Liviya eager to share other secrets, like how she was grateful for him, grateful she'd get to know him better. She swallowed those thoughts away. "I think King Herrick started that fire."

Michael came back to the table and sat down, brow furrowed. "Herrick's in Barlow."

"Maybe he sent someone. Maybe he has a contact here. I don't know." Liviya shrugged, wishing the words didn't sound so ridiculous.

Michael turned to the wide windows framing the large table. He pointed. "See those gates?" From the distance, the barred barrier was barely visible, but she had traveled through them before. They were heavily guarded. The guards saw everything. "The only person here from Barlow is you."

Liviya knew he was right, but Herrick hated her. That fire had taken people she loved. It was personal. It was cruel. Attacks that vicious only came from Herrick. A deep exhale blew a strand of loose hair into her face.

Michael placed a hand on her bandaged arm. His courage seeped into her soul. "I'll look into it," he said.

Liviya forced her forehead to soften. Spies and lies and darkness. Those were demons from Barlow. Saunder was different. Saunder was safe. Herrick couldn't hurt her here. She replayed the words in her mind, waiting for them to sound true.

"Thank you," she said finally.

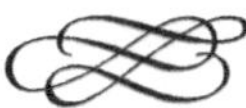

CHAPTER 22

The sky was still gray the next morning when Liviya crossed the dew-filled grass to the archery ring in the far east corner of the palace grounds. She had just a few hours until her schedule became full. Later that day, she would be hosting the noble women for tea. It was the first in a series of scheduled events to help heal the division between the people of Barlow and the people of Saunder. Until then, it would be only her and Michael.

With a deep breath, she inhaled the scent of a summer night turning to day. The sun climbed the mountain, slowly changing the sky until it reached the summit. The mountain peak pierced the sun, shooting rays of light into the sky and bathing the world below in a sea of color.

Above, bleary-eyed birds peered down from their nests. Upon finding it morning, the trees erupted in a chorus of whistles and warbles, as if to make up for the few moments of morning without any song.

When Liviya walked across the grounds, Michael had already placed the archery targets a few yards from the fence. He looked up and smiled as Liviya approached. His white sleeves were rolled to his elbows, though the air still held the night's chill. He brushed his dark curls off of his forehead.

Liviya eyed the target and the red spot in its center, the size of a large button. Two bows leaned against the fence. One was large, almost the length of her entire body. The string pulled each end of the bow slightly inward. Liviya refrained from plucking the taut string, though she was curious about the music it would make. Probably a deep hum. The other bow was much smaller. Much plainer. Compared to the other, its string looked like thread and the bow like a stick. If it made music, it would be shrill. She had a child's bow. She shot Michael a look of disappointment.

Michael understood her narrow glare and shrugged. "This seemed safer."

He picked up his bow and placed an arrow against his string. He explained the different types of bows, the arrows, and the feathers that affected their flight. With remarkable detail, he showed her where to stand, how to hold the bow, and how to pull the string. Liviya did her best to follow. She placed a finger on her lip where he taught her to anchor the string. Before Michael even shot his first arrow, Liviya knew he had the expertise only earned after years of practice.

"Give it a try." Michael tossed her the bow.

Liviya held out the bow with her left arm and pulled the string with her third and fourth fingers as Michael had directed. Instead of an arrow, her bow held a stick padded on one end, which, unfortunately, wouldn't pierce the target, but she'd earn her real weapon soon enough. As she pulled the string to her lip, her left arm shook, upsetting her aim. She looked at the target and imagined a rabbit, remembering the days when she was hungry. She imagined defending herself against Herrick's guards, and looking at the target, she imagined killing King Herrick himself. For the first time, she had power over her enemies. When she released the arrow, she'd be free. Her entire land would be free. Liviya let go and watched the arrow fly. It traveled about as far as she could spit water from her mouth.

Liviya held up her empty hand, leaving the bow hung at her side.

"A solid first shot," Michael said, smiling like there was laughter waiting. He took his own bow, placed an arrow, and pulled the string. His muscles flexed beneath his shirt. His form was exactly as he described. Every movement precise. The arrow flew across the field and landed in the target with a solid thump.

"Maybe if you watch a few." Michael shot arrows toward the trees instead of the target. Each arrow pierced an apple, forcing it to the ground until the grass was littered with impaled fruit. His aim was impeccable, his form flawless. He never missed.

Liviya tried more shots, but each time her padded stick fell in front of her feet.

"Try this," Michael said. "The winning shot." He handed her a real arrow. The sunlight caught the edge of the sharp head.

Liviya placed the arrow on the string and pulled it back, still shaking. Michael stepped behind her and held her bow. Reaching around her shoulders, he helped her pull the string. His strength stilled Liviya's shaking. The rest of the world stilled, too. His slow breathing warmed her neck.

"Eye on the target," he whispered.

Without aiming, Liviya released the arrow, eager to step away. The arrow shot across the fields. It landed in the trunk of a nearby tree.

"A perfect shot!" Michael cheered.

Liviya punched his shoulder. It was a terrible shot, but secretly, she was pleased. At least she had pierced something. As she shook out her shaking arms, she was surprised to see the sun well above them. "I'd better get back. I need to get dressed for tea." She held up her arm. "And we should probably change the bandage."

Liviya helped him gather the fallen arrows. Birds still singing, she and Michael returned to the palace. In the kitchen, Michael shut the door, allowing them a little bit of privacy.

"May I?" When Liviya nodded, he lifted her sleeve and unwrapped the bandage.

Liviya peeked around his head, trying to catch a glimpse. The scar stared back, fierce and dark.

"I think it helped some," Michael said.

"I think you've just never gotten a good look in daylight," Liviya replied. "It looks the same as always."

Michael rubbed her arm. "It's softer though."

Liviya rubbed it as well. The ridges were still rough and high. Michael's calloused hand was softer than her scar.

"That's all right. We have a hundred other things to try." Michael rummaged through his supplies and pulled out a pouch. The first ointment had come from a physician. This came from Mrs. Maude. It was a concoction she kept in the kitchen for mild burns. He crushed the leaves and mixed it with water until it formed a paste.

Liviya wrinkled her nose. "It stinks."

When the paste covered the scar, Michael wrapped it in a fresh bandage.

For a moment, they sat in a comfortable silence.

"I suppose this is good night, then," Michael said. It wasn't even midday, but she wouldn't see him till tomorrow. "I hope you enjoy your dinner."

She'd enjoy it a lot more if Michael would be attending as well, but she couldn't find a way to phrase it without sounding too intimate. She simply felt more comfortable with him.

"If you're interested, I'd be happy to do more archery tomorrow," he offered.

"I'd love that." Liviya's heart swelled. For the first time since arriving in Saunder, Liviya was glad she would be there another day.

WHEN LIVIYA RETURNED TO THE PALACE, THE NOBLE WOMEN HAD already arrived. They talked about the fire and its devastation. Liviya didn't listen. She had lived it. Their words brought back memories of the people she had watched die.

Sarah brought in the tray and placed it on the table between the ladies. Liviya was the most uncomfortable in her role as a princess since the day at the ball. Lying to the palace maids was a lot different than lying to the wealthy women. As they chatted, Liviya tried to tell herself it was friendly conversation, but she couldn't help but feel she was on trial. Except this time, the punishment would be far worse than lashings.

The girls asked unending questions. Liviya lied as simply as she could about her hobbies and talents and education. Hobbies were few, education was limited, talents were yet to be discovered.

When asked about her family, she answered with what she knew about Barlow's royal family. Her mother was dead. She had no siblings. Friends were all but forgotten.

The girls were unimpressed.

"Goodness. Sounds rather sheltered," Gentry said after a dainty sip of tea.

"Well, things are very different in Barlow." Liviya's shaking hands made the teacup clink.

"You must be glad to be away from all . . . that," Bethany added.

"I'm very glad to be here." That one was partially true. If she were in Barlow, there'd be no alliance.

Soon enough, the conversation turned to more interesting things. The girls discussed recent parties, upcoming weddings, who had died and which heir would receive the inheritance. Liviya knew none of the names. For the most part, she ignored the conversation. She exhaled and adjusted the heavy jewels that dug into the back of her neck. Just another hour or so and then they'd leave. Hopefully she wouldn't have to do this often.

"Oh, I envy you," Victoria whispered.

Gentry and Bethany continued talking, but Victoria looked her way.

Liviya pulled her eyebrows together. She had lied better than she thought if someone as rich and as beautiful as Victoria envied someone as poor and as plain as Liviya. Victoria had far more than Liviya ever would, the only exception being the crown.

"Life as a princess is not all luxury, I assure you," Liviya said.

"No, not that." Victoria's eyes flicked to the window before returning to her tea. Michael waited on the other side of the glass. When he caught Liviya's eye, he winked.

Liviya's face flushed. "We're not—No. It's nothing." Liviya placed a hand over her beating heart as she took a sip of her tea. "He's just helping me with my requirements."

"Poor Michael. He always has been a fool. See, if you complete your requirements, then you'll marry the prince. If you fail, you're an eligible young woman." Victoria raised a suggestive brow.

Liviya took another sip of tea. Her cheeks were still warm. She glanced at the fire crackling in the hearth. After a deep breath, she offered a cheerful smile. "Then may I win the crown and may you win Michael."

Victoria lifted her tea cup and clinked it against Liviya's. "To us."

Liviya studied the women differently as she finished her tea. In all the success these women had, all the enriching experiences their money provided, they had probably never scaled a wall, ran from guards, or held a dying child. Liviya didn't have riches, but she had wealth in her own ways. She had courage, she had grit. She looked across the window and watched Michael disappear across the palace grounds. In a small way, she had Michael.

CHAPTER 23

here was no more talk of dissension. Not even a whisper.
The fire must have burned it all out. For three days now,
the people of the village lined up at the palace doors. Prince Daniel
provided food, and they all bowed. All except one, and she was as
vocal as ever.

Liviya stood behind the prince as he gave his latest speech.
Michael moved to her shoulder. The contempt was evident on her
face. Lips straight, eyes glaring.

"Would it kill you to smile?" Michael whispered, glancing around
to be sure the king couldn't overhear. "Look supportive, perhaps?"

"What is this?" Liviya demanded, voice uncomfortably loud.

"He's helping the people," Michael replied.

Liviya raised a brow. "And what about tomorrow? I suppose he'll
make them march out here and bow in the dirt before they're fed as
well." She shook her head, eyes locked on something in the opposite
direction.

Michael followed her gaze. On the edge of the crowd, an elderly
woman struggled to carry a bucket of water to her tent. Back bent and
barely moving, each small step spilled water out of the side.

The prince continued his speech. He spoke to them of their hardships and reminded them how he had helped. He assured them he would continue to help and told them of the tears he had shed for their losses.

Liviya voiced her disgust with a snort. "This is the most selfish display of charity I've ever seen. He'll bear their burdens all right, but only one day at a time, and only if everyone is watching."

Michael looked into the crowd and saw the scene through different eyes. The dirty and tired people, the prince and his extravagant robes, the well-prepared speech and carefully portioned provisions. There was enough to keep them alive, but it would keep them hungry. It would keep them dependent on their prince. Michael rubbed his face with both hands.

Prince Daniel's speech came to an end with weak applause.

"Thank the heavens," Liviya muttered. She stepped off the platform and walked out among the people. Placing a loving hand on the woman's arm, Liviya muttered some unheard words that brought a smile to the stranger's face. She hoisted the stranger's bucket and carried it to her makeshift shelter. As she passed, the people lined up on either side. They were quiet, bowing as she passed. The prince on the platform was entirely forgotten. He stood with his arms raised, collecting the praise he thought was for him.

The king waited until Michael looked back at him before speaking. "That girl is a gift."

"Some gift," Michael muttered sarcastically. He watched her walk back through the people and toward the palace. She was so infuriating and so terrifying and so wonderful and so beautiful. Despite how impossible it seemed, somehow, he just knew that girl was going to be queen.

MICHAEL AND LIVIYA FELL INTO AN EASY PATTERN. MOST MORNINGS they spent practicing archery, then they met in the kitchen to inspect the scar and try the latest treatment. It was getting better. If Michael looked long enough at it in just the right light, he could see that it was fading. Or so he told himself.

Each afternoon, Michael and Liviya assisted Prince Daniel in delivering food to the villagers. Every day Liviya complained that he should be doing more.

As the weeks passed, the world grew greener. The vibrant buds of spring became the thick, leafy growth of summer. The days were warm, the nights were light. There was no more talk of rebels, and Daniel and Liviya continued to make progress toward the crown. Life was nearly perfect. Except Liviya was still a princess, an ambassador with an important mission. Michael was a common man. Many times her work stole her away from him. Michael attended events with Liviya when he could. Some days they toured the villages or the local homes of the needy. On others, they joined friends for meals or activities. Often, she and the prince visited with other noble and royal people or traveled to the academies and cathedrals.

Most evenings, she met alone with King Josiah, who insisted she learn the legends of Saunder. More than once, Michael considered reading the book Geoffrey had showed him, the king's personal history. Each time, he talked himself out of it. The history was irrelevant.

One evening, Michael wandered the palace, unsure of how he had spent his time before Liviya came into his life. Liviya was away with the noble ladies and wouldn't be back for several hours. He sat in the kitchen for a while until Mrs. Maude shooed him away with an accusation of moping. With nothing else to do, he went to work in the stables. The tack was clean and organized and the horses well-groomed, but he brushed them anyway. The only thing out of place was a box of equipment waiting to be taken to the blacksmith for repairs.

For years, Michael had fought to continue working in the stables along with his other responsibilities. He would do whatever the king asked, as long as he could work in the stables as well. He had thought he'd never leave. Since Liviya arrived, he had barely been in there.

Thinking back on it, the sacrifice wasn't as painful as he had thought it might be.

The door squeaked as it opened. Michael looked up with a wide smile that slipped when he saw Geoffrey.

"Ah, Michael, it's been a while," Geoffrey said.

"Doesn't look like you've missed me." Michael had been surprised to find the stables in such sharp condition.

"Jacob's done a right fine job here," Geoffrey said. "I think he aims to take your job. Hope you got a good idea for something better do to."

Michael chose to ignore Geoffrey's comment. Weeks ago, Liviya had presented some concerns about Herrick and the fire. Michael had sent some spies to the border, but they returned with a report that nothing had changed. There were no signs of war, no signs of anything. Maybe Geoffrey had heard something. "Listen, you know anything about that fire?"

"Folks say they first saw the flames in Humphrey's house. Took them a long time to get him out. When they did, he had sucked in too much smoke." Geoffrey didn't need to finish. Michael had dug Humphrey's grave.

"Prince Daniel just about killed Humphrey a few weeks ago."

"Yes, he did," Geoffrey replied.

Michael rubbed his chin. "That's an awful lot of bad luck for a good man."

"Yes, it is." Geoffrey looked hopeful. "You got some suspicions about that fire?"

"Liviya does," Michael replied. "She thinks King Herrick is responsible."

"Huh," Geoffrey said. "Don't know why Herrick would burn the village. But don't know why he'd insist on sending us a maid either."

Neither did Michael. The thoughts stole away hours of sleep every night. Michael rubbed away the headache that was forming. "I'll feel a lot better about our alliance with Barlow when Herrick isn't their king." He was torn between wishing he had never suggested the alliance and being forever grateful that he had. Without the alliance, he never would have found Liviya. But it was the alliance that caused Saunder a lot of trouble and caused Michael a lot of pain. It was because of the alliance that Michael was helping the woman he loved become eligible to marry another man.

Prince Daniel's challenge was no closer than the day he received it, but Liviya was making remarkable progress. The divide was nearly healed. People began to discuss the wedding. As soon as both challenges were completed, Liviya and Daniel would be married. Geoffrey had guessed right. Michael wouldn't be in the stables forever. Eventually, Jacob would take his place. When that happened, Michael had a plan. He'd leave. He loved Saunder. He loved the prince. But, he was beginning to admit to himself that he also loved Liviya. He couldn't stay and watch her marry Daniel. He was running out of time to spend with her. He mourned that loss already.

Geoffrey placed a fatherly hand on Michael's shoulder. "Take care of yourself, you hear? You don't have to save us all by yourself."

The door swung shut as Geoffrey left. Michael was alone again with hours to watch crawl by.

Begrudgingly, Michael loaded the broken tack into a sack. He hesitated to send the boys alone to the blacksmith to get it fixed. He still liked to keep them close since the incident in the blizzard. Besides, maybe it would be good to have some time away from the palace, away from the prince, starving citizens, and impossible challenges. His only hesitation was that he hadn't seen Liviya all day. He wasn't thrilled about missing her company two days in a row.

A horse whinnied over the waist-high wooden gate. Michael rubbed her nose. She stamped her hooves and threw her head. Michael spent enough time there to know exactly what she wanted.

"You're right, beautiful," he crooned. "Let's take her with us."

CHAPTER 24

*L*iviya awoke early the next morning. The previous night, Michael had invited her to go with him to attend to some of his duties, but their destination was a surprise. Despite her many questions, he had only given three clues: Mrs. Maude was packing a picnic, she was to wear riding clothes, and he had given her a package wrapped in brown paper and a blue ribbon.

Sarah squealed when she heard the news that morning. She piled all of Liviya's gowns on her bed and rummaged through them. "This dress'll suit your picnic. It'll be plenty comfortable for riding, but it'll still flatter your figure. We'll just braid your hair down your back, then it's out of your face. There won't be anyone lookin', just Michael, and he'll like it all."

Mrs. Maude came in a few minutes later and handed her a basket covered with a checkered cloth. The smell of delicious food wafted from underneath it. "I packed you a lunch. There's plenty of food and water in here, so don't feel like you have to rush home for your meals. You just stay out and enjoy your day. You'll see that this land ain't so different from yours. Now have a wonderful time, and be safe. We'll be waitin' to hear all the details." Liviya escaped from her hug, thanked Mrs. Maude, and hurried down to the stables.

Jacob greeted her outside. "I've got your horse ready, Princess." A bay mare stood ready. "She's a real gentle ride. She'll treat you good."

"Do you know where he's taking me?" Liviya asked.

"Of course I know," Jacob said with a teasing smile. "But I swore I wouldn't tell ya, so don't bother askin'." He clipped the saddle bags closed. "When you get up there, ask Michael about his adventures in Follett Pass. That's a story you need to hear."

"I'll ask him." Liviya patted the horse on the nose. "Thank you, Jacob." She turned and saw Michael coming down the path. He looked handsome as he pushed his loose curls from his face, a whisper of whiskers on his cheeks. He carried a sack over his shoulder. His lips pursed with a whistle that she was still too far away to hear.

When Michael caught sight of her, his eyes scanned the length of her body. Liviya wore a simple riding gown in soft pink. Sarah had been right when she claimed the he would like whatever he wore. Liviya remembered back to the day in Barlow when she met him in the crowd with the magician. It was no secret that he had thought she was beautiful then as well.

When his eyes found her face, they lingered there. "Hello, Liviya."

In front of people, peasants or nobles, Michael was very professional. Almost too professional. He never let his gaze linger. He remained at arm's length or beyond. And he certainly never used her name, preferring "Princess" or "Your Highness."

When they were alone, which was rare, things became more relaxed, though it was nothing close to affection. Both remembered all too well that she would be marrying the prince. But Michael's brief moments of attention were far more than she had ever been given from Daniel. Liviya found herself wishing that Daniel looked at her the way Michael did. That he said her name like Michael did. In fact, she found herself wishing that Daniel were far more like Michael in practically every way.

Michael offered her his hand and helped her mount the horse. When she sat comfortably in her saddle, Michael hopped onto his. He clicked to the horses. With the clapping of hooves, their adventures began.

Michael and Liviya rode through the palace gates, past the cities, and into Saunder's countryside. Liviya had never seen so much green nor so many hills. From up above, the kingdom below was divided into squares of varying shades of brown and green, like a well-loved quilt.

By afternoon, Liviya's backside ached. Despite that, she was grateful to be away from the palace, and even more grateful to be with Michael. As the paved roads turned to rocky trails, he told stories about life growing up in the palace and about King Josiah as a younger man. His stories were outrageous. Liviya was never quite sure where the truth stopped and exaggeration began. She couldn't hold back her laughter, though she was certain it encouraged the stories.

Some hours later, they arrived in a small village where Michael delivered his sack to a local blacksmith. "He's the best there is," Michael said, "so it's worth the trip. Besides, I wanted a good excuse to bring you up here." He steered the horses down a path and through the trees.

"Where are we going?" Liviya asked.

"We're almost there." Beside a tree, he dismounted and tied the reins around a low branch. He helped Liviya down. With a hand on her back, he guided her through the trees as she limped the stiffness from her legs.

They hiked along a path, pushing through the bushes and weeds. When they turned a corner, they found a large body of water.

"It's beautiful," Liviya replied. But she wasn't quite sure why Michael brought her to see it. There were far more impressive landscapes in Saunder.

"You can open your present now," Michael said.

Liviya pulled the ribbon and tore off the paper. She lifted off the top of the box. Inside, a spyglass sat on satin. She lifted it from the box and peered through its lens.

"Look over there," Michael said pointing.

Liviya moved where he directed. There was nothing but a gravel hill holding in water.

"That's a dam," Michael said. "Do you know what's on the other side?"

Liviya shook her head.

"Barlow's river. This dam keeps it dry. A few well-placed explosives." Michael imitated an explosion with his hands. "Then Barlow will have water, too."

Breathlessly, Liviya studied the dam through the spyglass. She dreamed about water, but this helped shape it into a reality. Despite her homesickness and her extreme dislike of Daniel, she was eager to keep trying.

"Thank you, Michael," Liviya whispered. She touched his elbow, just a friendly expression of appreciation. "Thank you so much."

"My pleasure," Michael said. He cleared his throat and stepped back.

Liviya looked back through the spyglass and her home hiding behind the earthen wall.

Michael spread a blanket on the grass. When the feast was spread, they sat shoulder-to-shoulder.

"King Josiah used to bring a load of supplies to this village every winter. My mama was from around here. Guess he wanted to show me where I was from." Michael shrugged. "One year, he brought Daniel, too. The king had left us in the wagon while he took in the supplies. We spotted a sled beside one of the cottages. Of course we couldn't resist. We took turns pushing each other on the sled, but there weren't any hills steep enough to make two boys with a sled go as fast as they wanted to go. So Daniel got an idea. We unhitched a horse from the wagon and tied it to the sled instead. We both got on the sled, and Daniel slapped the horse's rear. That horse was madder than I've ever seen. He took off running right through the village, pulling the sled right behind it. But then the canyon got closer. The horse ran along the edge, and each time he weaved directions, the sled slid closer to the cliff. I knew pretty quickly that we were going to fall off the edge, but there wasn't much that could be done from behind the horse. Sure enough, one more turn, and the sled fell."

Michael was lost in thought, brow furrowed. The mountain was silent, except for the bugs and birds and the wind-rustled leaves.

"What happened?" Liviya prompted.

Michael softened his gaze and smiled, but there was still angst in his eyes. "Well, I grabbed hold of the rope, Prince Daniel grabbed a hold of me, and that good old horse held right on to the rim of the canyon with his front two hooves. Just like this." Michael held out his arms.

Liviya, drinking from a canteen, tried to not spit out her water. "You're lying," she said after a forced swallow.

"Not a bit," Michael said. "We were hollering for help, dangling off the edge, thinking we would die when a man spotted us. Well, he grabbed the horse's hooves and started pulling. But we were all a lot heavier than him, and we pulled him right to the edge. So now the man was grabbing onto the edge of the canyon, the horse is holding on to his waist, I'm clinging to the horse's legs, Daniel's holding mine, and we were all screaming."

Liviya tried to look skeptical, but she laughed a little.

Michael didn't break a smile. "A woman heard the ruckus and found us. So she grabbed a hold of the man's hands and tried to pull us up."

"Let me guess," Liviya said. "She fell down, too?"

"You're exactly right," Michael said. He leaned sideways and bumped her shoulder. "This woman held on to the rim of the canyon by the toes of her boots and the man held her hands. The horse held on to the man, I clung on to the horse, and Daniel gripped me."

Liviya swatted him with the empty canteen. "This is absurd."

Michael continued. "About that time, King Josiah heard us wailing and came running from the village. He was spitting mad and sure took plenty of time yelling at me before offering any help at all. Meanwhile, the woman's boots slipped, and we began to fall. But with a single hand, King Josiah grabbed the woman's leg and hoisted her back up followed by the man, then the horse, then me then Daniel."

"He did that all with one hand?" Liviya asked.

"He was much younger back then. Stronger, too," Michael replied.

Finally, Liviya laughed. Michael did, too. They sat on the blanket, breathing the mountain air. The crease returned to Michael's brow. Liviya was torn between wanting to hear what troubled him and wanting to allow him the privacy to process it.

"So what adventure happened in Follett Pass?" Liviya asked, eager to have him talking again.

This only troubled Michael more. Any trace of amusement left his face. "What?"

"Jacob told me to ask you about Follett Pass."

"Follett Pass is just a meadow down the mountain," Michael replied.

"Oh." She tried to catch Michael's eye, but he stared ahead

Finally, he spoke. "Jacob and some of the boys got caught in a blizzard up there right before spring. Had to go dig them out, is all."

"Was everyone okay?" Liviya asked.

"Just cold. Nothing that an hour by the fire couldn't cure."

Liviya knew that Michael was exaggerating again. "Your stories sure have a lot more detail when you're embellishing them."

"I suppose some stories are easier to tell when they're not entirely true," Michael replied.

Liviya could understand that. She had told her fair share of lies in life. "So what's the true story of the sled?"

"It's all true right up till the sled went off the edge. We were little boys. The horse stayed up on top, and we clung to the rope. King Josiah found us. He was mad, but he did haul us up. He gave me a beating so hard I spun in circles for days." He looked at Liviya sideways. "Even Mrs. Maude took pity on me, and she doesn't pity me often."

Liviya studied the man sitting next to her, the man who traveled with kings and rode in sleds with princes. She had gotten to know so much about him in the past months, but so much of him was a mystery. Liviya wondered if his life was a mystery to himself as well. "Why did you get in trouble instead of Daniel? It was his idea."

"King Josiah said I should have stopped him before things got so dangerous." Michael shrugged. "Guess I just didn't know how far he would go."

Too soon, it was time to return to the palace. They packed the horses and began the long ride.

"Thank you," Liviya said when they returned home. "I had a good time."

"It was my pleasure," Michael replied.

Tired and aching, Liviya crawled in bed. Memories of Barlow flooded her. She squeezed her eyes tight and refused to let them water her bed. It had been a wonderful day, but it was a cruel reminder that the border was the closest she would ever get to home, and that broke her heart.

CHAPTER 25

*E*very day, Liviya met with the king. She looked forward to it almost as much as archery with Michael.

Most people loved the king. They talked freely how he was Saunder's greatest ruler. But lately, there had been a lot snickering about him. Every day, the king grew more confused. Regardless, Liviya grew to love him. He was pleasant. Funny. His silly stories reminded her much of Michael. Apparently, the king taught Michael much more than archery. He taught him about humor as well.

The king and Liviya met in the library. Even though it was the middle of summer, with everyone else sweltering in the heat, a fire always roared on the hearth. Sometimes King Josiah asked Liviya to read aloud for him. During those times, Liviya offered up prayers of gratitude for Mrs. Wilde and the hours she spent teaching the girls to read by scrawling letters on the dirt floor.

Most days, King Josiah read Liviya the legends. There were legends about everything. Magic stones and granted wishes, flowering plants that healed any sickness and mirrors that would show the past. Liviya loved each one of them.

Everyone knew the legends. They were discussed like they were books of scripture. Parents read them to their children in their cradles. The priests shared them in their sermons. They were sung and chanted, repeated with daily prayers. The legends were holy.

That day in the library, the king sat in his chair and gave Liviya a book filled with portraits, one portrait summarizing each year. It went back centuries, it seemed.

After unfamiliar faces and strange dress, the pages grew more recent. Finally, Liviya found King Josiah in a military coat standing next to a horse. He was young and handsome. The background in the portrait showed him receiving the requirements to become king. The next page showed his coronation and wedding. The queen was beautiful. She had a kind smile. She clasped Josiah's hand. It was evident they were in love. Flipping through the paintings, Liviya saw just the two of them, slowly aging.

"I was a much older man when my son was born," King Josiah explained. "We prayed for him for decades. Many of our children died before their birth. Nathan, though, he survived."

Liviya turned the page. The king was alone, holding his infant son. "I'm so sorry," Liviya whispered, the lack of his wife enough evidence to determine she had died during childbirth.

King Josiah didn't reply. Liviya continued to look at the pages. Several portraits depicted Prince Nathan as he grew from a baby to a boy to a man. Liviya stopped, admiring the handsome prince who stood in the ballroom to receive his requirements as well. But after, there was no coronation. No wedding.

Pages and pages and pages were left blank.

"What happened?" Liviya asked, scanning the empty section.

"We fought," King Josiah said. "He abdicated his throne and ran away to marry the woman he loved."

Judging by the king's ducked head and low voice, Liviya realized that very few people in the kingdom knew that fact.

With the first detail spilled, the king spoke more easily. "I spent years searching for him. When I found him, I attempted to make amends. Before I could, a beast attacked his family. It was seven feet tall. Teeth like knives. Claws like daggers. It killed his wife. His child saw it all. The loss drove Nathan mad."

Liviya shuddered. She wanted to tell herself that the beast wasn't real, but King Josiah remembered. She saw the fight replay in his lost gaze.

"That was the last time I saw my son." The king's voice was quiet. Liviya had to strain to hear him. "A few years later, a princess fled to my kingdom with her baby. She had married Prince Nathan and borne a son. Shortly after, Barlow destroyed the prince. The man who ruled in his place was vile. Cruel. She pleaded for help."

Liviya felt the familiar guilt for Nathan's death even though that was before she was even born.

"She left the baby here and disappeared, certain the new king would find her and kill her, too."

King Josiah was silent for a long time. The memories seemed to suck away the life within him, leaving him cold and ragged in his chair.

"Have peace, Your Majesty," Liviya said. "I'm sure Prince Nathan knows you didn't mean for it to end like that."

King Josiah opened his blue eyes. "Darling, it hasn't ended yet."

Whatever fight he'd had with his son, Liviya saw he relieved it every day.

King Josiah glanced to the window. "The villagers are here. They'll need your help with the food."

Already, the people lined up in the courtyard. Prince Daniel and Michael waited with the bagged supplies.

Liviya patted he king's arm, understanding her dismissal, but feeling no offense. She had experienced enough grief to know that sometimes it was best swallowed alone.

"Good day, Your Majesty."

MICHAEL INHALED DEEPLY AS HE WALKED ACROSS THE PALACE

courtyard. He loved summer. The smell of cut hay. Long, warm, nights. Skipping up the stairs, he whistled.

The people were lined up to receive their food for the day. Liviya still hated that. Every day, she begged Michael to convince the prince to help them in other ways. Michael tried, but Daniel refused.

It was only Michael's place to follow orders, so he did as he was told. He tried to not form opinions, but truthfully, he didn't like the situation either. Something seemed wrong about making people in need stand outside for hours for food rather than clean up their fields and let them plant their own.

However, the people receiving their food created a stretch of hours of every day that he got to see Liviya. Although he had spent the entire day with her before, he looked forward to seeing her again.

Most afternoons, Michael tried to make Liviya laugh. Often, he succeeded. He prided himself on bringing smiles to Liviya's face when so often one was missing.

Michael's own smile disappeared when he reached the balcony. Prince Daniel sat there alone.

"Where's the princess?" Michael asked.

"Who knows? Probably out waving with the ladies." Prince Daniel kept his gaze locked on the crowd.

Michael's hackles raised. The prince made comments like this often. Michael found them disrespectful of the work the princess did. "She's doing far more than waving to the crowds," Michael argued. "Her role here is an essential part of you getting the crown. Without her—"

Prince Daniel flicked his gaze from the crowd to Michael. Michael noticed the prince's tight jaw and steely gaze and decided to stop mid-sentence. He sat down. Without a word, Prince Daniel turned back to the crowd. He seemed to be inspecting each of the faces one at a time.

As the people formed a line, Michael noticed something he had been too distracted to notice on the days he had sat there with Liviya.

Fewer people were there.

Michael scanned the crowd, estimating that only half had arrived. He wanted to tell himself that it was only his imagination. A mistake.

No. There was no denying it. The prince noticed it as well, and he was angry. Half the people receiving food meant half the people bowing to him.

"It's harvest now," Michael said. "The fields have food." It was a weak lie. The village was still ash. The closest market was a day's journey. Not a lot could be spared for travel and food when the people had no homes. As far as Michael could tell, they were staying home and staying hungry. Michael didn't bother to tell them that there were still over a hundred who had arrived. Prince Daniel wanted them all.

With a growl, Prince Daniel tipped his chair on its back two legs. "It's time for more aggressive measures. I want these rebels ended."

"What, like a war?" Michael asked. He hoped the prince was kidding. Daniel's expression made it clear he was not.

Michael inhaled through his teeth, planning his next words carefully. It was always dangerous to disagree with the prince. "We haven't seen a rebel sign in...." Michael motioned with his hands while he tried to think back. "Weeks. Months. They're refusing food, but they're not harming anyone. We simply can't justify an attack."

Prince Daniel brought all four legs of the chair back down. "You may think—" Prince Daniel began.

The door opened, and Liviya walked outside, looking as radiant as ever. With a smile, Michael stood up and bowed deeply. "It's a pleasure to see you, as always, Your Highness."

Michael pulled out a chair for Liviya and held the back while she sat down.

"Forgive my tardiness," she said.

Michael already had.

"I was meeting with the king." Her brow turned down. "He's quite strange."

Michael was well aware of this. "He gets confused," he explained, wondering what peculiar story he had told Liviya.

Liviya smoothed her skirt and adjusted her wide hat. When Michael sat back down, he found the prince studying him.

Then Michael remembered that the prince had been speaking before Liviya arrived. Michael cleared his throat. "You were saying."

Prince Daniel nodded a few times before replying. "Mark my words, Michael. One day these rebels' acts will become more violent. Then you'll march."

"When they're violent," Michael agreed, satisfied with the argument's end. There would be no violent acts. There was no rebellion. Everyone loved Liviya. He stole a glance at her. Everyone.

CHAPTER 26

*L*iviya rarely spoke to Prince Daniel beyond basic pleasantries. She learned long ago that he would never listen to her. She had no interest in wasting her words.

There were others, however, who listened to her as if she were already queen. Liviya had no shortage of what she considered great ideas. She didn't hesitate to share them.

"Fewer people are showing up for food," Liviya said. She had first noticed it weeks ago. She sat on a stool in the kitchen across from Mrs. Maude. Chancey sat next to Liviya, scrubbing at the sticky spots on the counter. The extra linen bags of food had been brought in from the courtyard and waited in the cooler kitchen.

Mrs. Maude stopped kneading the bread dough and wiped the loose gray hairs out of her face with her forearm. "Now, you know those people love you. This don't mean nothin' 'bout you or your crown."

"Oh, of course not." Liviya knew that this small defiance was directed at the prince and not her. In fact, she found it amusing how much it perturbed him. If she were in the village, she'd stay home as well, just to make him angry. But she wasn't in the village. She was in the palace, so she might as well be useful. "If there's extra food just sitting here, perhaps we can deliver it to the girls' home."

Her thoughts often returned to the girls in a situation so similar to what she had left behind in Barlow.

Mrs. Maude returned to her kneading, thumping the dough across the counter and sending great clouds of flour into the air. "I suppose nobody'd miss one or two of them. Chancey, when you're through here, take some of these bags to Livy's girls."

Chancey slumped against the counter. "That'll take the rest of the day!"

"I'll go with you," Liviya offered. She was always eager for a chance to leave the palace walls.

Chancey brightened considerably.

Michael walked into the kitchen. After a round of nods to everyone present, he washed his hands in a basin. "Where are you going?" he asked.

"We're going to deliver extra food to the girls' home," Liviya replied.

Michael cocked his head, disapproval already forming at his lips.

Liviya was ready with her arguments. "The food's just sitting there. Prince Daniel doesn't need it, and the people in the village don't want it. We can't just let it waste."

Still thinking, Michael dried his hands on a towel. His face always held a half smile, like he was amused. He passed the towel back and forth in his calloused hands, gaze locked on Liviya. Her thoughts returned to the day she met him. If she could go back, she would have danced with him. Liviya looked away so her expression wouldn't betray her thoughts.

"How about I send some guards with the food," Michael suggested. "You don't need to traipse all the way out there in the heat."

Mrs. Maude smacked him with the back of her hand. It left a dusty handprint on his chest. "If she wants to go, let her go!"

Michael threw up his hands like he wanted to argue, but decided against it. Liviya grinned. The kingdom of Sunder had such a strange hierarchy. Sometimes she couldn't quite tell who was in charge. It wasn't King Josiah. Not often, at least. When he spoke, everyone moved, but his words rarely came. Prince Daniel didn't seem to be in charge either. The orders he gave were often discouraged. At times it might be Geoffrey, but today, it was certainly Mrs. Maude.

As Liviya thought back on it, she discovered that most often, Michael seemed to make the decisions. He was a curious man. Born of a peasant woman, raised in an orphanage, commander of a castle. He could have his pick of any woman in the land, yet Victoria claimed he fancied her. The words from the conversation long ago made Liviya warm.

Michael always has been a fool...If you fail, you're an eligible young woman.

If Michael fancied her, like Victoria claimed, then why help her become eligible to marry the prince? Maybe, Liviya considered, thinking back on all their adventures, maybe he enjoyed his time with Liviya as much as she enjoyed spending time with him. Maybe he wasn't such a fool after all. How else could a peasant man spend so much time with a princess without raising the suspicion of those in the palace? Liviya let this thought warm her heart. She liked Michael. He was pleasant, kind, and handsome as the devil. But did she spend her time with him because she enjoyed it or because it would help her earn her crown? She had been so focused on her requirements that she had taken Michael's help for granted. If he offered nothing but his company, would she still spend time with him? It would be a good thing to ponder as she walked to the girls' home.

"When shall we leave?" Liviya asked.

LIVIYA AND CHANCEY LEFT WITH BAGS OF FOOD IN PACKS ON THEIR backs. Liviya was strong. She felt the muscles in her arms from weeks of training with Michael. Her face glowed. Her stomach was full and mouth wet with as much water as she could drink. She was also finding her place in the new kingdom. At times, it almost felt like home. Friends, she learned, were just as important as food.

Chancey skipped along the road, hopping over rocks. She chatted about things in the palace, the projects Mrs. Maude let her help with, and the ribbons she was saving her wages for.

Most people recognized Liviya. The faces were becoming familiar, the baker and the butcher. A parade of sorts formed behind them. In only a few steps, her hands were full of tokens—flowers, ribbons, delicacies. She placed many in her bag to share with the girls in the home.

Liviya scanned the crowd as they journeyed, fighting the urge to cover her head. Something seemed wrong. At the crossroads, she took a moment to look all around her. Someone, she sensed, was following her. Liviya was in a sea of smiling faces. Most people loved her. The prejudice against Barlow was weakening. But that didn't mean she no longer had enemies. Despite the sun overhead, she shuddered. She should have allowed Michael to send the guards.

"Let's walk quickly," Liviya said.

A carriage crossed the road, kicking up dust behind it. Liviya jogged past with Chancey close behind.

As they turned on the left fork toward the girls' home, the crowds thinned. Soon the road was empty. Too empty. Too quiet. In either direction, nobody was in sight. Her instincts screamed. She didn't know which way to turn. Up ahead, two horses appeared, their riders dressed in black. One of them drew a sword.

"Run!" Liviya screamed.

From the other direction, two more horses advanced.

Liviya pulled on Chancey's arm. They dove off the trail and into the woods. The horses gained on them quickly. The girls wove through the trees, tearing past the branches hanging low. They ran until they reached a ravine. Panting, they skidded to a stop, sending rocks down the hill. It was too steep for them to run down. Liviya looked behind them. The horses grew nearer. They couldn't run down it either.

Liviya wrapped her arms around Chancey and dove down the hill. They rolled over briars and boulders. With each bump, the girls cried out. Finally, they reached the bottom. Liviya helped Chancey stand up.

"Come on. The stream."

A small stream cut through the forest. Bruised and limping, they waded through the stream, hoping the water would hide their tracks. In the deepest shadows, Liviya separated a bush's branches and helped Chancey crawl inside. She held Chancey's head on her shoulder, urging her gently to stay silent. On the other side of the stream, Liviya watched the horsemen scan for tracks. When night fell, they rode away, a rebel flag flying behind them.

WHEN LIVIYA FELT IT WAS SAFE, SHE AND CHANCEY LEFT THE SHELTER of the shrubbery.

Liviya cradled her shoulder as she walked. Any movement sent a searing pain down her arm. Chancey cried the entire way out of the forest, thick sobs echoing around the large trees.

In the distance, Liviya saw torches and heard people shouting her name.

"Here!" she hollered. "We're here!"

Guards helped them onto horses and raced them back to the palace. It seemed the entire kingdom was out looking for them. Dozens of people escorted them back home.

Inside, Mrs. Maude rushed to Liviya and Chancey. "What in the world happened?" she asked in that frantic urgency that sounded like anger. It sent Chancey into tears again.

Mrs. Maude brought a cool rag. Sarah knelt on the stone floor and gently pulled off Chancey's wet cloak.

Michael arrived soon, hair blown wild by a fast ride on a horse. It matched his wild eyes. "Are you all right?" He peeled back the rag that Liviya held on her shoulder.

"Just a bruise," Liviya said. She moved, gently twisting her arm. It caught painfully, making her wince. "I might be away from archery for a day or two."

"That's a shame," Michael replied, "you need the practice." He smiled weakly, but it didn't mask his fear.

"What happened?" Prince Daniel asked.

Michael stepped back. Liviya cleared her throat. She hadn't even noticed him there.

Word spread faster than she had thought possible in the palace if it reached him all the way in the locked room with his jewels.

Prince Daniel pulled at her cloak. Liviya twisted to keep her scar covered. "We were chased off the road."

"Who did this?" he asked. "What did they look like?"

They were men, based on the voices shouting the insults. They rode black horses, sleek and strong. They waved swords as they ran. The horses came both from both directions on the road. Liviya knew now that these were the men she felt following her in the market. She didn't know who they were or why they had targeted her. The only thing she knew for certain was that it wasn't the rebels. If anyone heard about the flag the men carried, the rebels would be beaten again. Probably killed. She had told a lot of lies in her time in Saunder, but this was the most important.

Liviya swallowed. "It was a beast. Seven feet tall. Claws like knives."

"Oh, good heavens," Mrs. Maude cried.

Prince Daniel leaned closer and looked into Liviya's eyes, but not at all the way Michael often did. He knew she was lying.

"I swear on my life," Liviya said. "It stalked us for miles before it attacked. I could see its eyes in the bushes. When it charged, we dove into the forest. We lost it down a ravine."

Michael, a few steps behind the prince, cocked his head. He knew very well she was lying as well, but was kind enough to give no accusation.

"I have statements from witnesses claiming it was men on horses. They chased you," Prince Daniel said.

Witnesses? The road was empty! Except for the men on horses.

"No, it was a beast," Liviya said. "Like a bear, but bigger. Heavens, if there were men on horses, they could have saved us. We were entirely alone."

Prince Daniel pushed Liviya aside. Chancey hid behind her skirts. "What color were the horses?"

It was probably the first time that Chancey had ever heard the prince speak to her. She was terrified. She erupted into tears. But at least she didn't deny Liviya's story.

"The princess is delusional," Daniel said. "She must have hit her head. Take her to her room. Keep her monitored." He motioned to Chancey. "Take her, too."

Chancey became hysterical, sobbing, screaming, grabbing at Liviya's arms. Chancey didn't deserve any more trauma this evening. Liviya wanted to protect the rebels, but not if Chancey got punished instead. With Prince Daniel, it seemed that someone was always being punished.

"Wait, I remember the horses," Liviya admitted.

Prince Daniel smiled, an artificial, arrogant line on his face that Liviya would have pummeled off of him if he were anyone other than the prince and if they were anywhere else than Saunder. "They were black," she offered.

Michael scratched his head, obviously confused.

"I heard snarling," Liviya explained weakly. "I thought it was a beast."

"What else?" Daniel said.

He offered no threats, but his fixed gaze communicated accurately enough that he was through with games.

Liviya brought both hands to her face and closed her eyes. She was silent for a long time. There seemed no way to avoid the detail that Daniel was looking for.

"They carried the rebel flag."

Prince Daniel stood up. "Organize the troops. I want them found."

"She's mistaken, Your Highness," Michael said.

"I know what the rebel flag looks like," Liviya snapped. She had already tried lying and it didn't work. She wouldn't let Michael ruin the truth.

"Send men to all the cities. I want everyone who's ever breathed a word of rebellion strung up in the streets," Daniel ordered.

"No," Michael said again. "I've been monitoring the rebels. I haven't heard a word of their movement in weeks."

Prince Daniel leaned toward Michael, his face inches away. His words were low. "Maybe you missed it when you were out frolicking with my princess."

Michael's body turned rigid. He pointed a finger at Daniel. "Every moment I have spent with her has been to help get you the throne! She has requirements, too, remember? You think she can do that alone? I have never acted outside my realm of responsibility."

Like a fist to the mouth, that was the most painful blow of the evening. Liviya had spent every day with Michael for weeks. She had thought they were friends. She had thought they might be more. She was wrong. Liviya didn't have Michael. She was his responsibility. The prince had Michael.

Liviya sniffed away her anger. There were more important matters at hand. The prince wanted to attack the rebels. But she had seen the rebels in the village up close. They were regular men and women. They lacked the equipment and skills of her would-be captors.

"These weren't the rebels," Liviya said when she could speak again. "These were guards. They rode in formations with trained horses, and they were expert trackers."

Prince Daniel did not like her answer. "Then how did you manage to avoid all of six of them?"

Liviya almost corrected him. There were only four horsemen. But she'd let him think there were six. She'd let him think something else as well.

She shrugged innocently. "Perhaps they let me escape. They may be rebels after all, rebelling against the coward who sent them. Next time, whoever wants to capture me should come do it himself."

The prince's jaw tightened dangerously. Restraining herself from any more words, Liviya walked to the door. Michael called her name, but she ignored him. She didn't need his help. She didn't need anything from Michael.

LIVIYA SAT IN HER ROOM WITH A BASIN OF WATER. SHE FURIOUSLY scrubbed her scar with one of Mrs. Maude's wide bristled brushes. It left her skin red and raw.

Liviya didn't hear Michael come in. He yanked the brush from her hands. "Easy, Liviya."

She grabbed for it back. "I need this gone. Now."

Things were growing dangerous. Someone had tried to capture her. What if it was because they knew she was lying? What if they knew that the entire alliance was a lie? She needed to marry the prince. She needed King Herrick dead.

Liviya had been toying with an idea for a while. She was ready to execute it. "I'm going to burn my arm again."

"No," Michael said. "We still have more ointments to try."

"They're not working!" Liviya said. "I'll just brush my arm against a pot in the kitchen."

"And how would we explain what you were doing in the kitchen? Most princesses don't spend time in there."

Liviya growled and scratched at her arm again. Michael swatted her hand down.

"Then I'll spill hot soup or accidentally light my sleeve on a lantern."

Michael was incredulous. "You're serious? No."

"This is outside your realm of responsibility," Liviya snapped, repeating Michael's hurtful words.

The pain registered in his eyes. "Liviya, I—"

"Just get out."

Michael left without a word. He did, however, take the brush with him, shutting the door behind him.

Liviya sank onto her bed. How stupid had she been to think that the people would serve her? Even if she were a princess, she was from Barlow. The divide would never be healed. She would never be queen. Her people would never be free.

CHAPTER 27

The next morning, Liviya remained in her bed. Gray clouds gathered outside her window. It was just as well. She wouldn't be doing archery anyway. She was still upset with Michael.

The winds began to howl, whipping her curtains around her room. She rushed to the window and pulled it closed just as the clouds broke open and rain sprayed down.

In a matter of moments, the thick rain formed puddles across the courtyard. She laid on her bed watching drops slide down the window. Maybe the storm was large enough that it was raining in Barlow, too.

A knock at the door stole her attention. She opened it to find Michael leaning against the doorframe. Without a word, she returned to her bed. She wasn't ready to talk to him yet.

Michael let himself in. He ran his fingers through his hair. "Liviya, I'm sorry."

Liviya pulled her pillow over her face.

"I was angry yesterday when I was talking to Daniel. I should have spoken more carefully. The words I chose made it sound—" He paused. "They made it sound like I didn't care for you."

Liviya slipped a hand beneath the pillow to wipe a tear from her cheek.

"I felt like the prince was accusing me, so I told a lie. Maybe you can understand that."

Liviya certainly understood the need to lie. She hadn't thought much about Michael and his role in their plan. He sacrificed his life just as much as she did by helping her get the crown.

"I had to lie because the truth is dangerous," he explained. "But since I know your secret, I'll tell you mine." He placed a gentle hand on her back. "I love you, Liviya. I love you more each day, and I hate that Daniel gets you. If there were any other way to seal this alliance, I'd do it and keep you for myself. But you deserve far more than I could ever give you."

Liviya kept her face covered with the pillow, afraid to meet Michael's gaze, afraid she might confess out loud that she loved him, too. She couldn't afford that kind of distraction.

"You know what I love most about you?" Michael asked. She could tell that the words came through mischievous smile. "I love how your cheeks turn red when you're embarrassed." He tugged on the pillow. "Is that what you're hiding under there?"

Liviya launched the pillow at him. She sat up and shot him an exaggerated eyeball. "Don't flatter yourself, Michael. I can barely tolerate you. However," Liviya said, "I understand your difficult position, and I appreciate you lying to the prince." With a small smile, she looked at Michael. "And in the interest of behind honest about our dishonesty, I'll confess that saying I'm a princess is not my only lie."

Liviya loved him. She had for a long time. Not being able to tell him was the biggest sacrifice she had made in Saunder.

Michael grinned and threw up his hands. "Good heavens, Liviya. You lie as much as you steal!"

They sat in the comfortable discomfort that came from confessing feelings that could never become more.

"I suppose there will be no more archery," Liviya said. Not after Prince Daniel's complaints about their friendship. A sad sigh escaped her lips.

"Of course we'll still do archery," Michael replied. "There are bandits after you. You'll need to learn to defend yourself. Frankly, you need a lot more practice."

Smiling, Liviya looked to the window. "It's too bad about the rain."

Michael nodded then said, "I wonder if you've even been given a proper tour of the palace. It will soon be yours, after all."

"Mrs. Maude showed me around when I first got here," Liviya replied.

"But did she show you its secrets?" He held out his hand.

Tentatively, Liviya accepted it. With the touch of his hand came the confirmation Michael didn't have much, but he had always given her all he had.

As they walked through the palace, Michael opened every door along the corridors. Many led to empty rooms, others led to closets filled with trunks and supplies. He told of visiting dignitaries from faraway lands, the strange languages they spoke, and the unusual foods and tokens they brought with them. He showed her the window he had broken as a boy when he was throwing rocks in the courtyard, and he showed her the tunnels between the walls where he had hidden until Mrs. Maude wasn't as angry.

Michael told her about the architects who had constructed the new wing of the palace and the artists who painted the murals on the wall. He shared stories of the men who arranged colored glass into the designs that filled the largest windows.

Then Michael led Liviya through the back corridors and to a set of stairs that Liviya had never seen. The stairs wound around and around and were so steep that Liviya had to hold her skirts to keep from stepping on them. At the very top of the stairs, a bent wooden door led outside. Raindrops seeped through the cracks and the wind roared behind it.

"This is the top of the tallest tower," Michael said. "The balcony here overlooks the entire kingdom. That's where, according to legend, the kings of Saunder stood to watch their people."

"Can you really see the entire kingdom?" Liviya asked. She pushed lightly against the door. With the help of the wind, the door blew open, slamming against the side of the tower. She stepped into the rain. The drops poured on her, dripping down her hair and soaking through her gown. She lifted her face to the clouds, letting the rain run across her face. The rain washed away the weight of her lies, the weight of becoming queen, the weight of marrying a man she didn't love. When all of that was gone, she found a small piece of herself again. She hadn't realized how much she had missed who she used to be.

Michael followed behind her, holding his coat above his head. He stood next to her. The coat did little to block out the rain. Beside them the wind howled, but it was the safest she had felt since the time she arrived in Saunder.

"I can't see the kingdom," Liviya shouted.

"I don't think they came up here in a storm." The thunder drowned out his reply.

Rain dripped off Michael's nose. His hair hung in his face. It soaked through his white shirt, making it cling to his skin. Liviya eyes found Michael's lips. She wished that he would kiss her. If this alliance failed, maybe she and Michael could be together. Maybe there was a way to save her people without breaking her heart. Another flash of lightning cut through the sky. When the thunder boomed, Liviya jumped. It was stupid to be outside in such a storm, and even more stupid to pretend that Michael could have a part in her future. She needed to marry Prince Daniel. She could only save people if she were queen. She looked to the clouds one more time, allowing a few more drops to tickle her face, then hurried back inside.

Inside, Liviya wiped her face. The rain had soaked her entire gown. Puddles formed beneath where she and Michael stood.

Michael led the way back down the rickety stairs and back to her room. They walked slowly, leaving a trail of water behind them.

"Can you believe this dreadful rain?" Sarah asked, running to close windows.

Liviya smiled. She loved every drop.

MICHAEL RETURNED TO HIS ROOM AND CHANGED INTO DRY CLOTHES. Walking down the corridor, he spotted King Josiah sitting alone in the darkened dining room in front of a plate of untouched food. Michael stepped inside and sat down beside the king. Michael rubbed stray raindrops from his hair.

"You're wet," King Josiah said.

"It's raining," Michael replied. As if on cue, lightning lit the sky and thunder made the windows rattle.

Michael hadn't spoken with the king in a while. Truthfully, he had been avoiding him, or rather, the insinuations he would make of Michael taking the crown. However, the king was a wise man, the closest thing to a father Michael ever knew, and Michael needed advice. He needed help getting Liviya the crown.

King Josiah's skinny legs stuck out beneath the blanket on his lap. The grizzly scar wound its way across his leg. It was the injury he had gotten while fighting to save his son.

"Did you ever try to erase that scar?" Michael asked.

"You can't erase a scar," the king said.

Michael puffed out his cheeks. He knew each attempt grew even more ridiculous.

"But you can change the story it tells," King Josiah whispered. "That's what all the legends are. Just stories I didn't want to tell."

Whatever the king was remembering seemed to haunt him.

Michael regretted sitting next to the king. With a smile, he attempted to lighten the mood. "They're just stories?" he asked with fake incredulity. "Then the canyon's not really a grave?"

King Josiah shook his head so slightly that Michael barely noticed. "But a girl did die there. It was your mother. I killed her."

Michael had already had far too many painful confessions that evening. He wouldn't listen to that as well. He stood up. "Geoffrey!" he called. "The king's confused again."

"Blast it, Michael! I'm not confused!" the king shouted.

"Geoffrey!" Michael didn't want to hear anymore. The king was wrong. He was remembering a different person. A different time.

Even if he had, Michael struggled to finish the thought. Even if the king had killed his mother, he would have mentioned it. After all these years, the king would have said something. He would have explained.

Geoffrey came running, along with Mrs. Maude. The king swatted them away. "I am not confused!" The words stiffened King Josiah's body.

Geoffrey gently lifted the old man out of his chair.

"You said he was ready!" King Josiah's voice cracked. Michael didn't know if it was the strain of the anger or if the old man was crying.

Michael ran his fingers through his hair, staring at the king. He paced beside the window, confused, scared, pleading that the king was wrong. Michael remembered the day the king arrived in the boys' home. He remembered how he studied each boy. He was looking for a boy who showed promise, he had said. But no. He had come for Michael. Because the king had killed his mother.

Mrs. Maude reached for his elbow. "D'you wanna talk about this?"

Michael pulled away from her touch. He needed space, air. He needed to think in peace.

"What's wrong with Michael?" Chancey whispered to Mrs. Maude as he left.

Mrs. Maude squeezed her in a side hug. "He's just scared is all, honey. He's just scared."

THE MAIDS WHISPERED ABOUT MICHAEL UPSETTING THE KING. LIVIYA hadn't seen it, but she heard all about it. They said that Michael was angry. Liviya could hardly imagine it. She couldn't imagine the king provoking that anger, either. The king barely spoke. When he did, it was mostly unintelligible.

Both Michael and the king missed dinner. The palace was strangely quiet. Mrs. Maude looked like she had been crying; Chancey was somber. Sarah looked pale. Liviya felt quite alone, unable to understand the extent of the grief she sensed.

That evening, Michael still wasn't around. Liviya wandered the palace grounds alone. The summer was slowly changing to autumn. The air was just cool enough to make it comfortable. The leaves began to change color, dusting the world with gold. The sounds of humming bees and chirping birds provided a cheerful song. The sweet scent of blossoms hung in the air. The entire scene was a majesty unmatched by anything in the palace. And Liviya loved it—almost.

Every time she found joy or beauty, a piece of her heart reminded her that she could have found that in Barlow. Every meal, every scene, every memory, she found herself loving it—loving the idea of recreating it at home.

She stopped in a garden and sat on a bench in the day's last bit of sun. Liviya plucked a flower and brought it to her nose.

At the sound of whistling, Liviya looked up. As she had guessed, Michael appeared around the corner. She was equally thrilled and relieved to see him. His early angst seemed gone. He was his usual self again, with a cheerful smile and a mischievous gleam in his eye.

He sat next to her on the bench and pulled her into a gentle side squeeze, a welcome reassurance that he was back and feeling better. For a moment, the only sound was Liviya's pounding heart.

"Have I ever told you the legend of Saunder's first princess?"

Liviya thought she had been in Saunder long enough to learn all the legends, but this one was new.

"Centuries ago, the kingdom of Saunder was weak. The people had no food, no army. Enemies advanced on every side. The king had a daughter. At her birth, it had been prophesied that she would save her people.

"When the enemy armies approached the palace, the people hid. But the princess stood at the top of the palace steps, fearlessly facing her foe. She lifted her bow and pulled the only arrow from her quiver." Michael paused to demonstrate. "Behind her, the people murmured. This girl couldn't destroy these seasoned warriors, not with a single arrow. As the leader drew his sword, the princess released the arrow, shooting it high into the sky.

"The arrow pierced the cloud, drawing out lightning. It descended in a line of fire that destroyed the entire army."

Michael took Liviya's hand. "That same fire kissed the arm of the princess, leaving her with the mark of a P, forever identifying her as princess, and more importantly, as protector. It's rumored," Michael continued, "that every few hundred years, a princess is born with the mark of a P, and with it, the mission the save the world."

Michael grinned, looking rather pleased with himself. The grin slipped when he saw Liviya's face. "You don't like it?"

"It's a cute story, I suppose," Liviya said slowly. "But nobody's going to believe it's true."

"It doesn't have to be true," Michael said. "You don't owe anybody the details to a story that you're not ready to share."

Liviya pulled up her sleeve and looked at her scar. She imagined standing on stone steps, facing an enemy with a single arrow and calling down lightning from the sky. She liked the story, but she had one hesitation. "It doesn't explain things very well. This mark isn't rare. There are hundreds of us back home with the very same scar."

Michael raised his brow. "Then Barlow isn't cursed at all. It's a blessed nation with a powerful army." He took Liviya's hand and kissed it. "I pity the man who ever marches against them."

As the maids helped Liviya undress for bed that night, Liviya pondered Michael's new legend. In the past, she had been careful to keep her scar hidden, squirming and twisting. But after months, she grew tired of hiding.

She slipped her arm out of her sleeve, baring her scar.

"Whoa!" someone said. "What happened?"

"You've never seen that before?" Chancey asked. "Guess not. They're quite rare. It's a mark from the heavens. It means 'Protector.'"

A crowd gathered around her, and Liviya let them look. She didn't hear the things they said and barely noticed them touching her. She only felt Michael's lips against her hand and heard his gentle words. *Barlow isn't cursed at all.*

CHAPTER 28

*M*ichael spent every spare moment trying to find the men who had attacked Liviya and Chancey. Liviya claimed it was random, that they were simply in the wrong place at the wrong time. Michael pretended to believe her, just for the sake of relieving her fear about another attack.

It was late morning. Liviya sat in the drawing room with the noble women. Michael watched carefully from across the corridor. He couldn't hear what they were saying, but he could see Liviya's smile. She was becoming more comfortable every day. More beautiful, too. More like a queen. Like hundreds of others, the noble women had come to offer love and support to their princess and future queen after her attack.

Michael busied himself by folding a napkin into a bird. There hadn't been any more threats, but he had guards following Liviya everywhere. For each day she didn't notice them, he offered a substantial reward, paid from his own pocket. She would be angry, but Michael couldn't be with her every second, although he certainly tried. If Prince Daniel expressed any more concern with their relationship, Michael would simply explain that he was keeping Liviya safe. Her attackers could come again at any moment.

That, however, was only part of the truth. Michael formed one wing, then flipped the bird over to form the other one. Even with the mysterious horsemen, the divide was healing. Soon, it would be complete. Michael's days with Liviya were coming to an end. The wedding was only delayed by Prince Daniel making the ruby clear.

Michael dropped the napkin. The fabric unfolded, leaving no trace of what he had created. Where was the prince? Michael hadn't seen him for several days. How long had it been? The last time was the night Liviya was attacked, but that was over a week ago. With the prince, a lot could happen in a single week.

Michael motioned to Geoffrey. He took Michael's place discreetly guarding Liviya. Two at a time, Michael took the stairs leading to the Daniel's room.

Michael knocked on the prince's door, not waiting for a reply before pushing it open. Prince Daniel had moved his bed to the side of the room. The room was full of chairs, each occupied. They men looked up as Michael entered. At the front of the room, Daniel stopped mid-sentence.

"Pardon the interruption," Michael said.

Prince Daniel stepped to the side, blocking whatever was hung on his wall. Several of the men moved their hands over the papers in front of them. Nobody spoke. Michael spotted Lord Drake and another of the barons. Two guards who worked under Michael ducked their heads. Many of the faces, he didn't recognize.

It was clear they were holding a meeting. Michael had not been invited. Nor had the king, Michael noticed. Whatever this was, Michael was sure it would cause more problems. The meeting needed to end, or at least be supervised. Prince Daniel cleared his throat, motioning to the door.

Movement outside the window caught Michael's eye. New recruits marched around the training fields, wooden sword slung over their backs.

"The king has asked for your assistance with training," Michael replied.

It was a bold-faced lie. Sometimes, one had to tell lies, though. He learned this from Liviya, and recently he had learned it from the king. Michael wouldn't leave the prince alone with those gluttonous, pig-faced fools. There were too many dangerous things happening in his kingdom for him to not know what was being discussed.

"Immediately," Michael added.

Even as the prince, Daniel was bound to follow the king's orders.

"We'll adjourn for now, gentlemen," Prince Daniel said. "Take note of your orders and see that you complete them quickly."

The men filed out the door. Prince Daniel and Michael were alone in the room.

"Just discussing the ruby," Prince Daniel said. "You were busy with the princess."

"She's at the archery fields every morning at sunrise. How about you meet her tomorrow and I'll help you with all this?" Michael held his hand toward the desk and the concealed papers.

"Not necessary." Prince Daniel straightened the stack of papers and placed them in a drawer, locking it when it closed. "To the training field."

THE RECRUITS TRAINED ON THE BATTLE FIELDS DAILY. MOSTLY, THERE were ignored. That afternoon, Michael and Daniel joined them. They walked down the corridor, backs straight, coats sharp, steps even, like they were marching to battle.

Everyone in the palace stopped as they passed.

When they were outside, King Josiah spoke first. "Help me up. I need some fresh air."

Geoffrey helped him stand. Together, they shuffled outside.

Mrs. Maude set a basket of laundry on her hip. "Gonna go hang this to dry.

"We'll help," Sarah said. She and Chancey followed.

Liviya looked around the nearly empty dining room. There didn't seem to be much else happening in the palace, so she followed the group outside.

In the fields, lines of boys swung their swords to the command of the officers. "One. Two. Three. Four."

Michael and Daniel leaned against the fence to watch. The group was surprised to see them, and even more surprised to see the king. The officers barked more loudly; the boys' held their swords straighter.

Liviya sat beside King Josiah in the shade of a large tree. It was unusually warm. Liviya fanned a breeze across her face. The king sat with a blanket over his legs.

Several real swords waited against the wall. Prince Daniel grabbed one and tossed it to Michael then grabbed one for himself. "Let's show them a real fight."

The boys scattered to the far wall, leaving plenty of room in the arena. Michael and Daniel, swords in hand, hopped the fence.

"Welcome, boys!" Michael said. "You're doing well. In a matter of weeks, your skills will be at the level—"

Prince Daniel lunged at Michael.

Liviya and the boys gasped.

Michael blocked the attack. "You'll be at the level where you can do that. Excellent demonstration, Your Highness."

Prince Daniel struck again, hard and fast, leaning against Michael's blade.

"Slowly, so the they can see," Michael said.

Prince Daniel slapped Michael's face with the side of his sword.

Michael's face twitched with a tiny bit of anger. "What are you doing?"

"I have work waiting for me," Daniel replied. "To finish it, I'll have to remove you." With a fake to the right, Daniel dove left, blade swinging toward Michael's abdomen.

Michael blocked it again, sending a loud *clang* across the fields. There was no more stopping, no more talking. The swords beat against each other again and again. The men's fast-moving feet clouded them in a dusty haze.

"They're fighting!" Liviya said in a panic.

Mrs. Maude only rolled her eyes. "These boys. Been fighting like this since they could walk."

While that might have been true, Liviya was certain they didn't fight with swords. She turned to the king. "Maybe you should stop them."

"It's just a squabble," the king replied. He watched closely, though Liviya wondered how much he could see.

The recruits cheered, but the fighting was too fast for Liviya to follow. "Who's winning?"

"Technically, Daniel," the king said. "Michael's too afraid to fight."

"He's fighting now," Liviya said, wincing against the harsh dings of their blades.

"This isn't fighting. This," he said, motioning to the arena, "is just to entertain Daniel." King Josiah stared across the courtyard, his gaze reaching farther than the arena. "I've been too afraid to fight for a long time, as well. I'm unworthy of the crown I wear." King Josiah sat with his hands folded in his lap. He moved his gaze to his knees. He muttered words Liviya couldn't hear. If it weren't for his moving lips, Liviya wouldn't have known he was speaking. Despite the heat, chills ran down her arms.

Liviya patted his hand. "It's dreadfully warm, Your Majesty. I wonder if we should return indoors."

The haze surrounding the arena grew thicker, a result of feet moving faster, more aggressively. The sounds changed, too. Instead of the clink clang clink it became clink clink clink clink clink, high and fast.

"There is no beast," the king said.

"I know," Liviya replied. It was a silly lie. She never should have said it. "They were men on horses. I was just scared."

"No." King Josiah paused and touched his lip. He saw Liviya's worried gaze and tried to smile, but the smile drooped. "The beast didn't kill my son's wife. I did." The king's words slurred.

"Michael?" she called. But her worried voice was lost in the clanging of swords.

"I tried to make it right." The king's voice was barely a whisper. "I hear the child screaming in my sleep." The king slumped to the side, face gray and eyes rolled back.

"Michael!" Liviya screamed.

Michael twisted away from the prince's attack and ran, hopping over the wall.

"He was talking," Liviya said. "It was nonsense. And then he—"

Michael scooped the old man into his arms. He ran into the palace. Liviya followed.

"We need help!" Michael yelled.

Sarah rushed inside, throwing pillows from the sofa. Michael laid the king onto the cushions. His open eyes saw nothing. His body hung limply.

Prince Daniel entered a few paces behind everyone. He peeked over Michael's shoulder and hooted a laugh. "The old man's finally gone." He raised his hands into the air. "I'm king!"

Liviya whirled around and slapped Prince Daniel's face. "You're vile!" she screamed.

She moved to hit him again, but Michael held her arm and shoved Prince Daniel back. "Get out!"

Prince Daniel looked startled. Liviya guessed that he had never been slapped before. That was a shame. She was certain he deserved it more than once.

Liviya sank to the floor in a daze. "I should have taken him inside. He was acting strange. He was saying things." The memory of the king's words haunted Liviya, but she didn't repeat them. *The beast didn't kill my son's wife. I did.*

Michael sank next to Liviya on the floor and pulled her into a hug. She rested her head against his chest. Her palm still stung from the force of hitting Daniel. She rubbed it against her thigh.

"He'll be alright. He's just warm." Michael's heart beat in a steady, slow rhythm, calm as always, even in chaos. Liviya watched the maids rush about bringing water and linens. They stripped off the king's clothes and washed his face with a towel. Throughout their care, he remained motionless. Liviya wished she could cry, but no matter what tragedy she faced, she was always more scared than she was sad—this time, scared for the life of the king she had come to love and more so, scared about what story his was hiding.

Liviya wanted to tell Michael how much she hated Prince Daniel and how much she dreaded her life with him, but he watched the king with furrowed brows. Despite how calmly his heart was beating, he was scared. Besides, he knew enough of Liviya's secrets. She didn't need to burden him with more.

CHAPTER 29

The next morning, Michael peeked into the king's bedroom where they had moved him the previous evening. Liviya sat by his bed holding his hand. She had stayed by his side all through the night.

Michael placed his hand on top of theirs. "Mrs. Maude insists you go down for breakfast. I tried to convince her to let you stay in here for days with no food and no rest, but she refused."

It was a lie. Michael had spent the entire night in the stables cleaning whatever would take his mind off of the king. He hadn't even seen Mrs. Maude yet. In fact, he had gone to great lengths to avoid her. But if he had seen her, that's what she would have said.

"I'll sit with him while you're gone."

Liviya left without much argument. Michael took her seat. The king's cheeks were gray, and his lips were dry. His breath came in raspy inhales that barely lifted his chest.

Michael enjoyed the silence for only a moment until it was interrupted by Mrs. Maude. Without a word, she placed a tray of food at the table beside Michael.

Geoffrey peeked his head through the doorway. "How's he doing?"

"He's alive," Michael replied. It was the only positive thing he could find.

At the sound of Geoffrey's voice, the king forced open his eyes. He coughed a few times and tried to lift his hand.

"I got some soup here for ya, Yer Majesty," Mrs. Maude said. She dipped a spoon in the bowl.

"Wait," Michael said. He moved to the foot of the bed where the king could see him without moving his head. "Who crowns the next king if you're dead?"

King Josiah closed his eyes again. "The legends—"

"The legends aren't real," Michael replied impatiently. "It's time to crown the prince."

Grimacing with pain, the king exhaled. "No one has completed the requirements."

"The princess has," Michael said.

The king shook his head. "There's still a hole."

"Everyone loves her!" Michael demanded. "Everyone wants her here!" He paced away from the bed, rubbing his hands over his face.

The king coughed. "Not everyone."

Michael sat back down, hand cupped over his forehead. There was no way to heal the divide. He had spent all summer watching Prince Daniel try to win the loyalty of every single person. It just wasn't possible.

Geoffrey spoke up from the corner. "Michael's right," he said. "It's time to crown a new king."

Slowly, Michael lifted his head. He had never been so grateful for Geoffrey's input.

"I can have the Heart of Saunder clear in an hour if you'll let me help," Geoffrey said.

The king didn't reply.

"It won't hurt near as bad as you think it will," Geoffrey said gently. "And they all deserve the truth."

Michael suddenly wasn't quite sure what Geoffrey was talking about.

The king was quiet for a long time. Michael wondered if he had fallen asleep.

"Very well," he said finally.

Michael perked up. After months, the end was in sight. Prince Daniel could be crowned within an hour.

"What do you need?" Michael asked. Tools, equipment, money. Whatever it was, Michael would find it.

"We just need a quiet place to talk," Geoffrey said.

The hair on Michael's neck raised. "How does that help Daniel get the throne?"

Geoffrey stood up and placed a hand on Michael's shoulder. "I'm not aiming to help Daniel get the throne. I'm going to get you there."

Michael cocked his head. He had been suspicious that Geoffrey knew the king's invitation, but this confirmed it.

"Those words sound mighty treasonous," Michael said.

Geoffrey met his gaze with a challenging stare. "You've said that before. How much can I say before you arrest me?"

Michael looked away. Geoffrey was playing a game. Michael didn't want to join.

"Michael the Brave is scared," Geoffrey taunted. "You're a coward."

Michael's temper flared. "I have done everything the king has ever asked me to do."

"The king isn't asking you to *do* anything. He's asking you to *be* something."

Michael turned around. "No. No, no, no."

"Yes," Geoffrey said. "This has been the plan from the very beginning. You were always to be king. And Prince Daniel has reinforced that decision with every stupid, selfish, reckless—"

Michael slammed his fist against Geoffrey's face. Geoffrey toppled backward and knocked over a chair. Blood spurted from his nose and dripped across his lips.

"Guards, arrest him for treason."

"Michael!" Mrs. Maude scolded.

"This coronation will happen at week's end," Michael said to everyone listening. "Prince Daniel will be king. Get everything ready."

NEWS OF THE UPCOMING CORONATION SPREAD QUICKLY. THE VILLAGERS gathered and travelers began to arrive. Tents filled the city square. What was announced as a coronation became a banquet, a ball, and a fair. At week's end, the prince would be crowned, but Liviya still needed to complete her requirements.

Michael found Sarah in the dining room cleaning up supper.

"You come to arrest me, too?"

"I came for help," Michael said.

"Don't think I owe you any." Sarah stacked the dirty dishes on a large platter and avoided looking at him.

"Tell me about the maids," Michael said. "Is there anyone who doesn't like Liviya?"

"They all love her," Sarah relied.

"What about the stable hands? Do you hear anything there? People in the village?"

"Everyone loves her."

"See, that's not quite true," Michael said. "The king says the divide isn't filled. That means someone doesn't want her in Saunder. She can't be queen until does."

Sarah sighed and sat down. Michael hid his grin. She may have been mad at him, but like others, she would do whatever it took to help Liviya become queen. "I think the only person that wishes Liviya was back in Barlow is Liviya herself."

Michael's entire core hummed with a confirmation that Sarah was right. Still, his mind questioned it. Michael had been to Barlow, and he would never go back. It was filthy. The people starved. Liviya was a maid. She should be grateful to be in Saunder. This alliance saved her life.

Strangely, he was offended, hurt, that the life he had worked so hard to provide for Liviya wasn't enough. Michael laced his fingers behind his neck while he thought. "What else does she need?" Michael asked.

"I ain't gonna pretend to know what she wants," Sarah said. "Just tellin' you what I noticed."

Sarah was right. Michael had learned a lot about Liviya over the summer. He knew her favorite food, her favorite story, her favorite song. He knew what jokes would make her laugh and which jokes would make her cringe. He knew her favorite seat by the window where she read her favorite book, and he even knew that Liviya loved him.

But he didn't really know Liviya. He didn't know about her family, her friends, or about her life in Barlow and all that she had left behind. He didn't know what her struggles had been, or how she had survived. While Liviya made an excellent princess, inside, she was the same scared girl he had met months ago in Barlow. *Princess* Liviya wouldn't be able to tell him how he could help. He'd need to ask the real Liviya. But to talk to the real Liviya, he'd need to get her out of the palace. Michael looked around at the bustling maids. He had just the idea.

CHAPTER 30

In the four days since it was announced that Prince Daniel would be crowned, Liviya had spent nearly every moment confined to her room. The work it took to transform a maid into a princess was minimal compared to the work required to transform a princess into a bride and a queen. She was fitted for multiple gowns—a day dress for the festivities, an evening gown for the prince's coronation ball, and a wedding dress for the ceremony to follow. Hopefully both she and the prince would have their requirements completed. The hole still wasn't filled. The ruby was still red.

In her room, the seamstresses pinned and tucked and trimmed. They would pause and inspect Liviya from across the room. Shaking their heads, they'd return. More ribbons, more lace, more beads. It wasn't good enough, and Liviya wondered if it ever would be, just like her. But it was only fair. Liviya would never be quite satisfied with Daniel either, only she wanted less. Less anger, less arrogance, less agitation.

All of Liviya's gowns had long sleeves, but eventually Daniel would see her arm. She only prayed that word of the legend had reached his ears, or that the alliance was sealed and water sent before the scar was discovered.

Liviya watched the preparations outside from her window. Nobles wandered through the palace grounds. The peasants waited in tents that spotted the city. Dozens of people worked to decorate the palace. But inside, the people were quiet, somber even. They mourned, and whether it was for the king they would soon lose or the king who would replace them, she didn't know. Maybe they mourned, as she did, for her life spent with Daniel.

Finally satisfied with the gown, the seamstresses left her to undress and wait for others who would come to tend to her hair and skin. Liviya sat on the edge of her bed. She held her head in her hands propped on her knees. It was really happening. Liviya sighed. She had thought that after all this work, she would feel relieved. Instead, she felt empty.

A tapping sound pulled Liviya's attention to the window. Clutching her robe, she crossed the room. Michael waved from the other side of the glass, balancing on the ivy-covered lattice that spanned the wall. Liviya pushed the window open.

"Thought you could use some help escaping," he said.

Liviya glanced around her room. Soon, someone would return to size the gown again, or curl her hair, or help her bathe. At some point, she needed to become a queen inside as well as out, and queens didn't sneak out of their palaces. "They'll be back soon."

Michael shook his head. "Mrs. Maude has every woman in the palace down fitting the servants for new work clothes. She won't have her maids strutting around in dirty dresses during a coronation. If I know Mrs. Maude, and I have my entire life, they've forgotten all about you." Michael grinned. "I'll wait while you change."

Smiling, Liviya shut the window and pulled on the plainest gown in her armoire. By the time she had dressed, Michael was back on the ground. He held the lattice as Liviya descended. Arm in arm, they crossed the palace grounds and climbed under the wall.

On the other side of the wall, the city was a kaleidoscope of activity. There were performers and vendors, music and food. Michael tossed a coin to a woman at the first cart they passed and selected the ugliest shawl from a mix of knitted clothing. The disguise wouldn't fool anybody. It was more of a plea for privacy, which the people respected. As they walked, they were left alone. Instead of the usual clamor of well-wishes, tokens, and bows that followed Liviya whenever she left the palace gates, today people only winked or gave knowing nods. They seemed to understand that this was her last ordinary day. Graciously, they allowed her to enjoy it in peace.

Michael and Liviya wove through the carts. Some sold wood carvings of delicate animals with detailed features, some sold pottery in varying shapes and colors. Other arts displayed jewelry and ornaments made of glass. Dried and pressed flowers filled another cart. They were held behind glass and organized to display colorful scenes of oceans or sunsets.

"Tell me about Barlow," Michael said.

"It's windy there," Liviya replied.

Michael nodded and kept walking.

"What about your family?"

Liviya was silent for a few paces. "My father enjoyed reading." It was the only detail that wasn't attached to painful memories. She was grateful that Michael didn't press for more information. Her scar had healed and no longer caused pain, but the wounds of losing her family burned again with every breath and lit a fire with every memory.

"Did you have a beau?" Michael asked with a sly grin. "Because I heard some men talking about you in the fields. They said you were beautiful. Eyes like stars."

Liviya shoved his arm and sent him stumbling sideways a few steps.

"I was kind enough to warn them that you were ill-tempered," he said with a laugh.

"Only in ill-company," Liviya replied.

Michael laughed, then turned serious again. "The king says that the divide isn't completely healed yet. It's been suggested that it's because you don't really want to stay."

He was right. Given the choice, she'd still return home. Unfortunately, that wasn't an option. She wouldn't return home and subject her people to starvation simply because she was homesick.

"If you could pick one thing from Barlow to bring back to Saunder, what would it be?"

Liviya pondered a few steps. She thought back to Bicka and how she wished she could have buried her. She thought about King Herrick and his tyranny. The alliance would change all that. So why was she still hesitant to stay? Michael was a dear friend, one who had made a lot of sacrifices to help her reach her goals. He deserved an answer, but Liviya truthfully didn't know.

Nearby, musicians began plucking their fiddles. Couples slowly began to dance on a ballroom floor of flattened grass.

Michael and Liviya stood beside each other, mostly listening to the music, but occasionally meeting the other's gaze.

"Do you intend to dance with Prince Daniel when you're married?" Michael asked.

When they were married, Prince Daniel would be king. He would have the honor of the first dance, as she claimed was custom in her land during the ball the first night she arrived.

"I don't know how," Liviya said. The honest words were refreshing to speak. No lies, no excuses, and no judgment from Michael.

Michael folded an arm over his waist and bowed. "Then may I have the pleasure?" He pulled Liviya into his arms and counted the steps as they twirled slowly between the paintings. Liviya stared at her feet, too embarrassed to look Michael in the eye. They were inches apart. She was very aware of the touch of his hand on her back. As the evening darkened, they danced beneath the decoration of the stars, to the whistling of the wind, to the hum of the fireflies. Though crowds surrounded them, they danced like they were alone. She looked over Michael's shoulder at the land of Saunder as it spun around her. If every night in Saunder like this, then she would have stayed even if staying offered nothing else.

They moved slower until they finally stopped, but Michael still held her in his arms.

"I wish," Liviya began, forcing out the uncomfortable words. Michael had listened to all her lies for months. This time, he deserved the truth. "I do wish Daniel loved me."

"Liviya," Michael said, pain in his eyes. "He loves you. He's just been busy."

True, he was busy. Liviya had been, too. But Daniel never looked at her the way Michael did.

"I wonder if we should return home," Michael whispered. "Might be they're missing you, and there's one more thing I need to do for Prince Daniel."

Michael dropped his arms. The world was cold outside his embrace. Liviya shivered, this time with grief. She had already lost so much. Soon, she would lose Michael, too.

CHAPTER 31

The moon had long since replaced the sun's shine when Michael escorted Liviya back to the side palace wall. He held the edges of the lattice while she climbed to the top. Liviya pulled herself through the window and waved before closing it. Michael entered the palace through the servant's entrance, being careful to wipe his boots. Mrs. Maude sat on a stool in the kitchen.

"How'd it go?" Michael asked.

"Didn't even notice she was gone, and I got my girls new clothes."

"Thank you," Michael said.

"D'you have a good time?"

"I did," Michael said. "And I've got one more idea. Where's the prince?"

Mrs. Maude hesitated before answering. "He's up in his room. Has been all day."

"Thanks." Michael started toward the kitchen door.

"Michael, if that idea don't work, I got one more fer ya," Mrs. Maude said.

Michael turned and smiled. "This one will work."

Michael opened Daniel's door without knocking. The first thing he noticed was the overwhelming smell of body odor trapped behind thick curtains. The lights were dim. Dirty dishes were stacked in the corner. Clothes were strewn across the floor, and books covered his bed. Prince Daniel sat at his desk surrounded by various tools, and in the center laid the ruby.

Prince Daniel didn't look up. "I'm close."

He claimed that, but the ruby remained as red as the day Daniel received the challenge.

Michael pulled a chair to the desk and sat down. "The princess is homesick."

Prince Daniel nodded, but it seemed more a confirmation that he was aware that Michael was talking. He made no indication that he heard the actual words.

"I wonder if your future bride would benefit from a token of your affection."

Prince Daniel rummaged through the tools. "What for?"

"So she knows that you love her. Women need these things." Michael shrugged.

"She'll marry me regardless." Prince Daniel held a chisel along the edge of the ruby.

The answer made Michael angry. He breathed it away. "The divide isn't filled yet because there's a hole in her heart. If she knew you loved her, it would heal her." Michael moved a sheet of parchment toward the prince. "Just a quick note with a few affirmations will do."

"She's beautiful," Prince Daniel admitted. He picked up the magnifying glass and inspected the ruby.

"Good. And what else?"

Prince Daniel returned the magnifying glass to the table and picked up a smaller chisel. "And her father has no other heir." For the first time he met Michael's eyes. "By marrying her, I'll become king of my land and hers. Can you imagine the power of these two lands combined?" Prince Daniel gave a sly grin.

"You'll be king of Barlow?" Michael asked.

Prince Daniel turned back to the ruby. "If I complete his challenge. I need to unite my land."

Michael felt the same tingles he knew well, the ones that warned him of danger he couldn't see. Daniel met him with a gaze that dared him to voice any suspicions. Michael chose not to. Instead, he cleared his throat.

"If you'll be king of two lands, then it's doubly worth your time to ensure Liviya stays forever." He tapped a finger against the parchment. "It's not difficult. 'Dear Liviya, If I had known that becoming king would have given me a life with you, I would have accepted my challenge without hesitation, because I have loved you since the day we met.'" Michael pushed the jar of ink closer. "Then sign your name."

Prince Daniel picked up the magnifying glass again, but this time studied Michael. "I have yet to defeat an enemy for Herrick." He placed the magnifying glass back on the table and picked up the quill. "He warned me of the enemy who claimed to be my friend."

The tingles surged again. "You'll write the letter?" Michael asked.

"Of course I will," Daniel said. "I think our princess needs to hear this."

Michael left Prince Daniel's room with more problems than he had when he arrived. King Herrick was setting up some sort of trap. Herrick knew Liviya wasn't a real princess. It was impossible to think that he would truly let her return and rule his land with the prince she had married. But most disturbing, he had given Prince Daniel the very same requirements as King Josiah, and Prince Daniel intended to fulfill them, no matter the cost.

 evening, she stopped by the king's room. Her slippered feet softened her steps, but the king looked up as she appeared in the doorway. He opened his mouth with what Liviya assumed was a greeting, though only a groan emerged.

Liviya crossed the room. She sat in the high-backed chair beside his bed. He looked much better than the day he fainted in the sun, but he looked frail compared to the days and weeks before. His bony arms stuck out from his night clothes and his skin sagged off his cheeks. He squeezed her hand gently.

"Liviya."

"Yes, Your Majesty," Liviya replied.

The king tried to sit up. Liviya helped him adjust the pillows behind his head. "Physician thinks I'm sick." The king shook his head. "I'm faking. I do this to accumulate the beautiful people I know."

"It's effective. There's hardly any room when I come to visit." The wedding plans had prevented her from visiting as much as she would have liked, but the room was often full when she did peek in.

"There's always room for you." King Josiah closed his eyes. "You'll be married tomorrow."

Liviya nodded.

"I never liked arranged marriages," King Josiah said. "I lost my son over an arranged marriage. He didn't love her."

Liviya remembered the story, the prince who gave up his throne to marry his love rather than marry another.

"Why are you here?" the king asked.

"I wanted to see how you were feeling," Liviya replied.

"No," the king said weakly, "why are you here in Saunder?"

The king waited patiently while she considered his question. Why was she there? She had been given opportunities to escape, yet she remained. "I want to free my people. I need to be queen."

"I've had many problems in the years I've lived," the king said, "but I've never had a problem that was solved simply because I wore the crown."

"But if I were queen—" Liviya began. The money, the food, the power. It would give her everything her people lacked.

King Josiah opened his eyes. "You don't need a crown; you need a friend." He reached out his other hand and placed it on top of hers. "Why not just ask the prince to free your people?"

"Prince Daniel needs the alliance," Liviya explained. That was what kept her in Saunder. Without the required marriage, Liviya would have been forgotten by him long ago.

"Ask the other prince," the king said weakly.

Liviya wasn't certain she heard the words correctly. The other prince? One by one, all of the king's strange stories and confused ramblings became clear. Prince Nathan who had run away to marry his love. King Josiah, the beast, who killed her, the child left screaming.

"Michael is Prince Nathan's son," King Josiah said.

Liviya brought her hands to her cheeks. Her mind raced too quickly to process her thoughts. Michael was Prince Nathan's son. He was heir to the throne. Maybe she didn't have to marry Daniel. Maybe she could seal the alliance by marrying Michael instead. If he completed the requirements, he'd be king.

King Josiah seemed to read her thoughts. "I offered Michael the crown. He refused."

Liviya peered at the king between her fingers.

"Not everybody is so courageous to accept their call to greatness as quickly as you were."

If Michael were king, he could defeat a different enemy. He would spare the people of Barlow, but still be brave enough to fight against King Herrick's regime. And if life were like the legends where fairies granted wishes and animals spoke and magic fell upon the land in a golden glitter, then it would be Michael that Liviya was marrying tomorrow. Her heart swelled in her chest at the thought. But the legends were simply tales told to children to protect them from the real dangers that assailed them in the dark nights.

"He won't take the throne?" Liviya asked, hating how much hope filled her voice.

"He refused today, but tomorrow will come, and with it, another opportunity." King Josiah smiled. "May the morning sun bless Michael with courage."

The king's eyes closed. Liviya sat beside him for a long time. She pondered what to do with the information the king had shared, but her thoughts quickly turned to dreams of how her life would be so different if Michael were king of Saunder and if there was anything she could do to convince him to take the crown.

CHAPTER 32

The next day began earlier than Liviya expected. She woke up to women barging into her room to help her dress. The day was filled with festivities—performances, tournaments, entertainment. She was expected to attend all of them, and she was expected to look flawless.

The guards had opened the palace gates. The entire kingdom filled the palace grounds. It was the only time Liviya had ever seen the rich and the poor mingle.

Liviya spent the morning being dragged from one activity to the other. Prince Daniel joined her with some but abandoned her at many. The ruby wasn't clear. He had only hours remaining.

Liviya waved when she was told to, smiled when it was suggested, and tried her best to look like a princess. In every group, she scanned the crowd for Michael's face. She didn't know what she'd say, but she hoped that her words would change the day's plans.

Nearby, a man announced the start of the archery tournament. Liviya's companions escorted her to the stands on the hillside where she had spent so much time with Michael all summer. Her seat was in the front row beneath an awning. Victoria and the other noble girls joined her. It seemed the whole kingdom gathered to watch. Even

King Josiah, weak as he was, had asked to be carried outdoors and sat on a chair in the shade.

Men young and old lined up on the grass, bows slung across their backs. Prince Daniel had reappeared. Michael accompanied him. Liviya's heart skipped. Her face flushed. She didn't know if she wanted to catch his eye or remain hidden in the crowd. Michael's gaze moved across the stands. He found her quickly and nodded in her direction.

The tournament official stood atop a tower and announced the start of the tournament. The people leaned over the gates, waving handkerchiefs and blowing kisses to their favorite competitors. It was a far different experience from the quiet mornings Michael and Liviya had spent on the field.

The first group took their places along the line and released their arrows. The whoosh-thump of the arrows was followed by groans and cheers. Those advancing from the first mark were ushered to the right side, those who lost exited the arena and joined their families in the stands.

After several waves, Michael stepped to the line. Liviya's heart pounded, though she knew he'd hit center. After taking careful aim, he released his string. Every woman in the stands seemed to scream his name. A blanket of handkerchiefs fell to the field. Liviya applauded politely.

Prince Daniel was next. Liviya had never seen him shoot a bow, but many people bet on him as the winner. Many others, Liviya included, believed Michael would win. Prince Daniel hit the center easily.

The archers moved back ten yards and the tournament repeated itself. The first group shot their arrows. Those who advanced moved aside, those who lost returned to the stands. It continued wave after wave, dozens eliminated each time, but Michael and the prince continued. The crowd was louder now. One by one, the men left until Michael and Prince Daniel stood alone. From the side, in their matching blue coats, they looked identical, exactly like the brothers they didn't know they were. They drew their bows with the same form and held their anchors in the same places, obviously taught by the same man, King Josiah.

Half of the people cheered for Daniel, the future king. The other spectators cheered for Michael, the friend to many. Among them, Baron Van Cleef and Victoria.

The people's cries neutralized each other until all that was heard was a deafening roar. It seemed to shake the stands and stir the leaves of the trees. Liviya applauded, giving no clues as for whom she cheered.

Despite the crowd's screams, the men's voices carried to the stands.

"Care to make a wager?" Prince Daniel asked.

Michael pulled an arrow from the quiver. "No, sir."

"Money," Prince Daniel said. "All the gold in my treasury."

Michael cocked his head to the targets. "It's your turn."

"Land. I'll make you lord over an entire village."

The crowd quieted and leaned forward, straining to hear. Michael didn't bother to answer.

"If you win, I'll give you my crown," Prince Daniel said.

Michael's eyes narrowed. "What game are you playing?"

Prince Daniel faced the crowd and raised his voice. "Every time I compete against Michael, I fear he loses on purpose. I want a real fight. I want a real victor. But what will motivate him to compete?" Prince Daniel stroked his chin and moved his gaze slowly up to the sky and back down until it landed on Liviya. "Ah, here's an idea." He turned back to Michael. "Winner gets Liviya."

Heat rose into Liviya's cheeks. Prince Daniel cackled. The sound made her cringe.

"What did your letter say?" Prince Daniel reached into his pocket and pulled out a folded paper. "'Dear Liviya, If I had known that becoming king would have given me a life with you, I would have accepted my challenge without hesitation, because I have loved you since the day we met. Love, Michael.'"

The crowd remained silent, and nobody moved. Liviya hoped her anger looked like humiliation, certain that was Daniel's goal. She already knew Michael loved her. That wasn't why her cheeks flushed. She was angry that he had been offered the throne and refused even though he loved her.

Michael looked neither surprised nor embarrassed. He simply looked calm. He turned to Liviya with a sly smile that she had seen so many times. "Let's let Liviya play." He held out an arrow. "If you win, you can pick between us."

Liviya's temper sparked. This was not a game. The lives of the people in two kingdoms were at stake. She had sacrificed too much to have her heart held so cruelly as a wager. "If you hand me an arrow I'll shoot you," Liviya spat.

Michael held up his hands apologetically. "Then it's you against me, Daniel. Winner takes the crown, and winner takes the princess."

Prince Daniel pulled out an arrow. "And now we will determine a real victor." With the snap of the string, his arrow sailed to the center of the target. Nobody cheered. Nobody breathed.

Liviya's heart pounded as if in slow motion, each pulse sending thick blood slowly through her body.

Michael raised his bow much more cautiously than Daniel, but with equal power. The arrow hit the target. The crowd remained in perfect silence. Not even the announcer said a word.

Prince Daniel stepped back ten yards and shot his arrow. The sound of the vibrating string hummed across the archery ring. Then Michael. Liviya didn't need to watch. She knew he'd hit the center.

The men were impossibly far away now. It seemed they were under water. Every motion was slow and every sound muddled. Arrow after arrow, the men competed, until finally, the distance disrupted Daniel's aim. His arrow struck just off-center. The crowd gasped.

"Whoever is closest wins," he said.

Michael placed his toe against the line and winked at Liviya. "This is the winning shot."

Liviya buried her face in her hands, but nothing happened. She peeked up to see Michael watching her, seeming to wait for an answer to a question she couldn't read.

"For Liviya." Michael released his arrow, but at the last second, pulled up his bow. The arrow soared across the sky and toward the trees. It sailed across the trees, piercing an apple and sending it to the ground.

Prince Daniel raised his hands above his head, like Michael had missed. Liviya knew, though, that he had aimed for that on purpose. He had been given an opportunity for the crown, for Liviya, and he had chosen to lose. The people cheered politely for their prince, the victor.

Liviya stood up and stormed away, shimmying through the narrow rows past the spectators. Michael followed behind her, but she didn't slow until she found at least a little bit of privacy on the busy palace grounds.

In the thick trees of the palace gardens, Liviya whirled around and stuck a finger into Michael's chest. "You lost on purpose!"

"Oh," Michael said slowly, with a teasing gleam in his eye. He stepped forward and stroked Liviya's cheek. "Did you want me to you win your hand?"

Liviya slapped his hand away. "I wanted you to win the crown."

Michael rolled his eyes. "The prince wouldn't have really given me his crown."

"King Josiah would have."

The color drained from Michael's face. "Where did you hear that?"

"King Josiah himself told me," Liviya said.

Michael stepped away, and Liviya was grateful for the space between them. "The king gets confused."

"He wasn't confused!" Liviya nearly shouted. "He meant every word he said. He said you were a coward."

Michael groaned. "Oh, come on, Liviya. I can't be king."

"But if you completed the requirements—"

"Requirements don't make someone royal!" Michael shouted. "I won't stand before my people and ask them to bow if I wouldn't be willing to bow to someone just like me—a nobody wearing a crown."

The words nearly knocked Liviya down. Back in Barlow, King Herrick had a punishment that he reserved for the criminals he hated the most. He tied those people to beams, sliced them open with a knife, and ripped their beating hearts from their chests. She was still under King Herrick's control, and he was still punishing her. Today, he tore out her heart. It hurt worse than Liviya had imagined.

Michael must have read the pain in her eyes. He tried to retrieve his words, but it was too late. "I didn't mean that, Liviya. You're different. I'd bow to you. The whole land will bow."

Liviya stepped away.

Michael reached out for her arm. "Just listen for a minute."

Liviya pushed him away. "Leave me alone!" she screamed. "I hate you!"

Michael held his hands up in surrender. Tears pooling, Liviya ran. She didn't know where she'd go, but she knew she didn't want to see Michael.

Liviya found space in the stables. She had told a thousand lies since she had arrived in Saunder. She had lied about her history, her home, her family, her land, her skills, her talents, her interests. She would have lied about the very color of her blood if she thought it shouldn't be red. She lied until she enjoyed it. She lay awake at night, rehearsing her lies so as to be able to repeat them the next day, and the next, and so she could repeat them as she lay an old woman, dying with the crown of Saunder on her head. But she had just told Michael she hated him, and that was the most difficult lie she had ever spoken. Liviya brought her hands to her face and wept every tear she had saved since arriving in Saunder.

Michael returned to the archery ring. Prince Daniel seemed to be waiting for him, one elbow resting on the fence around the field. Michael shoved the prince backward with both hands. "You're an imbecile. You almost lost your crown."

Prince Daniel raised his face to the sky and sighed. "Oh, Michael. It was a test."

Michael scoffed. "You thought Liviya loved me more than you?"

"No, I thought the king loved you more than me." He leaned forward. "I was worried he had offered you the crown."

"Even if he had," Michael said between clenched teeth, "I would have refused."

"I know that now." Prince Daniel put his arm around Michael's shoulders. "You'd lie on your face in the mud and allow me to stand on your back if you thought those few inches would help me reach the throne. Isn't that right?"

It was right. The realization was like walking down a flight of stairs, but another step remained when Michael thought they had ended. Now he was falling, except he wasn't sure how wrong he was, how many steps he had missed, or how far he would fall.

"I needed to know how much I could trust you. I need your help." Prince Daniel motioned for Michael to follow him. Michael felt uneasy, but he followed the prince. The prince had created a lot of problems in his life, but there had never been a test of loyalty before asking for Michael's help. Michael feared what he'd be asked to do.

Prince Daniel led Michael to the empty shed in the farthest corner of the palace grounds. He jiggled a key in the lock and opened the door. A smell assaulted them. Coughing, Michael peered inside. The stench threatened to devour him from the inside, burning his nose and his lungs. He pulled his coat's lapel over his nose.

Prince Daniel stepped inside. Michael followed. A large pot sat inside a wooden bucket on top of an altar of bricks. Liquid oozed from tiny holes in the bottom of the bucket, scarring the bricks with tiny burnt pocks. And oh, the smell.

"What is that?" Michael asked, near very real panic. "Daniel, what is that?"

"Acid," Prince Daniel replied. With long tongs, he picked up a rock from a pile near him and lowered it into the bucket. The yellow liquid sizzled and spat and threatened to boil over with a thick yellow foam. Droplets splashed onto the wooden floor. Where they landed, tiny streams of smoke rose like charmed snakes. Just before the foam ran down the edges, Prince Daniel removed the tongs. His timing was precise. He had done this before.

The tongs were now twisted and charred, but still grasped the rock, and the rock was now clear. It was like looking into a pool of perfect water. But the rock began to melt. It spun toward the ground in a thin stream, shattering when it hit the wooden floor.

Prince Daniel grinned, eyes showing his delight. "Did you see that?" When Michael didn't reply, he explained, "It was clear. I made it clear."

"Daniel," Michael said, "No. I won't help you with that."

"This is finished," Daniel said. "I need your help with Liviya."

Prince Daniel said her name like he was issuing a hex. Darkness and evil were very real, and Daniel had found it.

"You're right. There's a hole in her heart. But if she were to be frightened or hurt then I could save her. Then she would love me."

Michael took a small step back, fearful that anything faster would tip the pot, or worse, upset the prince. "What are you suggesting?" Michael eyed the pot suspiciously.

"Whatever feels right to you. But make sure she's actually caught this time." Prince Daniel grumbled his annoyance. "I don't know how those idiots let her escape."

Michael repeated the words in his head, praying he misunderstood. "The horsemen," he asked. "You sent them? You attacked your own princess."

"It wasn't an attack," Prince Daniel said, immediately defensive. "They were just supposed to capture her for a day. Then I'd have full support in attacking the rebels. I didn't know she'd dive into a ravine. It's her fault she got hurt."

Michael brought his hands to his head. Prince Daniel had risked Liviya's life in order to justify political moves, and he was planning on doing it again. Michael struggled to voice the next suspicion he had, but he needed to know the answer.

"And the fire?"

"Yes, well, that got out of hand, didn't it?" Prince Daniel chuckled. "I almost burned down my palace."

"Seventeen people died in the fire!" Michael bellowed.

"And all the survivors bowed. Small price to pay for a crown."

Michael took a shaky inhale, desperate to stay calm. He had been falling, and he just hit the ground. It was painful landing. "I'll take care of it," he said to appease the prince. "Make your ruby clear. I'll take care of the princess."

Prince Daniel pulled the ruby from his pocket and grasped it with the twisted tongs. He lowered it into the boiling liquid. Droplets splattered and sizzled. Michael left. He needed to warn Liviya. He needed to get her to safety. He needed to stop Prince Daniel, and he needed to—

Michael leaned against a tree, sucking in fresh air, forcing out the toxins with each exhale. When his head cleared, Michael stood up straight. He needed to defeat an enemy and complete the challenge. Michael needed to be king.

CHAPTER 33

Michael paced around the palace grounds as he tried to develop a plan. The ruby was gone, melted in Daniel's pot. He'd need a replacement, or at least some type of replica in order to complete the challenge. But he'd worry about that after finishing the other requirement—defeating his enemy. He had at least a dozen friends who were now enemies and even more foes who were a direct threat to the kingdom, but only one person came to mind. Liviya. Her words echoed in his mind. *I hate you.* She had said it before, but coming after their months of friendship, the words hurt. He needed to fix that. Most importantly, the alliance still required a marriage. He'd like to be on the best of terms with Liviya before he asked for her hand.

Michael found Liviya beside the pond. She leaned over the bridge and tossed pieces of bread to the ducks in the water. An occasional tear slipped down her cheek.

"There's a legend about this pond, you know," Michael said.

Liviya kept her face toward the water. The ducks quacked for more bread. Liviya tossed another piece into the water.

"Legend tells that tears cried here never leave. Hundreds of people over hundreds of years have stood on this very spot and drained their frustrations." Michael shrugged. "I've even contributed a tear or two myself in my time, but only when I think the fish look thirsty."

Liviya almost laughed, but she quickly pulled her mouth back to a frown.

Michael tried to hide his smile. "It's a real difficult problem we all have to consider. When too many tears are added, the pond overflows, and the flooding is a real mess. Can you swim, Highness?'

"You're lying."

"Perhaps." Michael reached into his pocket and passed her a handkerchief. "But if I'm not, it would be best for us all if you would dry your tears."

The tears had already stopped, but Liviya wiped the remaining residue from her cheeks. With a sniff, she tossed a few more crumbs to the water.

Michael placed a hand on her arm. "Liviya, I'm so sorry. How can I make this right?"

Liviya furrowed her brow. She pulled off another piece of bread and rolled it between her fingers. "I don't want to marry the prince. I want Herrick dead." Liviya tossed the bread into the water. "And I want to go home."

Selfishly, Michael had hoped she would stay and that the wedding planned would be for them. He thought that if he took the kingdom then he could have Liviya as well. Stupidly, he was wrong.

Michael puffed out his cheeks with his exhale. "I'm just a man. I have a handful of misfit rebels, and I've offended most of my friends."

Liviya nodded her understanding.

"But I'm going to be king," Michael added quickly. The words were difficult to speak out loud, but when he did, he was surprised how right they sounded. "When I'm king, I'll march against Herrick, and then—and then I'll take you home." Those words, though also difficult to speak, brought no relief to him. Instead, they pierced his heart with an agonizing pain.

Liviya wrapped him in a hug and buried her face against his shoulder, laughing and crying at the same time.

"The pond," Michael reminded, his heart breaking. "Be mindful of the pond." He needed to be certain there was room for the tears he'd cry later.

Liviya pulled away. Smiling, she wiped her tears. "It seems Saunder has a legend for everything. Some truer than others."

"The legends are how we share our stories and teach our children," Michael explained. "They're our very center, they're our very core. The legends are—" Michael cupped his hand and tapped it against his chest while he thought.

"The legends are the heart of Saunder," Liviya said.

"Exactly," Michael said. "The legends are the heart of Saunder." Then like a light that had just been lit, Michael understood the challenge. Make the Heart of Saunder clear. He didn't need a ruby. He didn't need to change its color. He needed to learn the legends, learn the stories and the secrets they hid. Michael pulled Liviya against his chest and held her tightly.

He had defeated his enemy by reconciling with Liviya. He knew how to complete the challenge. Tonight, he would be crowned. But he had agreed to take Liviya home. Michael had always known that becoming king would require sacrifices. He hadn't known how painful they would be.

THE PALACE GROUNDS BEGAN TO CLEAR AS PEOPLE MOVED INDOORS. They gathered in the ballroom for the coronation ball. So far, neither candidate was eligible yet, but Michael at least understood and could begin. He started toward the dungeon. He needed advice and a friend.

Michael found Geoffrey in the first cell on a straw cot with a thin blanket. Water dripped from the ceiling and plinked into puddles on the stone floor. Michael had a hundred things he needed to say. There wasn't a lot of time, and Michael needed to be careful about what he said, especially in front of the guards. Some people were still loyal to the prince.

"How are you?" Michael asked.

"Accommodations aren't as bad as I thought. We should rethink this as a punishment." A mouse scurried across the floor and disappeared in the straw. Michael shuddered. Geoffrey stood up. He propped his elbows on the iron bars. "How's the kingdom?"

"Storm's coming," Michael said.

"Been brewing for a while. You finally see the dark clouds?"

"I saw dark clouds, lightning, and brimstone steps descending to purgatory."

Geoffrey stuck out his chin. "I figure you're about to risk your life to ride off into this storm to save your people."

"That's my plan," Michael said, even though it sounded stupid the way Geoffrey said it.

Geoffrey inhaled between his teeth. "It's a fool's mission alone."

"I'm hoping I'm not alone. Looking for help. Wondering where you stand."

Geoffrey fixed Michael with a stern eye. Michael rubbed the back of his neck. He should have started with an apology.

"That's a stupid question," Geoffrey said. "I stand with my people. I stand with the man who serves them, and I stand with my sword lifted against the man who does not." He pulled on the bars. "Open this up. Let's go."

Relief filled Michael's chest. He inserted the key into the lock and opened the cell door.

"The legends," Michael said as they crossed the palace grounds.

Geoffrey nodded with a proud smile.

"I've remembered each one I could, but the connection's not clear." Michael shook his head. "But someone needs to stop Daniel. I'm expecting an altercation."

"Tell me what to do," Geoffrey said.

"Find Liviya. Don't let her leave your side." He looked at Geoffrey. "Do we have more than just us?"

Geoffrey put a hand on Michael's shoulder. "We got quite a few."

"Good. Get them in place in the ballroom. Make sure they're armed."

"And what are you going to do?" Geoffrey asked.

Michael sighed and shifted his weight. "I figure I'm going to start in the library. Read the words of every legend." Michael groaned. "It's going to take me all night!"

Geoffrey squeezed Michael's shoulder. "You're overlooking a simple solution." He waited until Michael was looking at him. "Go ask the king. It was never intended that you solve this alone."

Michael tilted his head back, letting the slight breeze fan away some of his anxiety. The king would help him. The crown was within his reach.

The palace grounds were completely empty now. Music drifted from the palace windows. Michael looked down at his dirty clothes. He'd need to change before he was crowned. He was going to be late.

CHAPTER 34

*L*iviya dressed for the ball. After hours of alterations, the wedding gown was finally finished, but it waited in the box on her bed. She wasn't getting married tonight. She was going home. But first, she'd dance with Michael, the future king of Saunder. Her heart fluttered, already dancing.

Instead of the wedding gown, Liviya chose a blue gown. Flowers climbed the bodice and wrapped around her back. Her hair fell down her back in wide curls. She pinned a few of them behind her ear with a jeweled pin. She looked in the mirror and smiled at her reflection. For the first time in months, she recognized herself. She looked beautiful.

Liviya walked down the stairs to the ballroom. The long tables were lined with crisp linens. Bright flowers were arranged in crystal vases that reflected the light of the chandeliers. At the top of the stairs, King Josiah sat on his throne.

The musicians played in the corner, but nobody danced. Although a royal feast was spread along the tables, nobody ate. The celebration wouldn't begin until the future king arrived. Prince Daniel hadn't completed his requirements. If Michael wasn't there, he hadn't either.

Liviya walked up the stairs and curtsied before sitting beside the king. Geoffrey stood behind the throne and nodded. Last she knew, he was imprisoned. Michael had been busy since his decision to take the crown.

The king, though, looked worse than she had seen. With a pained smile, he patted her knee. "That is the smile of a girl whose broken heart has healed. The divide has been filled, and you are ready to be queen." His voice croaked. The old man, sick as he was, beamed.

"Your Majesty," Liviya said. "I'm not going to be queen."

His face fell. "You're not?"

Liviya shook her head. "Michael said he'd take me home."

"He what?" The king paled more with each word spoken. His eyes darted back and forth.

"He said he'd take me home," Liviya repeated. She leaned forward and whispered, "After he gets the crown. He's going to complete the requirements."

As if on cue, Michael walked through the doors, still buttoning the cuff of his sleeve. He looked so much like an ordinary man and so much like a king at the same time. Skipping every other step, he climbed the stairs. He caught Liviya's eye and winked before bowing. "Your Majesty, I need help with the challenge."

"You're late," King Josiah mumbled.

"I got here as fast as I could," Michael replied.

"No. You're too late for the challenge. Daniel approached me not a half hour ago and asked for help."

Michael sank into the chair on the king's opposite side.

"I sent him to my room to read my personal history where he will find a clue that will answer his questions. I'll tell you now if you're curious."

Michael buried his face in his hands. "Sure."

"Herrick is my son."

Liviya reeled. She was sure her expression matched Michael's. She was confused. Michael looked like he'd vomit.

"You have two sons?" Michael asked.

"No. I have one son," the king said. "Prince Nathan. At eighteen years old, he abdicated the throne, ran away with his love, and was married in secret. I didn't see him for years. When I finally found him," the king said, "he was working on a farm, like a common man." The king choked out a derisive laugh. "I begged him to come home and take the crown that was his. He refused. We fought."

"You killed his wife," Liviya said. She had spent hours patiently listening to the king and his stories, but Prince Daniel would be arriving at any moment. She needed this story to end.

"It was an accident," the king replied. "Their young son watched." He turned his gaze away. "That was you, Michael. You are Nathan's son."

Michael brought his hands to head face and sank lower into the chair. Liviya had learned this the previous night and had processed it. Michael, though, was shocked.

"And—" Liviya prompted. Somehow the beloved Prince Nathan of Saunder became the King of Barlow who had nearly killed her entire people.

"That was the last time I saw him," the king said. "He was wounded when I left. I thought he had died."

"He went to Barlow," Liviya said, slowly making sense of the news. It was the story she had heard as a child. "Prince Nathan went to Barlow and married the princess." Tears filled her eyes.

King Josiah nodded.

"He killed her father, Herrick the first."

King Josiah nodded again.

The man who had killed her people and starved them, the man who had burned a mark into her arm. That was the beloved Prince Nathan, King Josiah's son.

The king peered at a spot on the floor in front of him. "The princess escaped with her infant son and pleaded for me to help her. I couldn't," the king whispered. "I couldn't attack my own son. But I took his child, raising him as my heir. That child is Prince Daniel."

"So it was all a lie," Michael said, finally finding his voice. "Barlow didn't kill your son. Your son killed the people of Barlow."

"The man that princess described was not my son," the king said. "He was a vile beast."

The group was quiet.

"I couldn't tell my people the truth. So I told them the legends. Soon, they became part of our history. They became the heart of my kingdom. But it's time my people know the truth. Prince Nathan is alive. He is seeking his revenge. Michael is heir to the throne."

"This will start a war," Michael said, panicked. "What are you going to do?"

"I'm too old to do anything," the king said. "What are you going to do?"

The ballroom door slammed open, stopping Michael's reply. Prince Daniel stood in the doorway. He pointed at Liviya. "You lied to me." He stared with an anger she recognized and feared. "Who are you?"

The entire ballroom quieted. It was the first time all summer that Prince Daniel had asked her to speak. Everybody waited to hear what she would say. Her gag had been loosened, but her words would lead her to the gallows.

If after all this time, the king could speak the truth, then Liviya could as well. "My name is Liviya," she began. "I'm from Barlow. I was a maid in the palace."

The crowd erupted into whispered comments. Prince Daniel's face twisted.

She might as well share the rest of the story, the part that not even Michael knew.

"I was caught stealing from the king."

Another wave of disbelief. Tears filled Liviya's eyes. She was scared, but mostly she was ashamed of the lies she had told and the person she really was. "I was to be punished with death, but instead, he sent me here to play the role as his princess and marry the prince." Liviya stared at her feet, unable to meet anyone's eyes. "There is no princess of Barlow." She had been killed. By King Josiah's son. Liviya couldn't look the king in the eye. He had lied.

"You made me a fool," Daniel snarled. He drew his sword, but Michael stepped in front of him.

"Get her out of here," Michael ordered.

Geoffrey took Liviya's arm. She pulled away from his grasp.

Fire filled Daniel's eyes. He swiped his sword across a table, scattering dishes onto the floor. The people backed against the wall. "I've lost my kingdom. I've lost both kingdoms!" He turned over another table then held his sword's point toward Michael. "You knew."

Geoffrey lifted Liviya from her seat and carried her toward the door.

"Let me go!" she shouted.

Michael reached for his own sword. "Please, Daniel. Don't make me kill you. You're my brother!"

Daniel roared. "Your brother? I'm your master. I am your king!"

"Be careful," Michael warned. "I will not lose."

Daniel lunged forward. Michael blocked the attack. The swords clanged together, the sound deafening in the silence-shocked ballroom.

Before either moved again, Josiah stood up, unassisted. "Drop your swords!"

Michael waited until Daniel dropped his sword before dropping his own. Arms raised, Michael turned toward the king who stood at the top of the stairs. Slowly, Michael bent to one knee.

Daniel knelt too. On the ground, he retrieved a dagger from his boot. He lunged forward and forced the blade into Michael's back.

"Michael!" Liviya screamed.

Michael met her eyes. Slowly, he fell forward.

At the top of the stairs, Josiah collapsed under the weight of his unsupported body. He tumbled down each of the steps with a sickening thud and landed on the floor.

Liviya screamed again. She kicked at Geoffrey, clawed at him with her nails, and drove her elbows to his gut, but he held her back.

King Josiah and Michael lay next to each other on the floor. Blood seeped from underneath each of the men into one large pool. From her view above, Liviya couldn't tell which blood came from which man.

Screaming, Liviya fought against Geoffrey. She wouldn't watch another friend die. Michael needed help. But Geoffrey dragged her out of the room. As she left, the sounds of a battle began. This had been Herrick's plan all along. His alliance had started a war.

CHAPTER 35

Geoffrey, with the help of Jacob, carried Liviya to her room. She fought them as best she could, but they forced her inside and shut the door, locking her in. Their footsteps echoed down the hall as they joined the fight in the ballroom.

Liviya screamed and beat her fists against the door, but it didn't open. When her fists ached, she stopped only to throw her belongings around her room. She returned to the door. "Please, Jacob!" she screamed, but he didn't listen.

There was a war downstairs. Michael and Josiah were both injured, maybe dead, and people were fighting. She sat on her bed and ran her hands through her hair, scratching her scalp to keep from screaming. This was her fault. She never should have come to Saunder. She never should have lied. She was stupid to think that she ever could have become queen, stupid to think that Prince Daniel would never find out, stupid to think he wouldn't care that he would be married to a maid. Screaming again, she grabbed a bottle of perfume and threw it across the room. It shattered against the window.

Liviya hid her face in her hands. Prince Daniel would find her. He'd kill her and everyone else in Barlow. Liviya needed to warn them. Not just about the war, but about everything. Prince Daniel was the rightful heir to the throne of Barlow. He was worse than King Herrick. She lifted her eyes to the window across the room. She could still escape. Finally, she was going home.

Liviya waited until it had been dark for several hours before leaving her hiding spot beneath the roots of a rotted tree. War raged in Saunder. It was safer to travel at night. She crept out of her hole and pulled at the long grasses nearby, hoping for food at its root. She hadn't eaten in the day and a half since she had left the palace, and there wouldn't be food when she crossed the border to home. Hunger ate at her stomach. It was worse than she had remembered. The nights grew chilly. Liviya ripped the layers from underneath her gown and wrapped them around her bare arms. The shoes that were made for dancing were poor shoes to wear when fleeing. She opted instead to go barefoot. Briars and branches cut at her feet. She limped along. She was almost home. Just as the sun began to rise, Liviya reached the canyon. Barlow waited for her on the other side. The rope bridge spanned the canyon. Closing her eyes, she stepped onto the bridge. The bridge creaked and swayed, but she continued. She focused on each breath, making them smooth and intentional. Peeking her eyes open, she saw Barlow only a few steps away. She ran, stumbling a little at the end, and arrived in Barlow on her knees.

Liviya was exhausted and terrified, but she walked as if in a daze. The tears she had cried leading up to her departure had used up what stores she had. Her eyes remained dry. Once again, her heartbreak hurt more than her fear.

The land of Barlow was even dryer and more desperate than it had been when Liviya left. Even the roads seemed to have aged. They were overgrown with weeds. Bits of garbage caught in the dried leaves. On the entire road to the palace, Liviya didn't see any other person.

Finally, the palace came into view. Liviya's only home and family were with Mrs. Wilde and the other maids in the servants' shack. She kept her eyes focused on the palace's leaning towers and continued home.

When she arrived, she rested a hand against the weathered door.

"Oh, what is it?" Mrs. Wilde grumbled. She opened the door and stumbled back. "Liviya."

Liviya gingerly stepped inside.

"Your feet!" Mrs. Wilde gasped. Each step left tracks of blood on the floor. She eased Liviya into a chair.

The rest of the action happened in a blur. The girls bustled about bringing clean clothes and fresh linens. Someone brought Liviya some soup, which Liviya drank gratefully. At some point, the apothecary arrived. He inspected Liviya's feet through his thin glasses, then tossed some herbs into warm water.

A few girls helped Liviya undress, gently peeling off the near unrecognizable ballgown. Most faces Liviya recognized. Some were new, but several were missing. Liviya's heart didn't have the room to hear what had happened to them.

Liviya looked around the servants' shack. It was just the same as she had left it. Winter would be arriving soon, and the girls had no wood. The little food they had they fed to Liviya. An orange film covered the water in the buckets, and everyone looked scared. After all the sacrifices Liviya gave to help them, nothing had changed. Everything she had endured had been for nothing.

"What happened?" Mrs. Wilde asked.

There was so much to tell, but so much of it even Liviya didn't understand. She had almost become queen. Michael had almost become king. He was going to save her people. But King Josiah had kept a terrible secret. King Herrick was his son. The beloved Prince Nathan of Saunder was the foreign prince who arrived in Barlow and killed the royal family. The baby prince that Liviya had hoped would one day return and save them was none other than Prince Daniel. He was even worse than Herrick. There would be no hero for Barlow, and an alliance wouldn't save them. Saunder was just as evil.

"I escaped," Liviya said simply. She lay down on the mat. Throughout the night, Liviya's dreams were punctuated by nightmares, all of which included Michael falling to the floor, knife in his back. He's not dead, she told herself. She'd know if he were dead.

For months Liviya had cursed the silence in her palace bedroom, but now she struggled to sleep among the servants. The girls coughed through the night. The mice in the shack nibbled crumbs and scurried across the floor. The wind whistled through the holes in the wall. Liviya's body ached. Her fingers were like ice, and winter hadn't even arrived yet.

Mrs. Wilde stayed awake all night. She sat in a chair positioned directly in front of the door. She probably feared that Liviya would escape. In another time, Liviya would have, but she had learned that sometimes the cost was too great.

Early in the morning, Liviya awoke to the steady shuffle of someone's feet. There was a gentle knock on the door. A woman entered. Liviya struggled to see in the dim light. She recognized the dog first, sores covered in pus.

It was the old blind woman who begged on the sides of the streets.

"Welcome home, Your Highness." Bones creaking, she offered a stiff bow. She held a package in her arms. With a smile, she gave it to Liviya. "A young man dropped this off months ago and asked that I deliver it."

Confused, Liviya pulled the string. Inside, there was food and a folded note.

"Dear Liviya,
It was a pleasure to meet you. I must confess, I was bluffing when I said that I knew how the magician accomplished his trick. I was only trying to win a dance with you. I haven't the slightest idea how he did it. However, I do know that magic is real. But most often, we must make it ourselves. So take the coin and make a wish. You have everything you need to make it come true.
Until Next Time
~Michael.

A coin slipped from the folded paper and landed in Liviya's palm. She remembered that day in the street with Michael. He had offered her a coin to make a wish to the magician. She never had, claiming she didn't believe in magic, especially not magic bought with a single coin. But maybe Michael was right about magic. Maybe he was right about other things as well. She remembered more of his words, his legend about the princess protecting her land with a single arrow, his musings about Liviya's people, literally scarred by their king. *Barlow isn't cursed. They have a powerful army.*

"What are you thinking?" Mrs. Wilde asked nervously.

Liviya sniffed, wiped her eyes, then kissed the coin. She took a stick and drew the rebel sign on the ground. "Herrick's tyranny ends tonight."

CHAPTER 36

*A*s it always did, word spread quickly. The people assembled with weapons and supplies. For a country that had little, they made a decent army.

Liviya had thought her time in Saunder was to make her a princess so the prince would come save her people. She was wrong. Her time in Saunder was to make her a soldier so she would save them herself.

The wind blew icy cold, but this time, Liviya was grateful. It made their rebel flag fly proud. Head held high, Liviya led her band of rebels to the front door of the palace. Outnumbered, the guards at the gates lowered their weapons. As they progressed, more souls joined them. It was the most rag-tag bunch of misfits that Liviya had ever seen, but they were strong.

Liviya left her army outside and took a handful of soldiers in the palace with her.

"Remember," she said, "we won't spill blood until necessary. First, we offer him the chance to stand down."

Liviya marched into the palace and threw open the doors. King Herrick dined in the ballroom at a table by himself. He was considerably more ill than when she had left six months earlier. By her estimation, he had two weeks or so before he died, and that was with the help of Ruttamon. His skin was thin and yellow, eyes blue and sagging.

The guards at his side lunged forward when Liviya stepped in, but Herrick called them back. He did not look at all threatened by the army behind her. "Welcome home. Come, sit."

Liviya did not sit. "Take your hatred somewhere else, Nathan. We're not part of your war."

"I'll not stop till that tyrant is dead," the king replied.

"Josiah's not the tyrant. You are!"

"Josiah is a tyrant!" King Herrick roared. He leapt to his feet and pushed the table away from him. It tipped to the floor with a crash that sent her soldiers back few steps. Liviya kept her gaze fixed on the king.

"Josiah is a tyrant," King Herrick said again. "Did you learn nothing there?"

"I learned it all!" Liviya said. "I know you're Prince Nathan. I know you left your throne to marry your love and that Josiah killed her. But nobody else needs to die!" Liviya's voice caught as she remembered the sight of Josiah on the ballroom floor, lying next to Michael in a puddle of blood. "Nobody else needs to die."

"You learned only part of the story," King Herrick said. "Barlow's river is dry because Josiah dammed it. Every day, under the eyes and command of your beloved king, thousands of slaves filled it. Slaves burned with a mark, just like yours. Do you want to know the number of men who died? I know!" he shouted again. "Because I watched it as a boy. I watched Josiah kill them."

"No," Liviya said.

"Yes. In time, I received the requirements to become king. Josiah sent me to Barlow to defeat my enemy. It was a scheme dreamed up by my power-hungry father. We were to seal an alliance, and I was to marry their princess. Once we were married, I would kill the royal family. He probably would have killed me next. Then he would rule Saunder and Barlow."

Liviya looked away. It was all a lie. It had to be.

"I didn't want to marry the princess of Barlow," King Herrick said.

"I loved another girl. A peasant. I brought her to Josiah and asked to marry her instead. He refused."

"He knew it was a ploy to overthrow him," Liviya said.

"He knew I loved her!" King Herrick shouted. "And it would foil his plan to rule both kingdoms. I left my father to plunder and war by himself and wed my love. Josiah found her and killed her."

"It was an accident," Liviya argued.

King Herrick crossed the room. He grabbed the collar of her dress and pulled her so close that the spittle from his words sprayed her face.

"Josiah sliced her open with his sword. Then he pierced me and left me to die. I watched him ride away with my child." He sneered at her. "I trust you met Michael."

"He's not at all like you," Liviya said.

"My father needed to be stopped," Herrick said, eyes focusing in the distance as he remembered the past. "I wanted to free my people from the murderous king. But I had no army. I had no country. So I used my father's plan, and it went perfectly. I married the princess. I killed Barlow's king. I would have killed my wife as well, but she escaped to save the child she carried. She took him to Saunder!" King Herrick roared with laughter, but his face showed his anger. "She begged protection from the man who had sent me to kill her. And Josiah, that hypocrite, took her in. Raised her child to be heir to my throne.

"I waited for an opportunity to attack, but Saunder marched to me with an alliance instead." King Herrick laughed again "I sealed an alliance with Josiah based on the very terms he had set forth years ago: the prince of Saunder would marry the princess of Barlow. Just like years ago, I sent him a peasant girl to rule his land. Michael is the rightful heir to that throne. I set the pieces in place to make that happen."

"You started a war there as well," Liviya said. "Michael might be dead. The land is in ruins."

"It's a war, princess," King Herrick said without remorse. "I expected casualties."

An arrow sped across the room and pierced King Herrick, pinning him to him throne.

"No!" Liviya shouted. She looked at her army, but none of them had fired.

Liviya looked to the king, eyes wide, blood filling between his teeth. The arrow had struck the center of his heart. There was only one man who could aim like that and kill that cruelly.

Shouts sounded from outside. Liviya looked to the window. An army approached, led by Daniel.

"We're under attack!" Liviya screamed.

Liviya pulled out her bow. Standing in the protection of the window, she shot arrows toward her enemy, the man she had nearly married. Swords clanged, bowstrings snapped, blood spilled, and screams filled the air.

Liviya's small army fought bravely, Daniel's men marched through them without slowing down. They held torches against the buildings as they passed. The houses and shops turned to flames. Smoke stained the sky. All around, people were screaming. Blood began to puddle in the streets. Dead bodies lay broken in the street, crudely trampled by the enemy's horses.

Soon, Daniel's army reached the palace. In the dining room, a soldier lit the drapes on fire. Flames climbed the walls. Smoke filled the room.

"Run!" Liviya screamed. She pushed everyone out the back door of the palace. Before they had escaped, one of the flame-eaten walls collapsed, crushing Liviya beneath it. She screamed, the weight of the stone pinning her legs. The fire teased sparks toward her hair.

Someone hauled the stones off of her. Still screaming, Liviya crawled out. Lights shone against the backs of Liviya's eyelids and warm blood oozed down the sides of her face.

Her land was destroyed. King Herrick was dead. Why was Daniel still here? Why were his men still attacking? As soon as Liviya asked the question, the answer came. He was looking for her. He'd kill everyone until he found her. An entire village had been beaten before in order to protect Liviya. She wouldn't let her entire kingdom be slaughtered as well.

Liviya climbed to the top of the palace steps, flames roaring behind her.

"You won't win!" she yelled. She wiped the blood-soaked hair from her eyes.

Prince Daniel stopped. Turning slowly, he pulled his sword from a dead body and held the bloody tip toward her. "You."

"I've heard this story before, Daniel, and you don't win." Liviya placed the arrow against the string and pulled back. "With this arrow, I will call down lightning from the sky that will obliterate your army and leave your bones a pile of ash."

It was just a legend created days ago by Michael, but Daniel hesitated. Whether he feared the legend or her skill with a bow, Liviya didn't know. Behind her, the scared people arose.

Prince Daniel studied them for a minute then sheathed his sword. "I don't have to fight a war. Winter will destroy you far better than I can." He motioned to his men. "Burn the city."

The men retreated, but as they did, they tossed their torches to the remaining structures. Inside the palace, something exploded. Liviya heard the crash before she felt it. It blasted her off the palace steps. In seemingly slow-motion, she hurtled through the air, crashing against the ground behind Daniel's retreating armies.

All through the night, Liviya and the others watched their kingdom burn. When the flames died, people searched through the palace debris for anything to salvage. Other moved the bodies from the road.

Weak and exhausted, the survivors gathered in the shelter of a tent next to the dry river bed.

A tear slipped from Liviya's cheeks into the mud below. Liviya squished her sandals in the grime. Then she scooped some up into her hand. The riverbed was muddy, but rain hadn't fallen. Water was flowing from somewhere. She looked down the river toward the border. Saunder must have broken the dam. The others began to realize it, as well. They cheered, dancing through the mud, running up high to watch the river fill. Liviya sat, stunned and grateful. She had succeeded. Herrick was dead. Barlow had water. It was everything she had ever wanted.

Mrs. Wilde approached, hands full of charred dishes. She also held the crown. After wiping it on her skirts, she handed it to Liviya.

Liviya turned away. "I'm done playing princess."

"We don't need a princess," Mrs. Wilde responded. "We need a queen."

CHAPTER 37

When Michael awoke, he kept his eyes shut. He was hot and confused, but he was very aware of the bandage wrapped around his chest. The wound pulsed. He wished for the peace of unconsciousness again. When it didn't come, he opened his eyes.

Geoffrey sat in a chair beside his bed. He leaned forward and held up his head with his hand. Mrs. Maude dipped a towel in the water and placed it on Michael's forehead.

"Where's Liviya?"

"She's gone," Geoffrey said. "She escaped."

Michael groaned. He had promised to protect her.

"Her people need her more right now than we do, and they've got water now. We blew up the dam."

Michael smiled weakly. "What about Daniel?"

"He fought here with a surprising number of followers," Geoffrey said. "We suffered significant losses but managed to drive him out."

Michael's head spun. He wanted to stop listening, but he had laid in bed too long. It was time to fix this. "How are the people?"

"Our land is filled with homeless widows and hungry children.

The people are divided. Some wait for Daniel to serve him when he returns, others wait to fight against him. He will return, Michael."

Michael nodded. He was aware of that already. This was just the beginning.

"And Josiah?"

"He's alive, but he's weak."

Michael tossed off his blankets. "I need to talk to him." He expected Mrs. Maude to step in front of him and demand he stay in bed, but she offered a tired smile. "Been waitin' a long time for this conversation."

Michael slowly made his way to the king. Shallow breathing barely lifted the old man's chest. Large bruises covered his forehead, and swelling forced his eyes shut.

Geoffrey gently lowered Michael into a chair beside the king's bed.

"You're alive," the king said.

"Barely," Michael said.

King Josiah furrowed his brow, then smiled like he had finally made peace with the painful past. Each word was separated by a long, pain-filled breath. "Prince Nathan is your father."

Michael rubbed his hands against his face. He was the orphan son of a peasant mother because King Josiah had killed her. His absent father was none other than the revered Prince Nathan, the King of Barlow.

Michael held up a hand, then dropped it to his lap. He didn't know if he was sad or confused or angry. He blamed the pain in his back for making him unaware of any other feeling.

"How did nobody know?" Michael asked.

"I lied," King Josiah said slowly. "Many never knew what had happened to Prince Nathan. I told them that he was destroyed in Barlow. In some ways, it was true. Other people, I paid. The money erased their memories, or at least silenced them. Those who knew never taught their children, and those who didn't know never asked. But it's time for the truth. You are the rightful heir. Will you take the crown?"

Michael shook his head. "I didn't destroy my enemy. Daniel

escaped. And Liviya—." She probably hated him still. He had failed her.

"Daniel was never your enemy," King Josiah said. "Your enemy was the voice in your head that kept telling you that you weren't worthy."

Michael dropped his head and sighed. He considered himself an exceptional soldier. He was wrong. In all the battle plans he had made, he had never figured out a way to fight against himself, to fight against fear. Had he defeated that voice long ago, maybe the entire war could have been avoided.

"Will you take the crown?" the king asked.

"It's not much of a kingdom now," Michael said. "The land is filled with widows and hungry children. I have half an army, and Daniel will return."

The king raised an eyebrow. "I wonder if we would benefit from an alliance with Barlow."

CHAPTER 38

The winter was long and difficult in Barlow. After months of freezing weather, the air finally held a hint of spring. Barlow had survived, thanks to the water from Saunder.

Liviya joined her people outside. They cleared the rubble from the fields and roads. The few horses left in the kingdom pulled plows through the dirt. They'd plant seeds. In the coming months, they'd have food.

In Saunder, it had been easy to pretend to be a princess. But becoming a real princess was a lot more difficult. Finally, she understood Michael's hesitation to accept the crown. The feeling of inadequacy was a difficult beast to fight.

Liviya grabbed one end of a large beam that had fallen from a house and helped haul it off the road, stopping to rest when Mrs. Wilde brought food. Several of the maids joined Liviya on a blanket.

"It was about this time last year that I was arriving in Saunder," Liviya said. She shook her head. It seemed so long ago now. "They had thrown a ball. Days after becoming a princess, I was presented to the people and was supposed to dance in a formal gown. I lied so I wouldn't have to dance. Only one person suspected the truth." The memory of Michael and the night at the ball made the words catch in her throat.

The girls smiled kindly and didn't push. Liviya rarely spoke about her time in Saunder. There were too many things she didn't understand and too much pain in the stories.

"You were never properly crowned," Mrs. Wilde said. "There's supposed to a ceremony and a ball."

In Saunder, a wedding followed. But not in Barlow. Not for Liviya.

Liviya studied the dirt beneath her fingernails. Again, she felt so far from being queen. But her people needed reason to celebrate.

"Spread the word," Liviya said. "We're having a ball."

THE FIRE HAD DAMAGED A LOT OF THE PALACE, BUT THE WEST WING still stood. The people gathered there for the ball. Poor and lame musicians gathered together with violins missing strings and bent flutes. The people danced. It was not the choreographed minuets from Saunder that the nobles learned and practiced, but a dance of poverty, a dance of the people, a dance of peace.

The once broken and fearful people feasted, cheered, sang. The celebration was more difficult than Liviya had imagined. Partway through, she slipped outside.

She studied the land below her. She had thought her broken heart would heal when she came home, but it still pulsed though the very same hole she had in Saunder.

Liviya had kept Michael's coin, attaching it to a chain around her neck. She rubbed its edges, making a wish without knowing what it was. She wanted to go home, but home appeared to not be in Barlow either. Maybe there was no home for a lost girl like Liviya.

Mrs. Wilde stepped through the glass door. "Congratulations, Your Majesty." Her voice was rough and aged. The war and winter had taken an effect on the old housekeeper as well, deepening the creases in her face, sinking her eyes into the hollows of her face.

Liviya should have been happy. She was ashamed that tears filled her eyes, instead.

Mrs. Wilde pulled her into a tight hug. "I always wondered why you didn't run away when you had the chance. You know what I think? I think you never ran away because it's scary to not know where you're going. Traveling to Saunder was terrifying, but not as much as running without a destination in mind. Now, I'm thinking to myself that you're not happy, and I can't help but wonder why you don't leave." Mrs. Wilde held her at arm's length. "You don't need all the answers right now, honey. Sometimes, you just need to go."

Liviya's tears fell so quickly that her fingers only smeared them across her face. Mrs. Wilde was right. Liviya's biggest fear was not knowing where she'd go. But if she wanted to heal her heart, she'd have to take that first step."

"Now, I didn't come out here to make you cry," Mrs. Wilde said. "There's a young man in there asking to dance with you. If you're not going back in, I'll go dance with him myself."

A shadow moved into the doorway. As he stepped through, the moonlight showed his face. Michael reached into his pocket and pulled out a handkerchief. "If I may, Your Majesty."

Liviya leapt into his arms. They stood in an embrace on the balcony for a long time. She nestled her face again his neck and savored the touch of his arms around her. Finally, she pulled away to look at him.

Michael put both of his hands on her cheeks and wiped away her tears. "I'm so sorry. I would have come sooner—" He stopped, but Liviya understood. He had almost died.

"I'm glad you're alive," Liviya said.

Michael escorted her to a bench facing the kingdom. He put his arm around her and pulled her close. "It's been a long time. How are you?"

Liviya inhaled. There was so much to tell. They had barely survived the winter, Daniel had destroyed her land, and King Herrick was dead. Liviya looked up. After all she had witnessed, one thing was more painful than the rest. "Herrick said terrible things about King Josiah. Are they true?"

Michael pulled her closer. "I don't know how. Time sometimes changes stories. All I know is that King Josiah died a great king. I can only hope that I'm strong enough and wise enough to rule greatly in the beginning as well."

Liviya nodded, leaning back against him. Then she sat up quickly. "Michael, you're king?"

Michael humbly held out his hands. "It's still unofficial. See, I'm supposed to be married."

He knelt to the ground and held out his mother's ring, the twisted piece of metal he wore around his neck.

"I don't have much to give, but I can make you a promise to love you every day of my life. Will you marry me?"

"Yes," Liviya said. "Of course." She wrapped her arms around him again.

He stroked her hair and whispered in her ear. "I loved you from the moment I saw you, and I've loved you more every moment since."

Liviya pulled away and looked into his eyes. "Are you exaggerating again?"

"Not in the least." Michael tilted his head toward her until their lips met.

In the ballroom, the spying people of Barlow cheered.

When they stepped apart, Michael held a hand toward the ballroom. "May I have this dance?"

"Only because you're king," Liviya teased, placing her hand in his.

As they twirled around Barlow's simple ball, Liviya's heart filled. For the first time in years, she had where she belonged. It wasn't in Saunder, and it wasn't in Barlow. She belonged with Michael.

MICHAEL, TRUE TO HIS PROMISE LONG AGO, HAD BROUGHT SUPPLIES. AS Liviya and Michael journeyed to Saunder, they stopped along the small villages, distributing food to the needy. The people, who for so long had been beaten and broken, celebrated. The winter was over, the war was over, and an alliance was sealed with Saunder.

In the palace in Saunder, Michael and Liviya sat beside the king's bed, holding hands. Michael's mother's ring rested on Liviya's finger. Around them, everyone bustled with wedding preparations.

Liviya touched the king's hand. "When Michael told me you were ill, I thought you were faking again."

The king smiled weakly. "What else did Michael tell you?"

"He told me you were the greatest king to ever rule Saunder."

"He was lying," the king said.

"He does do that sometimes," Liviya said. "But you're certainly the greatest king that I've ever known."

"What will you tell the people?" the king asked.

Michael inhaled as he thought. "I think we'll tell them a legend about the long ago king of Saunder who had gotten ensnared in heavy chains that threatened to pull him into darkness forever. We'll tell them that the king pressed forward, dragging his chains with him every day, but that he died a free man."

"It's a nice story," King Josiah said. "But be certain you tell them the truth, too."

He motioned to the book on his bedside, the same book Geoffrey had shown him in the stables weeks ago. The History of Saunder. "It's all written here."

Michael hadn't read it yet, but one day, he would. Then he'd share the story with others.

"I'm sorry you didn't live to see it resolved," Michael said.

"It's the perfect ending. You're king. Liviya's queen."

"But Daniel will come back," Michael said. "War is coming."

"War is always coming. Hold your family close and try to keep it out." As King Josiah's eyes closed, he whispered, "Your Majesty."

The End

ACKNOWLEDGMENTS

Many thanks to all those who helped this story come to life. An especially big thank you to:

My dad, for teaching me to tell stories.

My mom, for teaching me to find happily ever after.

Laura, for her detailed edits and constant encouragement.

My sister, Kara, for many, many detailed edits and an open ear for brainstorming.

My sister, Tessa, for always providing much-needed therapy.

The League of Utah Writers for reading my chapters again and again and teaching me how to improve them.

Countless beta-readers and critique partners who read the drafts of the book before it was any good and saw its potential.

And finally, for my husband Blake, who is the best companion I could ask for when writing a book, raising a family, living a life, and more.

ABOUT THE AUTHOR

Arielle Hadfield lives in Northern Utah with her husband and four children, her dog, seven chickens, and an ever-changing number of foster children.

She can be found on her website where she blogs about faith, family, and foster care:

www.ariellehadfield.com